# The Chorus Girl and Other Stories

Anton Chekhov

Translated by Constance Garnett

ESPRIOS DIGITAL PUBLISHING

THE TALES OF CHEKHOV

VOLUME 8

THE CHORUS GIRL AND OTHER STORIES

BY

ANTON TCHEKHOV

Translated by CONSTANCE GARNETT

CONTENTS

THE CHORUS GIRL

VEROTCHKA

MY LIFE

AT A COUNTRY HOUSE

A FATHER

ON THE ROAD

ROTHSCHILD'S FIDDLE

IVAN MATVEYITCH

ZINOTCHKA

BAD WEATHER

A GENTLEMAN FRIEND

A TRIVIAL INCIDENT

## THE CHORUS GIRL

ONE day when she was younger and better-looking, and when her voice was stronger, Nikolay Petrovitch Kolpakov, her adorer, was sitting in the outer room in her summer villa. It was intolerably hot and stifling. Kolpakov, who had just dined and drunk a whole bottle of inferior port, felt ill-humoured and out of sorts. Both were bored and waiting for the heat of the day to be over in order to go for a walk.

All at once there was a sudden ring at the door. Kolpakov, who was sitting with his coat off, in his slippers, jumped up and looked inquiringly at Pasha.

"It must be the postman or one of the girls," said the singer.

Kolpakov did not mind being found by the postman or Pasha's lady friends, but by way of precaution gathered up his clothes and went into the next room, while Pasha ran to open the door. To her great surprise in the doorway stood, not the postman and not a girl friend, but an unknown woman, young and beautiful, who was dressed like a lady, and from all outward signs was one.

The stranger was pale and was breathing heavily as though she had been running up a steep flight of stairs.

"What is it?" asked Pasha.

The lady did not at once answer. She took a step forward, slowly looked about the room, and sat down in a way that suggested that from fatigue, or perhaps illness, she could not stand; then for a long time her pale lips quivered as she tried in vain to speak.

"Is my husband here?" she asked at last, raising to Pasha her big eyes with their red tear-stained lids.

"Husband?" whispered Pasha, and was suddenly so frightened that her hands and feet turned cold. "What husband?" she repeated, beginning to tremble.

"My husband, . . . Nikolay Petrovitch Kolpakov."

"N . . . no, madam. . . . I . . . I don't know any husband."

A minute passed in silence. The stranger several times passed her handkerchief over her pale lips and held her breath to stop her inward trembling, while Pasha stood before her motionless, like a post, and looked at her with astonishment and terror.

"So you say he is not here?" the lady asked, this time speaking with a firm voice and smiling oddly.

"I . . . I don't know who it is you are asking about."

"You are horrid, mean, vile . . ." the stranger muttered, scanning Pasha with hatred and repulsion. "Yes, yes . . . you are horrid. I am very, very glad that at last I can tell you so!"

Pasha felt that on this lady in black with the angry eyes and white slender fingers she produced the impression of something horrid and unseemly, and she felt ashamed of her chubby red cheeks, the pock-mark on her nose, and the fringe on her forehead, which never could be combed back. And it seemed to her that if she had been thin, and had had no powder on her face and no fringe on her forehead, then she could have disguised the fact that she was not "respectable," and she would not have felt so frightened and ashamed to stand facing this unknown, mysterious lady.

"Where is my husband?" the lady went on. "Though I don't care whether he is here or not, but I ought to tell you that the money has been missed, and they are looking for Nikolay Petrovitch. . . . They mean to arrest him. That's your doing!"

The lady got up and walked about the room in great excitement. Pasha looked at her and was so frightened that she could not understand.

"He'll be found and arrested to-day," said the lady, and she gave a sob, and in that sound could be heard her resentment and vexation. "I know who has brought him to this awful position! Low, horrid creature! Loathsome, mercenary hussy!" The lady's lips worked and her nose wrinkled up with disgust. "I am helpless, do you hear, you low woman? . . . I am helpless; you are stronger than I am, but there is One to defend me and my children! God sees all! He is just! He will punish you for every tear I have shed, for all my sleepless nights! The time will come; you will think of me! . . ."

Silence followed again. The lady walked about the room and wrung her hands, while Pasha still gazed blankly at her in amazement, not understanding and expecting something terrible.

"I know nothing about it, madam," she said, and suddenly burst into tears.

"You are lying!" cried the lady, and her eyes flashed angrily at her. "I know all about it! I've known you a long time. I know that for the last month he has been spending every day with you!"

"Yes. What then? What of it? I have a great many visitors, but I don't force anyone to come. He is free to do as he likes."

"I tell you they have discovered that money is missing! He has embezzled money at the office! For the sake of such a . . . creature as you, for your sake he has actually committed a crime. Listen," said the lady in a resolute voice, stopping short, facing Pasha. "You can have no principles; you live simply to do harm—that's your object; but one can't imagine you have fallen so low that you have no trace of human feeling left! He has a wife, children. . . . If he is condemned and sent into exile we shall starve, the children and I. . . . Understand that! And yet there is a chance of saving him and us from destitution and disgrace. If I take them nine hundred roubles to-day they will let him alone. Only nine hundred roubles!"

"What nine hundred roubles?" Pasha asked softly. "I . . . I don't know. . . . I haven't taken it."

"I am not asking you for nine hundred roubles. . . . You have no money, and I don't want your money. I ask you for something else. . . . Men usually give expensive things to women like you. Only give me back the things my husband has given you!"

"Madam, he has never made me a present of anything!" Pasha wailed, beginning to understand.

"Where is the money? He has squandered his own and mine and other people's. . . . What has become of it all? Listen, I beg you! I was carried away by indignation and have said a lot of nasty things to you, but I apologize. You must hate me, I know, but if you are capable of sympathy, put yourself in my position! I implore you to give me back the things!"

"H'm!" said Pasha, and she shrugged her shoulders. "I would with pleasure, but God is my witness, he never made me a present of anything. Believe me, on my conscience. However, you are right, though," said the singer in confusion, "he did bring me two little things. Certainly I will give them back, if you wish it."

Pasha pulled out one of the drawers in the toilet-table and took out of it a hollow gold bracelet and a thin ring with a ruby in it.

"Here, madam!" she said, handing the visitor these articles.

The lady flushed and her face quivered. She was offended.

"What are you giving me?" she said. "I am not asking for charity, but for what does not belong to you . . . what you have taken advantage of your position to squeeze out of my husband . . . that weak, unhappy man. . . . On Thursday, when I saw you with my husband at the harbour you were wearing expensive brooches and bracelets. So it's no use your playing the innocent lamb to me! I ask you for the last time: will you give me the things, or not?"

"You are a queer one, upon my word," said Pasha, beginning to feel offended. "I assure you that, except the bracelet and this little ring, I've never seen a thing from your Nikolay Petrovitch. He brings me nothing but sweet cakes."

"Sweet cakes!" laughed the stranger. "At home the children have nothing to eat, and here you have sweet cakes. You absolutely refuse to restore the presents?"

Receiving no answer, the lady sat down and stared into space, pondering.

"What's to be done now?" she said. "If I don't get nine hundred roubles, he is ruined, and the children and I am ruined, too. Shall I kill this low woman or go down on my knees to her?"

The lady pressed her handkerchief to her face and broke into sobs.

"I beg you!" Pasha heard through the stranger's sobs. "You see you have plundered and ruined my husband. Save him. . . . You have no feeling for him, but the children . . . the children . . . What have the children done?"

Pasha imagined little children standing in the street, crying with hunger, and she, too, sobbed.

"What can I do, madam?" she said. "You say that I am a low woman and that I have ruined Nikolay Petrovitch, and I assure you . . . before God Almighty, I have had nothing from him whatever. . . . There is only one girl in our chorus who has a rich admirer; all the rest of us live from hand to mouth on bread and kvass. Nikolay Petrovitch is a highly educated, refined gentleman, so I've made him welcome. We are bound to make gentlemen welcome."

"I ask you for the things! Give me the things! I am crying. . . . I am humiliating myself. . . . If you like I will go down on my knees! If you wish it!"

Pasha shrieked with horror and waved her hands. She felt that this pale, beautiful lady who expressed herself so grandly, as though she were on the stage, really might go down on her knees to her, simply from pride, from grandeur, to exalt herself and humiliate the chorus girl.

"Very well, I will give you things!" said Pasha, wiping her eyes and bustling about. "By all means. Only they are not from Nikolay Petrovitch. . . . I got these from other gentlemen. As you please. . . ."

Pasha pulled out the upper drawer of the chest, took out a diamond brooch, a coral necklace, some rings and bracelets, and gave them all to the lady.

"Take them if you like, only I've never had anything from your husband. Take them and grow rich," Pasha went on, offended at the threat to go down on her knees. "And if you are a lady . . . his lawful wife, you should keep him to yourself. I should think so! I did not ask him to come; he came of himself."

Through her tears the lady scrutinized the articles given her and said:

"This isn't everything. . . . There won't be five hundred roubles' worth here."

Pasha impulsively flung out of the chest a gold watch, a cigar-case and studs, and said, flinging up her hands:

"I've nothing else left. . . . You can search!"

The visitor gave a sigh, with trembling hands twisted the things up in her handkerchief, and went out without uttering a word, without even nodding her head.

The door from the next room opened and Kolpakov walked in. He was pale and kept shaking his head nervously, as though he had swallowed something very bitter; tears were glistening in his eyes.

"What presents did you make me?" Pasha asked, pouncing upon him. "When did you, allow me to ask you?"

"Presents . . . that's no matter!" said Kolpakov, and he tossed his head. "My God! She cried before you, she humbled herself. . . ."

"I am asking you, what presents did you make me?" Pasha cried.

"My God! She, a lady, so proud, so pure. . . . She was ready to go down on her knees to . . . to this wench! And I've brought her to this! I've allowed it!"

He clutched his head in his hands and moaned.

"No, I shall never forgive myself for this! I shall never forgive myself! Get away from me . . . you low creature!" he cried with repulsion, backing away from Pasha, and thrusting her off with trembling hands. "She would have gone down on her knees, and . . . and to you! Oh, my God!"

He rapidly dressed, and pushing Pasha aside contemptuously, made for the door and went out.

Pasha lay down and began wailing aloud. She was already regretting her things which she had given away so impulsively, and her feelings were hurt. She remembered how three years ago a merchant had beaten her for no sort of reason, and she wailed more loudly than ever.

## VEROTCHKA

IVAN ALEXEYITCH OGNEV remembers how on that August evening he opened the glass door with a rattle and went out on to the verandah. He was wearing a light Inverness cape and a wide-brimmed straw hat, the very one that was lying with his top-boots in the dust under his bed. In one hand he had a big bundle of books and notebooks, in the other a thick knotted stick.

Behind the door, holding the lamp to show the way, stood the master of the house, Kuznetsov, a bald old man with a long grey beard, in a snow-white piqué jacket. The old man was smiling cordially and nodding his head.

"Good-bye, old fellow!" said Ognev.

Kuznetsov put the lamp on a little table and went out to the verandah. Two long narrow shadows moved down the steps towards the flower-beds, swayed to and fro, and leaned their heads on the trunks of the lime-trees.

"Good-bye and once more thank you, my dear fellow!" said Ivan Alexeyitch. "Thank you for your welcome, for your kindness, for your affection. . . . I shall never forget your hospitality as long as I live. You are so good, and your daughter is so good, and everyone here is so kind, so good-humoured and friendly . . . Such a splendid set of people that I don't know how to say what I feel!"

From excess of feeling and under the influence of the home-made wine he had just drunk, Ognev talked in a singing voice like a divinity student, and was so touched that he expressed his feelings not so much by words as by the blinking of his eyes and the twitching of his shoulders. Kuznetsov, who had also drunk a good deal and was touched, craned forward to the young man and kissed him.

"I've grown as fond of you as if I were your dog," Ognev went on. "I've been turning up here almost every day; I've stayed the night a dozen times. It's dreadful to think of all the home-made wine I've drunk. And thank you most of all for your co-operation and help. Without you I should have been busy here over my statistics till

October. I shall put in my preface: 'I think it my duty to express my gratitude to the President of the District Zemstvo of N——, Kuznetsov, for his kind co-operation.' There is a brilliant future before statistics! My humble respects to Vera Gavrilovna, and tell the doctors, both the lawyers and your secretary, that I shall never forget their help! And now, old fellow, let us embrace one another and kiss for the last time!"

Ognev, limp with emotion, kissed the old man once more and began going down the steps. On the last step he looked round and asked: "Shall we meet again some day?"

"God knows!" said the old man. "Most likely not!"

"Yes, that's true! Nothing will tempt you to Petersburg and I am never likely to turn up in this district again. Well, good-bye!"

"You had better leave the books behind!" Kuznetsov called after him. "You don't want to drag such a weight with you. I would send them by a servant to-morrow!"

But Ognev was rapidly walking away from the house and was not listening. His heart, warmed by the wine, was brimming over with good-humour, friendliness, and sadness. He walked along thinking how frequently one met with good people, and what a pity it was that nothing was left of those meetings but memories. At times one catches a glimpse of cranes on the horizon, and a faint gust of wind brings their plaintive, ecstatic cry, and a minute later, however greedily one scans the blue distance, one cannot see a speck nor catch a sound; and like that, people with their faces and their words flit through our lives and are drowned in the past, leaving nothing except faint traces in the memory. Having been in the N—— District from the early spring, and having been almost every day at the friendly Kuznetsovs', Ivan Alexeyitch had become as much at home with the old man, his daughter, and the servants as though they were his own people; he had grown familiar with the whole house to the smallest detail, with the cosy verandah, the windings of the avenues, the silhouettes of the trees over the kitchen and the bath-house; but as soon as he was out of the gate all this would be changed to memory and would lose its meaning as reality for ever, and in a year or two all these dear images would grow as dim in his consciousness as stories he had read or things he had imagined.

"Nothing in life is so precious as people!" Ognev thought in his emotion, as he strode along the avenue to the gate. "Nothing!"

It was warm and still in the garden. There was a scent of the mignonette, of the tobacco-plants, and of the heliotrope, which were not yet over in the flower-beds. The spaces between the bushes and the tree-trunks were filled with a fine soft mist soaked through and through with moonlight, and, as Ognev long remembered, coils of mist that looked like phantoms slowly but perceptibly followed one another across the avenue. The moon stood high above the garden, and below it transparent patches of mist were floating eastward. The whole world seemed to consist of nothing but black silhouettes and wandering white shadows. Ognev, seeing the mist on a moonlight August evening almost for the first time in his life, imagined he was seeing, not nature, but a stage effect in which unskilful workmen, trying to light up the garden with white Bengal fire, hid behind the bushes and let off clouds of white smoke together with the light.

When Ognev reached the garden gate a dark shadow moved away from the low fence and came towards him.

"Vera Gavrilovna!" he said, delighted. "You here? And I have been looking everywhere for you; wanted to say good-bye. . . . Good-bye; I am going away!"

"So early? Why, it's only eleven o'clock."

"Yes, it's time I was off. I have a four-mile walk and then my packing. I must be up early to-morrow."

Before Ognev stood Kuznetsov's daughter Vera, a girl of one-and-twenty, as usual melancholy, carelessly dressed, and attractive. Girls who are dreamy and spend whole days lying down, lazily reading whatever they come across, who are bored and melancholy, are usually careless in their dress. To those of them who have been endowed by nature with taste and an instinct of beauty, the slight carelessness adds a special charm. When Ognev later on remembered her, he could not picture pretty Verotchka except in a full blouse which was crumpled in deep folds at the belt and yet did not touch her waist; without her hair done up high and a curl that had come loose from it on her forehead; without the knitted red shawl with ball fringe at the edge which hung disconsolately on Vera's shoulders in the evenings, like a flag on a windless day, and in the daytime lay about, crushed up, in the hall near the men's hats or on a box in the dining-room, where the old cat did not hesitate to sleep on it. This shawl and the folds of her blouse suggested a feeling of freedom and laziness, of good-nature and sitting at home. Perhaps because Vera attracted Ognev he saw in every frill and button something warm, naïve, cosy, something nice and poetical, just what is lacking in cold, insincere women that have no instinct for beauty.

Verotchka had a good figure, a regular profile, and beautiful curly hair. Ognev, who had seen few women in his life, thought her a beauty.

"I am going away," he said as he took leave of her at the gate. "Don't remember evil against me! Thank you for everything!"

In the same singing divinity student's voice in which he had talked to her father, with the same blinking and twitching of his shoulders, he began thanking Vera for her hospitality, kindness, and friendliness.

"I've written about you in every letter to my mother," he said. "If everyone were like you and your dad, what a jolly place the world would be! You are such a splendid set of people! All such genuine, friendly people with no nonsense about you."

"Where are you going to now?" asked Vera.

"I am going now to my mother's at Oryol; I shall be a fortnight with her, and then back to Petersburg and work."

"And then?"

"And then? I shall work all the winter and in the spring go somewhere into the provinces again to collect material. Well, be happy, live a hundred years . . . don't remember evil against me. We shall not see each other again."

Ognev stooped down and kissed Vera's hand. Then, in silent emotion, he straightened his cape, shifted his bundle of books to a more comfortable position, paused, and said:

"What a lot of mist!"

"Yes. Have you left anything behind?"

"No, I don't think so. . . ."

For some seconds Ognev stood in silence, then he moved clumsily towards the gate and went out of the garden.

"Stay; I'll see you as far as our wood," said Vera, following him out.

They walked along the road. Now the trees did not obscure the view, and one could see the sky and the distance. As though covered with a veil all nature was hidden in a transparent, colourless haze through which her beauty peeped gaily; where the mist was thicker and whiter it lay heaped unevenly about the stones, stalks, and bushes or drifted in coils over the road, clung close to the earth and seemed trying not to conceal the view. Through the haze they could see all the road as far as the wood, with dark ditches at the sides and tiny bushes which grew in the ditches and caught the straying wisps of mist. Half a mile from the gate they saw the dark patch of Kuznetsov's wood.

"Why has she come with me? I shall have to see her back," thought Ognev, but looking at her profile he gave a friendly smile and said: "One doesn't want to go away in such lovely weather. It's quite a romantic evening, with the moon, the stillness, and all the etceteras. Do you know, Vera Gavrilovna, here I have lived twenty-nine years in the world and never had a romance. No romantic episode in my whole life, so that I only know by hearsay of rendezvous, 'avenues of sighs,' and kisses. It's not normal! In town, when one sits in one's lodgings, one does not notice the blank, but here in the fresh air one feels it. . . . One resents it!"

"Why is it?"

"I don't know. I suppose I've never had time, or perhaps it was I have never met women who. . . . In fact, I have very few acquaintances and never go anywhere."

For some three hundred paces the young people walked on in silence. Ognev kept glancing at Verotchka's bare head and shawl, and days of spring and summer rose to his mind one after another. It had been a period when far from his grey Petersburg lodgings, enjoying the friendly warmth of kind people, nature, and the work he loved, he had not had time to notice how the sunsets followed the glow of dawn, and how, one after another foretelling the end of summer, first the nightingale ceased singing, then the quail, then a little later the landrail. The days slipped by unnoticed, so that life must have been happy and easy. He began calling aloud how reluctantly he, poor and unaccustomed to change of scene and society, had come at the end of April to the N —— District, where he had expected dreariness, loneliness, and indifference to statistics, which he considered was now the foremost among the sciences. When he arrived on an April morning at the little town of N —— he had put up at the inn kept by Ryabuhin, the Old Believer, where for twenty kopecks a day they had given him a light, clean room on condition that he should not smoke indoors. After resting and finding who was the president of the District Zemstvo, he had set off at once on foot to Kuznetsov. He had to walk three miles through lush meadows and young copses. Larks were hovering in the clouds, filling the air with silvery notes, and rooks flapping their wings with sedate dignity floated over the green cornland.

"Good heavens!" Ognev had thought in wonder; "can it be that there's always air like this to breathe here, or is this scent only to-day, in honour of my coming?"

Expecting a cold business-like reception, he went in to Kuznetsov's diffidently, looking up from under his eyebrows and shyly pulling his beard. At first Kuznetsov wrinkled up his brows and could not understand what use the Zemstvo could be to the young man and his statistics; but when the latter explained at length what was material for statistics and how such material was collected, Kuznetsov brightened, smiled, and with childish curiosity began looking at his notebooks. On the evening of the same day Ivan Alexeyitch was already sitting at supper with the Kuznetsovs, was rapidly becoming exhilarated by their strong home-made wine, and looking at the calm faces and lazy movements of his new acquaintances, felt all over that sweet, drowsy indolence which makes one want to sleep and stretch and smile; while his new acquaintances looked at him good-naturedly and asked him whether his father and mother were living, how much he earned a month, how often he went to the theatre. . . .

Ognev recalled his expeditions about the neighbourhood, the picnics, the fishing parties, the visit of the whole party to the convent to see the Mother Superior Marfa, who had given each of the visitors a bead purse; he recalled the hot, endless typically Russian arguments in which the opponents, spluttering and banging the table with their fists, misunderstand and interrupt one another, unconsciously contradict themselves at every phrase, continually change the subject, and after arguing for two or three hours, laugh and say: "Goodness knows what we have been arguing about! Beginning with one thing and going on to another!"

"And do you remember how the doctor and you and I rode to Shestovo?" said Ivan Alexeyitch to Vera as they reached the copse. "It was there that the crazy saint met us: I gave him a five-kopeck piece, and he crossed himself three times and flung it into the rye. Good heavens! I am carrying away such a mass of memories that if I could gather them together into a whole it would make a good nugget of gold! I don't understand why clever, perceptive people crowd into Petersburg and Moscow and don't come here. Is there more truth and freedom in the Nevsky and in the big damp houses than here? Really, the idea of artists, scientific men, and journalists all living crowded together in furnished rooms has always seemed to me a mistake."

Twenty paces from the copse the road was crossed by a small narrow bridge with posts at the corners, which had always served as a resting-place for the Kuznetsovs and their guests on their evening walks. From there those who liked could mimic the forest echo, and one could see the road vanish in the dark woodland track.

"Well, here is the bridge!" said Ognev. "Here you must turn back."

Vera stopped and drew a breath.

"Let us sit down," she said, sitting down on one of the posts. "People generally sit down when they say good-bye before starting on a journey."

Ognev settled himself beside her on his bundle of books and went on talking. She was breathless from the walk, and was looking, not at Ivan Alexeyitch, but away into the distance so that he could not see her face.

"And what if we meet in ten years' time?" he said. "What shall we be like then? You will be by then the respectable mother of a family, and I shall be the author of some weighty statistical work of no use to anyone, as thick as forty thousand such works. We shall meet and think of old days. . . . Now we are conscious of the present; it absorbs and excites us, but when we meet we shall not remember the day, nor the month, nor even the year in which we saw each other for the last time on this bridge. You will be changed, perhaps . . . . Tell me, will you be different?"

Vera started and turned her face towards him.

"What?" she asked.

"I asked you just now. . . ."

"Excuse me, I did not hear what you were saying."

Only then Ognev noticed a change in Vera. She was pale, breathing fast, and the tremor in her breathing affected her hands and lips and head, and not one curl as usual, but two, came loose and fell on her forehead. . . . Evidently she avoided looking him in the face, and, trying to mask her emotion, at one moment fingered her collar, which seemed to be rasping her neck, at another pulled her red shawl from one shoulder to the other.

"I am afraid you are cold," said Ognev. "It's not at all wise to sit in the mist. Let me see you back *nach-haus*."

Vera sat mute.

"What is the matter?" asked Ognev, with a smile. "You sit silent and don't answer my questions. Are you cross, or don't you feel well?"

Vera pressed the palm of her hand to the cheek nearest to Ognev, and then abruptly jerked it away.

"An awful position!" she murmured, with a look of pain on her face. "Awful!"

"How is it awful?" asked Ognev, shrugging his shoulders and not concealing his surprise. "What's the matter?"

Still breathing hard and twitching her shoulders, Vera turned her back to him, looked at the sky for half a minute, and said:

"There is something I must say to you, Ivan Alexeyitch. . . ."

"I am listening."

"It may seem strange to you. . . . You will be surprised, but I don't care. . . ."

Ognev shrugged his shoulders once more and prepared himself to listen.

"You see . . ." Verotchka began, bowing her head and fingering a ball on the fringe of her shawl. "You see . . . this is what I wanted to tell you. . . . You'll think it strange . . . and silly, but I . . . can't bear it any longer."

Vera's words died away in an indistinct mutter and were suddenly cut short by tears. The girl hid her face in her handkerchief, bent lower than ever, and wept bitterly. Ivan Alexeyitch cleared his throat in confusion and looked about him hopelessly, at his wits' end, not knowing what to say or do. Being unused to the sight of tears, he felt his own eyes, too, beginning to smart.

"Well, what next!" he muttered helplessly. "Vera Gavrilovna, what's this for, I should like to know? My dear girl, are you . . . are you ill? Or has someone been nasty to you? Tell me, perhaps I could, so to say . . . help you. . . ."

When, trying to console her, he ventured cautiously to remove her hands from her face, she smiled at him through her tears and said:

"I . . . love you!"

These words, so simple and ordinary, were uttered in ordinary human language, but Ognev, in acute embarrassment, turned away from Vera, and got up, while his confusion was followed by terror.

The sad, warm, sentimental mood induced by leave-taking and the home-made wine suddenly vanished, and gave place to an acute and unpleasant feeling of awkwardness. He felt an inward revulsion; he looked askance at Vera, and now that by declaring her love for him she had cast off the aloofness which so adds to a woman's charm, she seemed to him, as it were, shorter, plainer, more ordinary.

"What's the meaning of it?" he thought with horror. "But I . . . do I love her or not? That's the question!"

And she breathed easily and freely now that the worst and most difficult thing was said. She, too, got up, and looking Ivan Alexeyitch straight in the face, began talking rapidly, warmly, irrepressibly.

As a man suddenly panic-stricken cannot afterwards remember the succession of sounds accompanying the catastrophe that overwhelmed him, so Ognev cannot remember Vera's words and phrases. He can only recall the meaning of what she said, and the sensation her words evoked in him. He remembers her voice, which seemed stifled and husky with emotion, and the extraordinary music and passion of her intonation. Laughing, crying with tears glistening on her eyelashes, she told him that from the first day of their acquaintance he had struck her by his originality, his intelligence, his kind intelligent eyes, by his work and objects in life; that she loved him passionately, deeply, madly; that when coming into the house from the garden in the summer she saw his cape in the hall or heard his voice in the distance, she felt a cold shudder at her heart, a foreboding of happiness; even his slightest jokes had made her laugh; in every figure in his note-books she saw something extraordinarily wise and grand; his knotted stick seemed to her more beautiful than the trees.

The copse and the wisps of mist and the black ditches at the side of the road seemed hushed listening to her, whilst something strange and unpleasant was passing in Ognev's heart. . . . Telling him of her love, Vera was enchantingly beautiful; she spoke eloquently and passionately, but he felt neither pleasure nor gladness, as he would have liked to; he felt nothing but compassion for Vera, pity and regret that a good girl should be distressed on his account. Whether he was affected by generalizations from reading or by the insuperable habit of looking at things objectively, which so often hinders people from living, but Vera's ecstasies and suffering struck him as affected, not to be taken seriously, and at the same time rebellious feeling whispered to him that all he was hearing and seeing now, from the point of view of nature and personal happiness, was more important than any statistics and books and truths. . . . And he raged and blamed himself, though he did not understand exactly where he was in fault.

To complete his embarrassment, he was absolutely at a loss what to say, and yet something he must say. To say bluntly, "I don't love you," was beyond him, and he could not bring himself to say "Yes," because however much he rummaged in his heart he could not find one spark of feeling in it. . . .

He was silent, and she meanwhile was saying that for her there was no greater happiness than to see him, to follow him wherever he liked this very moment, to be his wife and helper, and that if he went away from her she would die of misery.

"I cannot stay here!" she said, wringing her hands. "I am sick of the house and this wood and the air. I cannot bear the everlasting peace and aimless life, I can't endure our colourless, pale people, who are all as like one another as two drops of water! They are all good-natured and warm-hearted because they are all well-fed and know nothing of struggle or suffering, . . . I want to be in those big damp houses where people suffer, embittered by work and need. . ."

And this, too, seemed to Ognev affected and not to be taken seriously. When Vera had finished he still did not know what to say, but it was impossible to be silent, and he muttered:

"Vera Gavrilovna, I am very grateful to you, though I feel I've done nothing to deserve such . . . feeling . . . on your part. Besides, as an honest man I ought to tell you that . . . happiness depends on equality—that is, when both parties are . . . equally in love. . . ."

But he was immediately ashamed of his mutterings and ceased. He felt that his face at that moment looked stupid, guilty, blank, that it was strained and affected. . . . Vera must have been able to read the truth on his countenance, for she suddenly became grave, turned pale, and bent her head.

"You must forgive me," Ognev muttered, not able to endure the silence. "I respect you so much that . . . it pains me. . . ."

Vera turned sharply and walked rapidly homewards. Ognev followed her.

"No, don't!" said Vera, with a wave of her hand. "Don't come; I can go alone."

"Oh, yes . . . I must see you home anyway."

Whatever Ognev said, it all to the last word struck him as loathsome and flat. The feeling of guilt grew greater at every step. He raged inwardly, clenched his fists, and cursed his coldness and his stupidity with women. Trying to stir his feelings, he looked at Verotchka's beautiful figure, at her hair and the traces of her little feet on the dusty road; he remembered her words and her tears, but all that only touched his heart and did not quicken his pulse.

"Ach! one can't force oneself to love," he assured himself, and at the same time he thought, "But shall I ever fall in love without? I am nearly thirty! I have never met anyone better than Vera and I never shall. . . . Oh, this premature old age! Old age at thirty!"

Vera walked on in front more and more rapidly, without looking back at him or raising her head. It seemed to him that sorrow had made her thinner and narrower in the shoulders.

"I can imagine what's going on in her heart now!" he thought, looking at her back. "She must be ready to die with shame and mortification! My God, there's so much life, poetry, and meaning in it that it would move a stone, and I . . . I am stupid and absurd!"

At the gate Vera stole a glance at him, and, shrugging and wrapping her shawl round her walked rapidly away down the avenue.

Ivan Alexeyitch was left alone. Going back to the copse, he walked slowly, continually standing still and looking round at the gate with an expression in his whole figure that suggested that he could not believe his own memory. He looked for Vera's footprints on the road, and could not believe that the girl who had so attracted him had just declared her love, and that he had so clumsily and bluntly "refused" her. For the first time in his life it was his lot to learn by experience how little that a man does depends on his own will, and to suffer in his own person the feelings of a decent kindly man who has against his will caused his neighbour cruel, undeserved anguish.

His conscience tormented him, and when Vera disappeared he felt as though he had lost something very precious, something very near and dear which he could never find again. He felt that with Vera a part of his youth had slipped away from him, and that the moments which he had passed through so fruitlessly would never be repeated.

When he reached the bridge he stopped and sank into thought. He wanted to discover the reason of his strange coldness. That it was due to something within him and not outside himself was clear to him. He frankly acknowledged to himself that it was not the intellectual coldness of which clever people so often boast, not the coldness of a conceited fool, but simply impotence of soul, incapacity for being moved by beauty, premature old age brought on by education, his casual existence, struggling for a livelihood, his homeless life in lodgings. From the bridge he walked slowly, as it were reluctantly, into the wood. Here, where in the dense black darkness glaring patches of moonlight gleamed here and there, where he felt nothing except his thoughts, he longed passionately to regain what he had lost.

And Ivan Alexeyitch remembers that he went back again. Urging himself on with his memories, forcing himself to picture Vera, he strode rapidly towards the garden. There was no mist by then along the road or in the garden, and the bright moon looked down from the sky as though it had just been washed; only the eastern sky was dark and misty. . . . Ognev remembers his cautious steps, the dark windows, the heavy scent of heliotrope and mignonette. His old friend Karo, wagging his tail amicably, came up to him and sniffed his hand. This was the one living creature who saw him walk two or three times round the house, stand near Vera's dark window, and with a deep sigh and a wave of his hand walk out of the garden.

An hour later he was in the town, and, worn out and exhausted, leaned his body and hot face against the gatepost of the inn as he knocked at the gate. Somewhere in the town a dog barked sleepily, and as though in response to his knock, someone clanged the hour on an iron plate near the church.

"You prowl about at night," grumbled his host, the Old Believer, opening the door to him, in a long nightgown like a woman's. "You had better be saying your prayers instead of prowling about."

When Ivan Alexeyitch reached his room he sank on the bed and gazed a long, long time at the light. Then he tossed his head and began packing.

## MY LIFE

## THE STORY OF A PROVINCIAL

### I

THE Superintendent said to me: "I only keep you out of regard for your worthy father; but for that you would have been sent flying long ago." I replied to him: "You flatter me too much, your Excellency, in assuming that I am capable of flying." And then I heard him say: "Take that gentleman away; he gets upon my nerves."

Two days later I was dismissed. And in this way I have, during the years I have been regarded as grown up, lost nine situations, to the great mortification of my father, the architect of our town. I have served in various departments, but all these nine jobs have been as alike as one drop of water is to another: I had to sit, write, listen to rude or stupid observations, and go on doing so till I was dismissed.

When I came in to my father he was sitting buried in a low arm-chair with his eyes closed. His dry, emaciated face, with a shade of dark blue where it was shaved (he looked like an old Catholic organist), expressed meekness and resignation. Without responding to my greeting or opening his eyes, he said:

"If my dear wife and your mother were living, your life would have been a source of continual distress to her. I see the Divine Providence in her premature death. I beg you, unhappy boy," he continued, opening his eyes, "tell me: what am I to do with you?"

In the past when I was younger my friends and relations had known what to do with me: some of them used to advise me to volunteer for the army, others to get a job in a pharmacy, and others in the telegraph department; now that I am over twenty-five, that grey hairs are beginning to show on my temples, and that I have been already in the army, and in a pharmacy, and in the telegraph department, it would seem that all earthly possibilities have been exhausted, and people have given up advising me, and merely sigh or shake their heads.

"What do you think about yourself?" my father went on. "By the time they are your age, young men have a secure social position, while look at you: you are a proletarian, a beggar, a burden on your father!"

And as usual he proceeded to declare that the young people of to-day were on the road to perdition through infidelity, materialism, and self-conceit, and that amateur theatricals ought to be prohibited, because they seduced young people from religion and their duties.

"To-morrow we shall go together, and you shall apologize to the superintendent, and promise him to work conscientiously," he said in conclusion. "You ought not to remain one single day with no regular position in society."

"I beg you to listen to me," I said sullenly, expecting nothing good from this conversation. "What you call a position in society is the privilege of capital and education. Those who have neither wealth nor education earn their daily bread by manual labour, and I see no grounds for my being an exception."

"When you begin talking about manual labour it is always stupid and vulgar!" said my father with irritation. "Understand, you dense fellow—understand, you addle-pate, that besides coarse physical strength you have the divine spirit, a spark of the holy fire, which distinguishes you in the most striking way from the ass or the reptile, and brings you nearer to the Deity! This fire is the fruit of the efforts of the best of mankind during thousands of years. Your great-grandfather Poloznev, the general, fought at Borodino; your grandfather was a poet, an orator, and a Marshal of Nobility; your uncle is a schoolmaster; and lastly, I, your father, am an architect! All the Poloznevs have guarded the sacred fire for you to put it out!"

"One must be just," I said. "Millions of people put up with manual labour."

"And let them put up with it! They don't know how to do anything else! Anybody, even the most abject fool or criminal, is capable of manual labour; such labour is the distinguishing mark of the slave and the barbarian, while the holy fire is vouchsafed only to a few!"

To continue this conversation was unprofitable. My father worshipped himself, and nothing was convincing to him but what he said himself. Besides, I knew perfectly well that the disdain with which he talked of physical toil was founded not so much on reverence for the sacred fire as on a secret dread that I should become a workman, and should set the whole town talking about me; what was worse, all my contemporaries had long ago taken their degrees and were getting on well, and the son of the manager of the State Bank was already a collegiate assessor, while I, his only son, was nothing! To continue the conversation was unprofitable and unpleasant, but I still sat on and feebly retorted, hoping that I might at last be understood. The whole question, of course, was clear and simple, and only concerned with the means of my earning my living; but the simplicity of it was not seen, and I was talked to in mawkishly rounded phrases of Borodino, of the sacred fire, of my uncle a forgotten poet, who had once written poor and artificial verses; I was rudely called an addlepate and a dense fellow. And how I longed to be understood! In spite of everything, I loved my father and my sister and it had been my habit from childhood to consult them—a habit so deeply rooted that I doubt whether I could ever have got rid of it; whether I were in the right or the wrong, I was in constant dread of wounding them, constantly afraid that my father's thin neck would turn crimson and that he would have a stroke.

"To sit in a stuffy room," I began, "to copy, to compete with a typewriter, is shameful and humiliating for a man of my age. What can the sacred fire have to do with it?"

"It's intellectual work, anyway," said my father. "But that's enough; let us cut short this conversation, and in any case I warn you: if you don't go back to your work again, but follow your contemptible propensities, then my daughter and I will banish you from our hearts. I shall strike you out of my will, I swear by the living God!"

With perfect sincerity to prove the purity of the motives by which I wanted to be guided in all my doings, I said:

"The question of inheritance does not seem very important to me. I shall renounce it all beforehand."

For some reason or other, quite to my surprise, these words were deeply resented by my father. He turned crimson.

"Don't dare to talk to me like that, stupid!" he shouted in a thin, shrill voice. "Wastrel!" and with a rapid, skilful, and habitual movement he slapped me twice in the face. "You are forgetting yourself."

When my father beat me as a child I had to stand up straight, with my hands held stiffly to my trouser seams, and look him straight in the face. And now when he hit me I was utterly overwhelmed, and, as though I were still a child, drew myself up and tried to look him in the face. My father was old and very thin but his delicate muscles must have been as strong as leather, for his blows hurt a good deal.

I staggered back into the passage, and there he snatched up his umbrella, and with it hit me several times on the head and shoulders; at that moment my sister opened the drawing-room door to find out what the noise was, but at once turned away with a look of horror and pity without uttering a word in my defence.

My determination not to return to the Government office, but to begin a new life of toil, was not to be shaken. All that was left for me to do was to fix upon the special employment, and there was no particular difficulty about that, as it seemed to me that I was very strong and fitted for the very heaviest labour. I was faced with a monotonous life of toil in the midst of hunger, coarseness, and stench, continually preoccupied with earning my daily bread. And—who knows?—as I returned from my work along Great Dvoryansky Street, I might very likely envy Dolzhikov, the engineer, who lived by intellectual work, but, at the moment, thinking over all my future hardships made me light-hearted. At times I had dreamed of spiritual activity, imagining myself a teacher, a doctor, or a writer, but these dreams remained dreams. The taste for intellectual pleasures—for the theatre, for instance, and for reading—was a passion with me, but whether I had any ability for intellectual work I don't know. At school I had had an unconquerable aversion for Greek, so that I was only in the fourth class when they had to take me from school. For a long while I had coaches preparing me for the fifth class. Then I served in various Government offices, spending the greater part of the day in complete idleness, and I was told that was intellectual work. My activity in the scholastic and official sphere had required neither mental application nor talent, nor special qualifications, nor creative impulse; it was mechanical. Such intellectual work I put on a lower level than physical toil; I despise it, and I don't think that for one moment it could serve as a justification for an idle, careless life, as it is indeed nothing but a sham, one of the forms of that same idleness. Real intellectual work I have in all probability never known.

Evening came on. We lived in Great Dvoryansky Street; it was the principal street in the town, and in the absence of decent public gardens our *beau monde* used to use it as a promenade in the evenings. This charming street did to some extent take the place of a public garden, as on each side of it there was a row of poplars which smelt sweet, particularly after rain, and acacias, tall bushes of lilac, wild-cherries and apple-trees hung over the fences and palings. The May twilight, the tender young greenery with its shifting shades, the scent of the lilac, the buzzing of the insects, the stillness, the warmth—how fresh and marvellous it all is, though spring is repeated every year! I stood at the garden gate and watched the passers-by. With most of them I had grown up and at one time played pranks; now they might have been disconcerted by my being near them, for I was poorly and unfashionably dressed, and they used to say of my very narrow trousers and huge, clumsy boots that they were like sticks of macaroni stuck in boats. Besides, I had a bad reputation in the town because I had no decent social position, and used often to play billiards in cheap taverns, and also, perhaps, because I had on two occasions been hauled up before an officer of the police, though I had done nothing whatever to account for this.

In the big house opposite someone was playing the piano at Dolzhikov's. It was beginning to get dark, and stars were twinkling in the sky. Here my father, in an old top-hat with wide upturned brim, walked slowly by with my sister on his arm, bowing in response to greetings.

"Look up," he said to my sister, pointing to the sky with the same umbrella with which he had beaten me that afternoon. "Look up at the sky! Even the tiniest stars are all worlds! How insignificant is man in comparison with the universe!"

And he said this in a tone that suggested that it was particularly agreeable and flattering to him that he was so insignificant. How absolutely devoid of talent and imagination he was! Sad to say, he was the only architect in the town, and in the fifteen to twenty years that I could remember not one single decent house had been built in it. When any one asked him to plan a house, he usually drew first the reception hall and drawing-room: just as in old days the boarding-school misses always started from the stove when they danced, so his artistic ideas could only begin and develop from the hall and drawing-room. To them he tacked on a dining-room, a nursery, a study, linking the rooms together with doors, and so they all inevitably turned into passages, and every one of them had two or even three unnecessary doors. His imagination must have been lacking in clearness, extremely muddled, curtailed. As though feeling that something was lacking, he invariably had recourse to all sorts of outbuildings, planting one beside another; and I can see now the narrow entries, the poky little passages, the crooked staircases leading to half-landings where one could not stand upright, and where, instead of a floor, there were three huge steps like the shelves of a bath-house; and the kitchen was invariably in the basement with a brick floor and vaulted ceilings. The front of the house had a harsh, stubborn expression; the lines of it were stiff and timid; the roof was low-pitched and, as it were, squashed down; and the fat, well-fed-looking chimneys were invariably crowned by wire caps with squeaking black cowls. And for some reason all these houses, built by my father exactly like one another, vaguely reminded me of his top-hat and the back of his head, stiff and stubborn-looking. In the course of years they have grown used in the town to the poverty of my father's imagination. It has taken root and become our local style.

This same style my father had brought into my sister's life also, beginning with christening her Kleopatra (just as he had named me Misail). When she was a little girl he scared her by references to the stars, to the sages of ancient times, to our ancestors, and discoursed at length on the nature of life and duty; and now, when she was twenty-six, he kept up the same habits, allowing her to walk arm in arm with no one but himself, and imagining for some reason that sooner or later a suitable young man would be sure to appear, and to desire to enter into matrimony with her from respect for his personal qualities. She adored my father, feared him, and believed in his exceptional intelligence.

It was quite dark, and gradually the street grew empty. The music had ceased in the house opposite; the gate was thrown wide open, and a team with three horses trotted frolicking along our street with a soft tinkle of little bells. That was the engineer going for a drive with his daughter. It was bedtime.

I had my own room in the house, but I lived in a shed in the yard, under the same roof as a brick barn which had been built some time or other, probably to keep harness in; great hooks were driven into the wall. Now it was not wanted, and for the last thirty years my father had stowed away in it his newspapers, which for some reason he had bound in half-yearly volumes and allowed nobody to touch. Living here, I was less liable to be seen by my father and his visitors, and I fancied that if I did not live in a real room, and did not go into the house every day to dinner, my father's words that I was a burden upon him did not sound so offensive.

My sister was waiting for me. Unseen by my father, she had brought me some supper: not a very large slice of cold veal and a piece of bread. In our house such sayings as: "A penny saved is a penny gained," and "Take care of the pence and the pounds will take care of themselves," and so on, were frequently repeated, and my sister, weighed down by these vulgar maxims, did her utmost to cut down the expenses, and so we fared badly. Putting the plate on the table, she sat down on my bed and began to cry.

"Misail," she said, "what a way to treat us!"

She did not cover her face; her tears dropped on her bosom and hands, and there was a look of distress on her face. She fell back on the pillow, and abandoned herself to her tears, sobbing and quivering all over.

"You have left the service again . . ." she articulated. "Oh, how awful it is!"

"But do understand, sister, do understand . . . ." I said, and I was overcome with despair because she was crying.

As ill-luck would have it, the kerosene in my little lamp was exhausted; it began to smoke, and was on the point of going out, and the old hooks on the walls looked down sullenly, and their shadows flickered.

"Have mercy on us," said my sister, sitting up. "Father is in terrible distress and I am ill; I shall go out of my mind. What will become of you?" she said, sobbing and stretching out her arms to me. "I beg you, I implore you, for our dear mother's sake, I beg you to go back to the office!"

"I can't, Kleopatra!" I said, feeling that a little more and I should give way. "I cannot!"

"Why not?" my sister went on. "Why not? Well, if you can't get on with the Head, look out for another post. Why shouldn't you get a situation on the railway, for instance? I have just been talking to Anyuta Blagovo; she declares they would take you on the railway-line, and even promised to try and get a post for you. For God's sake, Misail, think a little! Think a little, I implore you."

We talked a little longer and I gave way. I said that the thought of a job on the railway that was being constructed had never occurred to me, and that if she liked I was ready to try it.

She smiled joyfully through her tears and squeezed my hand, and then went on crying because she could not stop, while I went to the kitchen for some kerosene.

## II

Among the devoted supporters of amateur theatricals, concerts and *tableaux vivants* for charitable objects the Azhogins, who lived in their own house in Great Dvoryansky Street, took a foremost place; they always provided the room, and took upon themselves all the troublesome arrangements and the expenses. They were a family of wealthy landowners who had an estate of some nine thousand acres in the district and a capital house, but they did not care for the country, and lived winter and summer alike in the town. The family consisted of the mother, a tall, spare, refined lady, with short hair, a short jacket, and a flat-looking skirt in the English fashion, and three daughters who, when they were spoken of, were called not by their names but simply: the eldest, the middle, and the youngest. They all had ugly sharp chins, and were short-sighted and round-shouldered. They were dressed like their mother, they lisped disagreeably, and yet, in spite of that, infallibly took part in every performance and were continually doing something with a charitable object—acting, reciting, singing. They were very serious and never smiled, and even in a musical comedy they played without the faintest trace of gaiety, with a businesslike air, as though they were engaged in bookkeeping.

I loved our theatricals, especially the numerous, noisy, and rather incoherent rehearsals, after which they always gave a supper. In the choice of the plays and the distribution of the parts I had no hand at all. The post assigned to me lay behind the scenes. I painted the scenes, copied out the parts, prompted, made up the actors' faces; and I was entrusted, too, with various stage effects such as thunder, the singing of nightingales, and so on. Since I had no proper social position and no decent clothes, at the rehearsals I held aloof from the rest in the shadows of the wings and maintained a shy silence.

I painted the scenes at the Azhogins' either in the barn or in the yard. I was assisted by Andrey Ivanov, a house painter, or, as he called himself, a contractor for all kinds of house decorations, a tall, very thin, pale man of fifty, with a hollow chest, with sunken temples, with blue rings round his eyes, rather terrible to look at in fact. He was afflicted with some internal malady, and every autumn and spring people said that he wouldn't recover, but after being laid up for a while he would get up and say afterwards with surprise: "I have escaped dying again."

In the town he was called Radish, and they declared that this was his real name. He was as fond of the theatre as I was, and as soon as rumours reached him that a performance was being got up he threw aside all his work and went to the Azhogins' to paint scenes.

The day after my talk with my sister, I was working at the Azhogins' from morning till night. The rehearsal was fixed for seven o'clock in the evening, and an hour before it began all the amateurs were gathered together in the hall, and the eldest, the middle, and the youngest Azhogins were pacing about the stage, reading from manuscript books. Radish, in a long rusty-red overcoat and a scarf muffled round his neck, already stood leaning with his head against the wall, gazing with a devout expression at the stage. Madame Azhogin went up first to one and then to another guest, saying something agreeable to each. She had a way of gazing into one's face, and speaking softly as though telling a secret.

"It must be difficult to paint scenery," she said softly, coming up to me. "I was just talking to Madame Mufke about superstitions when I saw you come in. My goodness, my whole life I have been waging war against superstitions! To convince the servants what nonsense all their terrors are, I always light three candles, and begin all my important undertakings on the thirteenth of the month."

Dolzhikov's daughter came in, a plump, fair beauty, dressed, as people said, in everything from Paris. She did not act, but a chair was set for her on the stage at the rehearsals, and the performances never began till she had appeared in the front row, dazzling and astounding everyone with her fine clothes. As a product of the capital she was allowed to make remarks during the rehearsals; and she did so with a sweet indulgent smile, and one could see that she looked upon our performance as a childish amusement. It was said she had studied singing at the Petersburg Conservatoire, and even sang for a whole winter in a private opera. I thought her very charming, and I usually watched her through the rehearsals and performances without taking my eyes off her.

I had just picked up the manuscript book to begin prompting when my sister suddenly made her appearance. Without taking off her cloak or hat, she came up to me and said:

"Come along, I beg you."

I went with her. Anyuta Blagovo, also in her hat and wearing a dark veil, was standing behind the scenes at the door. She was the daughter of the Assistant President of the Court, who had held that office in our town almost ever since the establishment of the circuit court. Since she was tall and had a good figure, her assistance was considered indispensable for *tableaux vivants*, and when she represented a fairy or something like Glory her face burned with shame; but she took no part in dramatic performances, and came to the rehearsals only for a moment on some special errand, and did not go into the hall. Now, too, it was evident that she had only looked in for a minute.

"My father was speaking about you," she said drily, blushing and not looking at me. "Dolzhikov has promised you a post on the railway-line. Apply to him to-morrow; he will be at home."

I bowed and thanked her for the trouble she had taken.

"And you can give up this," she said, indicating the exercise book.

My sister and she went up to Madame Azhogin and for two minutes they were whispering with her looking towards me; they were consulting about something.

"Yes, indeed," said Madame Azhogin, softly coming up to me and looking intently into my face. "Yes, indeed, if this distracts you from serious pursuits"—she took the manuscript book from my hands—"you can hand it over to someone else; don't distress yourself, my friend, go home, and good luck to you."

I said good-bye to her, and went away overcome with confusion. As I went down the stairs I saw my sister and Anyuta Blagovo going away; they were hastening along, talking eagerly about something, probably about my going into the railway service. My sister had never been at a rehearsal before, and now she was most likely conscience-stricken, and afraid her father might find out that, without his permission, she had been to the Azhogins'!

I went to Dolzhikov's next day between twelve and one. The footman conducted me into a very beautiful room, which was the engineer's drawing-room, and, at the same time, his working study. Everything here was soft and elegant, and, for a man so unaccustomed to luxury as I was, it seemed strange. There were costly rugs, huge arm-chairs, bronzes, pictures, gold and plush frames; among the photographs scattered about the walls there were very beautiful women, clever, lovely faces, easy attitudes; from the drawing-room there was a door leading straight into the garden on to a verandah: one could see lilac-trees; one could see a table laid for lunch, a number of bottles, a bouquet of roses; there was a fragrance of spring and expensive cigars, a fragrance of happiness—and everything seemed as though it would say: "Here is a man who has lived and laboured, and has attained at last the happiness possible on earth." The engineer's daughter was sitting at the writing-table, reading a newspaper.

"You have come to see my father?" she asked. "He is having a shower bath; he will be here directly. Please sit down and wait."

I sat down.

"I believe you live opposite?" she questioned me, after a brief silence.

"Yes."

"I am so bored that I watch you every day out of the window; you must excuse me," she went on, looking at the newspaper, "and I often see your sister; she always has such a look of kindness and concentration."

Dolzhikov came in. He was rubbing his neck with a towel.

"Papa, Monsieur Poloznev," said his daughter.

"Yes, yes, Blagovo was telling me," he turned briskly to me without giving me his hand. "But listen, what can I give you? What sort of posts have I got? You are a queer set of people!" he went on aloud in a tone as though he were giving me a lecture. "A score of you keep coming to me every day; you imagine I am the head of a department! I am constructing a railway-line, my friends; I have employment for heavy labour: I need mechanics, smiths, navvies, carpenters, well-sinkers, and none of you can do anything but sit and write! You are all clerks."

And he seemed to me to have the same air of happiness as his rugs and easy chairs. He was stout and healthy, ruddy-cheeked and broad-chested, in a print cotton shirt and full trousers like a toy china sledge-driver. He had a curly, round beard—and not a single grey hair—a hooked nose, and clear, dark, guileless eyes.

"What can you do?" he went on. "There is nothing you can do! I am an engineer. I am a man of an assured position, but before they gave me a railway-line I was for years in harness; I have been a practical mechanic. For two years I worked in Belgium as an oiler. You can judge for yourself, my dear fellow, what kind of work can I offer you?"

"Of course that is so . . ." I muttered in extreme confusion, unable to face his clear, guileless eyes.

"Can you work the telegraph, any way?" he asked, after a moment's thought.

"Yes, I have been a telegraph clerk."

"Hm! Well, we will see then. Meanwhile, go to Dubetchnya. I have got a fellow there, but he is a wretched creature."

"And what will my duties consist of?" I asked.

"We shall see. Go there; meanwhile I will make arrangements. Only please don't get drunk, and don't worry me with requests of any sort, or I shall send you packing."

He turned away from me without even a nod.

I bowed to him and his daughter who was reading a newspaper, and went away. My heart felt so heavy, that when my sister began asking me how the engineer had received me, I could not utter a single word.

I got up early in the morning, at sunrise, to go to Dubetchnya. There was not a soul in our Great Dvoryansky Street; everyone was asleep, and my footsteps rang out with a solitary, hollow sound. The poplars, covered with dew, filled the air with soft fragrance. I was sad, and did not want to go away from the town. I was fond of my native town. It seemed to be so beautiful and so snug! I loved the fresh greenery, the still, sunny morning, the chiming of our bells; but the people with whom I lived in this town were boring, alien to me, sometimes even repulsive. I did not like them nor understand them.

I did not understand what these sixty-five thousand people lived for and by. I knew that Kimry lived by boots, that Tula made samovars and guns, that Odessa was a sea-port, but what our town was, and what it did, I did not know. Great Dvoryansky Street and the two other smartest streets lived on the interest of capital, or on salaries received by officials from the public treasury; but what the other eight streets, which ran parallel for over two miles and vanished beyond the hills, lived upon, was always an insoluble riddle to me. And the way those people lived one is ashamed to describe! No garden, no theatre, no decent band; the public library and the club library were only visited by Jewish youths, so that the magazines and new books lay for months uncut; rich and well-educated people slept in close, stuffy bedrooms, on wooden bedsteads infested with bugs; their children were kept in revoltingly dirty rooms called nurseries, and the servants, even the old and respected ones, slept on the floor in the kitchen, covered with rags. On ordinary days the houses smelt of beetroot soup, and on fast days of sturgeon cooked in sunflower oil. The food was not good, and the drinking water was unwholesome. In the town council, at the governor's, at the head priest's, on all sides in private houses, people had been saying for years and years that our town had not a good and cheap water-supply, and that it was necessary to obtain a loan of two hundred thousand from the Treasury for laying on water; very rich people, of whom three dozen could have been counted up in our town, and who at times lost whole estates at cards, drank the polluted water, too, and talked all their lives with great excitement of a loan for the water-supply—and I did not understand that; it seemed to me it would have been simpler to take the two hundred thousand out of their own pockets and lay it out on that object.

I did not know one honest man in the town. My father took bribes, and imagined that they were given him out of respect for his moral qualities; at the high school, in order to be moved up rapidly from class to class, the boys went to board with their teachers, who charged them exorbitant sums; the wife of the military commander took bribes from the recruits when they were called up before the board and even deigned to accept refreshments from them, and on one occasion could not get up from her knees in church because she was drunk; the doctors took bribes, too, when the recruits came up for examination, and the town doctor and the veterinary surgeon levied a regular tax on the butchers' shops and the restaurants; at the district school they did a trade in certificates, qualifying for partial exemption from military service; the higher clergy took bribes from the humbler priests and from the church elders; at the Municipal, the Artisans', and all the other Boards every petitioner was pursued by a shout: "Don't forget your thanks!" and the petitioner would turn back to give sixpence or a shilling. And those who did not take bribes, such as the higher officials of the Department of Justice, were haughty, offered two fingers instead of shaking hands, were distinguished by the frigidity and narrowness of their judgments, spent a great deal of time over cards, drank to excess, married heiresses, and undoubtedly had a pernicious corrupting influence on those around them. It was only the girls who had still the fresh fragrance of moral purity; most of them had higher impulses, pure and honest hearts; but they had no understanding of life, and believed that bribes were given out of respect for moral qualities, and after they were married grew old quickly, let themselves go completely, and sank hopelessly in the mire of vulgar, petty bourgeois existence.

### III

A railway-line was being constructed in our neighbourhood. On the eve of feast days the streets were thronged with ragged fellows whom the townspeople called "navvies," and of whom they were afraid. And more than once I had seen one of these tatterdemalions with a bloodstained countenance being led to the police station, while a samovar or some linen, wet from the wash, was carried behind by way of material evidence. The navvies usually congregated about the taverns and the market-place; they drank, ate, and used bad language, and pursued with shrill whistles every woman of light behaviour who passed by. To entertain this hungry rabble our shopkeepers made cats and dogs drunk with vodka, or tied an old kerosene can to a dog's tail; a hue and cry was raised, and the dog dashed along the street, jingling the can, squealing with terror; it fancied some monster was close upon its heels; it would run far out of the town into the open country and there sink exhausted. There were in the town several dogs who went about trembling with their tails between their legs; and people said this diversion had been too much for them, and had driven them mad.

A station was being built four miles from the town. It was said that the engineers asked for a bribe of fifty thousand roubles for bringing the line right up to the town, but the town council would only consent to give forty thousand; they could not come to an agreement over the difference, and now the townspeople regretted it, as they had to make a road to the station and that, it was reckoned, would cost more. The sleepers and rails had been laid throughout the whole length of the line, and trains ran up and down it, bringing building materials and labourers, and further progress was only delayed on account of the bridges which Dolzhikov was building, and some of the stations were not yet finished.

Dubetchnya, as our first station was called, was a little under twelve miles from the town. I walked. The cornfields, bathed in the morning sunshine, were bright green. It was a flat, cheerful country, and in the distance there were the distinct outlines of the station, of ancient barrows, and far-away homesteads. . . . How nice it was out there in the open! And how I longed to be filled with the sense of freedom, if only for that one morning, that I might not think of what was being done in the town, not think of my needs, not feel hungry! Nothing has so marred my existence as an acute feeling of hunger, which made images of buckwheat porridge, rissoles, and baked fish mingle strangely with my best thoughts. Here I was standing alone in the open country, gazing upward at a lark which hovered in the air at the same spot, trilling as though in hysterics, and meanwhile I was thinking: "How nice it would be to eat a piece of bread and butter!"

Or I would sit down by the roadside to rest, and shut my eyes to listen to the delicious sounds of May, and what haunted me was the smell of hot potatoes. Though I was tall and strongly built, I had as a rule little to eat, and so the predominant sensation throughout the day was hunger, and perhaps that was why I knew so well how it is that such multitudes of people toil merely for their daily bread, and can talk of nothing but things to eat.

At Dubetchnya they were plastering the inside of the station, and building a wooden upper storey to the pumping shed. It was hot; there was a smell of lime, and the workmen sauntered listlessly between the heaps of shavings and mortar rubble. The pointsman lay asleep near his sentry box, and the sun was blazing full on his face. There was not a single tree. The telegraph wire hummed faintly and hawks were perching on it here and there. I, wandering, too, among the heaps of rubbish, and not knowing what to do, recalled how the engineer, in answer to my question what my duties would consist in, had said: "We shall see when you are there"; but what could one see in that wilderness?

The plasterers spoke of the foreman, and of a certain Fyodot Vasilyev. I did not understand, and gradually I was overcome by depression—the physical depression in which one is conscious of one's arms and legs and huge body, and does not know what to do with them or where to put them.

After I had been walking about for at least a couple of hours, I noticed that there were telegraph poles running off to the right from the station, and that they ended a mile or a mile and a half away at a white stone wall. The workmen told me the office was there, and at last I reflected that that was where I ought to go.

It was a very old manor house, deserted long ago. The wall round it, of porous white stone, was mouldering and had fallen away in places, and the lodge, the blank wall of which looked out on the open country, had a rusty roof with patches of tin-plate gleaming here and there on it. Within the gates could be seen a spacious courtyard overgrown with rough weeds, and an old manor house with sunblinds on the windows, and a high roof red with rust. Two lodges, exactly alike, stood one on each side of the house to right and to left: one had its windows nailed up with boards; near the other, of which the windows were open, there was washing on the line, and there were calves moving about. The last of the telegraph poles stood in the courtyard, and the wire from it ran to the window of the lodge, of which the blank wall looked out into the open country. The door stood open; I went in. By the telegraph apparatus a gentleman with a curly dark head, wearing a reefer coat made of sailcloth, was sitting at a table; he glanced at me morosely from under his brows, but immediately smiled and said:

"Hullo, Better-than-nothing!"

It was Ivan Tcheprakov, an old schoolfellow of mine, who had been expelled from the second class for smoking. We used at one time, during autumn, to catch goldfinches, finches, and linnets together, and to sell them in the market early in the morning, while our parents were still in their beds. We watched for flocks of migrating starlings and shot at them with small shot, then we picked up those that were wounded, and some of them died in our hands in terrible agonies (I remember to this day how they moaned in the cage at night); those that recovered we sold, and swore with the utmost effrontery that they were all cocks. On one occasion at the market I had only one starling left, which I had offered to purchasers in vain, till at last I sold it for a farthing. "Anyway, it's better than nothing," I said to comfort myself, as I put the farthing in my pocket, and from that day the street urchins and the schoolboys called after me: "Better-than-nothing"; and to this day the street boys and the shopkeepers mock at me with the nickname, though no one remembers how it arose.

Tcheprakov was not of robust constitution: he was narrow-chested, round-shouldered, and long-legged. He wore a silk cord for a tie, had no trace of a waistcoat, and his boots were worse than mine, with the heels trodden down on one side. He stared, hardly even blinking, with a strained expression, as though he were just going to catch something, and he was always in a fuss.

"You wait a minute," he would say fussily. "You listen. . . . Whatever was I talking about?"

We got into conversation. I learned that the estate on which I now was had until recently been the property of the Tcheprakovs, and had only the autumn before passed into the possession of Dolzhikov, who considered it more profitable to put his money into land than to keep it in notes, and had already bought up three good-sized mortgaged estates in our neighbourhood. At the sale Tcheprakov's mother had reserved for herself the right to live for the next two years in one of the lodges at the side, and had obtained a post for her son in the office.

"I should think he could buy!" Tcheprakov said of the engineer. "See what he fleeces out of the contractors alone! He fleeces everyone!"

Then he took me to dinner, deciding fussily that I should live with him in the lodge, and have my meals from his mother.

"She is a bit stingy," he said, "but she won't charge you much."

It was very cramped in the little rooms in which his mother lived; they were all, even the passage and the entry, piled up with furniture which had been brought from the big house after the sale; and the furniture was all old-fashioned mahogany. Madame Tcheprakov, a very stout middle-aged lady with slanting Chinese eyes, was sitting in a big arm-chair by the window, knitting a stocking. She received me ceremoniously.

"This is Poloznev, mamma," Tcheprakov introduced me. "He is going to serve here."

"Are you a nobleman?" she asked in a strange, disagreeable voice: it seemed to me to sound as though fat were bubbling in her throat.

"Yes," I answered.

"Sit down."

The dinner was a poor one. Nothing was served but pies filled with bitter curd, and milk soup. Elena Nikiforovna, who presided, kept blinking in a queer way, first with one eye and then with the other. She talked, she ate, but yet there was something deathly about her whole figure, and one almost fancied the faint smell of a corpse. There was only a glimmer of life in her, a glimmer of consciousness that she had been a lady who had once had her own serfs, that she was the widow of a general whom the servants had to address as "your Excellency"; and when these feeble relics of life flickered up in her for an instant she would say to her son:

"Jean, you are not holding your knife properly!"

Or she would say to me, drawing a deep breath, with the mincing air of a hostess trying to entertain a visitor:

"You know we have sold our estate. Of course, it is a pity, we are used to the place, but Dolzhikov has promised to make Jean stationmaster of Dubetchnya, so we shall not have to go away; we shall live here at the station, and that is just the same as being on our own property! The engineer is so nice! Don't you think he is very handsome?"

Until recently the Tcheprakovs had lived in a wealthy style, but since the death of the general everything had been changed. Elena Nikiforovna had taken to quarrelling with the neighbours, to going to law, and to not paying her bailiffs or her labourers; she was in constant terror of being robbed, and in some ten years Dubetchnya had become unrecognizable.

Behind the great house was an old garden which had already run wild, and was overgrown with rough weeds and bushes. I walked up and down the verandah, which was still solid and beautiful; through the glass doors one could see a room with parquetted floor, probably the drawing-room; an old-fashioned piano and pictures in deep mahogany frames—there was nothing else. In the old flower-beds all that remained were peonies and poppies, which lifted their white and bright red heads above the grass. Young maples and elms, already nibbled by the cows, grew beside the paths, drawn up and hindering each other's growth. The garden was thickly overgrown and seemed impassable, but this was only near the house where there stood poplars, fir-trees, and old limetrees, all of the same age, relics of the former avenues. Further on, beyond them the garden had been cleared for the sake of hay, and here it was not moist and stuffy, and there were no spiders' webs in one's mouth and eyes. A light breeze was blowing. The further one went the more open it was, and here in the open space were cherries, plums, and spreading apple-trees, disfigured by props and by canker; and pear-trees so tall that one could not believe they were pear-trees. This part of the garden was let to some shopkeepers of the town, and it was protected from thieves and starlings by a feeble-minded peasant who lived in a shanty in it.

The garden, growing more and more open, till it became definitely a meadow, sloped down to the river, which was overgrown with green weeds and osiers. Near the milldam was the millpond, deep and full of fish; a little mill with a thatched roof was working away with a wrathful sound, and frogs croaked furiously. Circles passed from time to time over the smooth, mirror-like water, and the water-lilies trembled, stirred by the lively fish. On the further side of the river was the little village Dubetchnya. The still, blue millpond was alluring with its promise of coolness and peace. And now all this—the millpond and the mill and the snug-looking banks—belonged to the engineer!

And so my new work began. I received and forwarded telegrams, wrote various reports, and made fair copies of the notes of requirements, the complaints, and the reports sent to the office by the illiterate foremen and workmen. But for the greater part of the day I did nothing but walk about the room waiting for telegrams, or made a boy sit in the lodge while I went for a walk in the garden, until the boy ran to tell me that there was a tapping at the operating machine. I had dinner at Madame Tcheprakov's. Meat we had very rarely: our dishes were all made of milk, and Wednesdays and Fridays were fast days, and on those days we had pink plates which were called Lenten plates. Madame Tcheprakov was continually blinking—it was her invariable habit, and I always felt ill at ease in her presence.

As there was not enough work in the lodge for one, Tcheprakov did nothing, but simply dozed, or went with his gun to shoot ducks on the millpond. In the evenings he drank too much in the village or the station, and before going to bed stared in the looking-glass and said: "Hullo, Ivan Tcheprakov."

When he was drunk he was very pale, and kept rubbing his hands and laughing with a sound like a neigh: "hee-hee-hee!" By way of bravado he used to strip and run about the country naked. He used to eat flies and say they were rather sour.

## IV

One day, after dinner, he ran breathless into the lodge and said: "Go along, your sister has come."

I went out, and there I found a hired brake from the town standing before the entrance of the great house. My sister had come in it with Anyuta Blagovo and a gentleman in a military tunic. Going up closer I recognized the latter: it was the brother of Anyuta Blagovo, the army doctor.

"We have come to you for a picnic," he said; "is that all right?"

My sister and Anyuta wanted to ask how I was getting on here, but both were silent, and simply gazed at me. I was silent too. They saw that I did not like the place, and tears came into my sister's eyes, while Anyuta Blagovo turned crimson.

We went into the garden. The doctor walked ahead of us all and said enthusiastically:

"What air! Holy Mother, what air!"

In appearance he was still a student. And he walked and talked like a student, and the expression of his grey eyes was as keen, honest, and frank as a nice student's. Beside his tall and handsome sister he looked frail and thin; and his beard was thin too, and his voice, too, was a thin but rather agreeable tenor. He was serving in a regiment somewhere, and had come home to his people for a holiday, and said he was going in the autumn to Petersburg for his examination as a doctor of medicine. He was already a family man, with a wife and three children, he had married very young, in his second year at the University, and now people in the town said he was unhappy in his family life and was not living with his wife.

"What time is it?" my sister asked uneasily. "We must get back in good time. Papa let me come to see my brother on condition I was back at six."

"Oh, bother your papa!" sighed the doctor.

I set the samovar. We put down a carpet before the verandah of the great house and had our tea there, and the doctor knelt down, drank out of his saucer, and declared that he now knew what bliss was. Then Tcheprakov came with the key and opened the glass door, and we all went into the house. There it was half dark and mysterious, and smelt of mushrooms, and our footsteps had a hollow sound as though there were cellars under the floor. The doctor stopped and touched the keys of the piano, and it responded faintly with a husky, quivering, but melodious chord; he tried his voice and sang a song, frowning and tapping impatiently with his foot when some note was mute. My sister did not talk about going home, but walked about the rooms and kept saying:

"How happy I am! How happy I am!"

There was a note of astonishment in her voice, as though it seemed to her incredible that she, too, could feel light-hearted. It was the first time in my life I had seen her so happy. She actually looked prettier. In profile she did not look nice; her nose and mouth seemed to stick out and had an expression as though she were pouting, but she had beautiful dark eyes, a pale, very delicate complexion, and a touching expression of goodness and melancholy, and when she talked she seemed charming and even beautiful. We both, she and I, took after our mother, were broad shouldered, strongly built, and capable of endurance, but her pallor was a sign of ill-health; she often had a cough, and I sometimes caught in her face that look one sees in people who are seriously ill, but for some reason conceal the fact. There was something naïve and childish in her gaiety now, as though the joy that had been suppressed and smothered in our childhood by harsh education had now suddenly awakened in her soul and found a free outlet.

But when evening came on and the horses were brought round, my sister sank into silence and looked thin and shrunken, and she got into the brake as though she were going to the scaffold.

When they had all gone, and the sound had died away . . . I remembered that Anyuta Blagovo had not said a word to me all day.

"She is a wonderful girl!" I thought. "Wonderful girl!"

St. Peter's fast came, and we had nothing but Lenten dishes every day. I was weighed down by physical depression due to idleness and my unsettled position, and dissatisfied with myself. Listless and hungry, I lounged about the garden and only waited for a suitable mood to go away.

Towards evening one day, when Radish was sitting in the lodge, Dolzhikov, very sunburnt and grey with dust, walked in unexpectedly. He had been spending three days on his land, and had come now to Dubetchnya by the steamer, and walked to us from the station. While waiting for the carriage, which was to come for him from the town, he walked round the grounds with his bailiff, giving orders in a loud voice, then sat for a whole hour in our lodge, writing letters. While he was there telegrams came for him, and he himself tapped off the answers. We three stood in silence at attention.

"What a muddle!" he said, glancing contemptuously at a record book. "In a fortnight I am transferring the office to the station, and I don't know what I am to do with you, my friends."

"I do my best, your honour," said Tcheprakov.

"To be sure, I see how you do your best. The only thing you can do is to take your salary," the engineer went on, looking at me; "you keep relying on patronage to *faire le carrière* as quickly and as easily as possible. Well, I don't care for patronage. No one took any trouble on my behalf. Before they gave me a railway contract I went about as a mechanic and worked in Belgium as an oiler. And you, Panteley, what are you doing here?" he asked, turning to Radish. "Drinking with them?"

He, for some reason, always called humble people Panteley, and such as me and Tcheprakov he despised, and called them drunkards, beasts, and rabble to their faces. Altogether he was cruel to humble subordinates, and used to fine them and turn them off coldly without explanations.

At last the horses came for him. As he said good-bye he promised to turn us all off in a fortnight; he called his bailiff a blockhead; and then, lolling at ease in his carriage, drove back to the town.

"Andrey Ivanitch," I said to Radish, "take me on as a workman."

"Oh, all right!"

And we set off together in the direction of the town. When the station and the big house with its buildings were left behind I asked: "Andrey Ivanitch, why did you come to Dubetchnya this evening?"

"In the first place my fellows are working on the line, and in the second place I came to pay the general's lady my interest. Last year I borrowed fifty roubles from her, and I pay her now a rouble a month interest."

The painter stopped and took me by the button.

"Misail Alexeyitch, our angel," he went on. "The way I look at it is that if any man, gentle or simple, takes even the smallest interest, he is doing evil. There cannot be truth and justice in such a man."

Radish, lean, pale, dreadful-looking, shut his eyes, shook his head, and, in the tone of a philosopher, pronounced:

"Lice consume the grass, rust consumes the iron, and lying the soul. Lord, have mercy upon us sinners."

## V

Radish was not practical, and was not at all good at forming an estimate; he took more work than he could get through, and when calculating he was agitated, lost his head, and so was almost always out of pocket over his jobs. He undertook painting, glazing, paperhanging, and even tiling roofs, and I can remember his running about for three days to find tilers for the sake of a paltry job. He was a first-rate workman; he sometimes earned as much as ten roubles a day; and if it had not been for the desire at all costs to be a master, and to be called a contractor, he would probably have had plenty of money.

He was paid by the job, but he paid me and the other workmen by the day, from one and twopence to two shillings a day. When it was fine and dry we did all kinds of outside work, chiefly painting roofs. When I was new to the work it made my feet burn as though I were walking on hot bricks, and when I put on felt boots they were hotter than ever. But this was only at first; later on I got used to it, and everything went swimmingly. I was living now among people to whom labour was obligatory, inevitable, and who worked like cart-horses, often with no idea of the moral significance of labour, and, indeed, never using the word "labour" in conversation at all. Beside them I, too, felt like a cart-horse, growing more and more imbued with the feeling of the obligatory and inevitable character of what I was doing, and this made my life easier, setting me free from all doubt and uncertainty.

At first everything interested me, everything was new, as though I had been born again. I could sleep on the ground and go about barefoot, and that was extremely pleasant; I could stand in a crowd of the common people and be no constraint to anyone, and when a cab horse fell down in the street I ran to help it up without being afraid of soiling my clothes. And the best of it all was, I was living on my own account and no burden to anyone!

Painting roofs, especially with our own oil and colours, was regarded as a particularly profitable job, and so this rough, dull work was not disdained, even by such good workmen as Radish. In short breeches, and wasted, purple-looking legs, he used to go about the roofs, looking like a stork, and I used to hear him, as he plied his brush, breathing heavily and saying: "Woe, woe to us sinners!"

He walked about the roofs as freely as though he were upon the ground. In spite of his being ill and pale as a corpse, his agility was extraordinary: he used to paint the domes and cupolas of the churches without scaffolding, like a young man, with only the help of a ladder and a rope, and it was rather horrible when standing on a height far from the earth; he would draw himself up erect, and for some unknown reason pronounce:

"Lice consume grass, rust consumes iron, and lying the soul!"

Or, thinking about something, would answer his thoughts aloud:

"Anything may happen! Anything may happen!"

When I went home from my work, all the people who were sitting on benches by the gates, all the shopmen and boys and their employers, made sneering and spiteful remarks after me, and this upset me at first and seemed to be simply monstrous.

"Better-than-nothing!" I heard on all sides. "House painter! Yellow ochre!"

And none behaved so ungraciously to me as those who had only lately been humble people themselves, and had earned their bread by hard manual labour. In the streets full of shops I was once passing an ironmonger's when water was thrown over me as though by accident, and on one occasion someone darted out with a stick at me, while a fishmonger, a grey-headed old man, barred my way and said, looking at me angrily:

"I am not sorry for you, you fool! It's your father I am sorry for."

And my acquaintances were for some reason overcome with embarrassment when they met me. Some of them looked upon me as a queer fish and a comic fool; others were sorry for me; others did not know what attitude to take up to me, and it was difficult to make them out. One day I met Anyuta Blagovo in a side street near Great Dvoryansky Street. I was going to work, and was carrying two long brushes and a pail of paint. Recognizing me Anyuta flushed crimson.

"Please do not bow to me in the street," she said nervously, harshly, and in a shaking voice, without offering me her hand, and tears suddenly gleamed in her eyes. "If to your mind all this is necessary, so be it . . . so be it, but I beg you not to meet me!"

I no longer lived in Great Dvoryansky Street, but in the suburb with my old nurse Karpovna, a good-natured but gloomy old woman, who always foreboded some harm, was afraid of all dreams, and even in the bees and wasps that flew into her room saw omens of evil, and the fact that I had become a workman, to her thinking, boded nothing good.

"Your life is ruined," she would say, mournfully shaking her head, "ruined."

Her adopted son Prokofy, a huge, uncouth, red-headed fellow of thirty, with bristling moustaches, a butcher by trade, lived in the little house with her. When he met me in the passage he would make way for me in respectful silence, and if he was drunk he would salute me with all five fingers at once. He used to have supper in the evening, and through the partition wall of boards I could hear him clear his throat and sigh as he drank off glass after glass.

"Mamma," he would call in an undertone.

"Well," Karpovna, who was passionately devoted to her adopted son, would respond: "What is it, sonny?"

"I can show you a testimony of my affection, mamma. All this earthly life I will cherish you in your declining years in this vale of tears, and when you die I will bury you at my expense; I have said it, and you can believe it."

I got up every morning before sunrise, and went to bed early. We house painters ate a great deal and slept soundly; the only thing amiss was that my heart used to beat violently at night. I did not quarrel with my mates. Violent abuse, desperate oaths, and wishes such as, "Blast your eyes," or "Cholera take you," never ceased all day, but, nevertheless, we lived on very friendly terms. The other fellows suspected me of being some sort of religious sectary, and made good-natured jokes at my expense, saying that even my own father had disowned me, and thereupon would add that they rarely went into the temple of God themselves, and that many of them had not been to confession for ten years. They justified this laxity on their part by saying that a painter among men was like a jackdaw among birds.

The men had a good opinion of me, and treated me with respect; it was evident that my not drinking, not smoking, but leading a quiet, steady life pleased them very much. It was only an unpleasant shock to them that I took no hand in stealing oil and did not go with them to ask for tips from people on whose property we were working. Stealing oil and paints from those who employed them was a house painter's custom, and was not regarded as theft, and it was remarkable that even so upright a man as Radish would always carry away a little white lead and oil as he went home from work. And even the most respectable old fellows, who owned the houses in which they lived in the suburb, were not ashamed to ask for a tip, and it made me feel vexed and ashamed to see the men go in a body to congratulate some nonentity on the commencement or the completion of the job, and thank him with degrading servility when they had received a few coppers.

With people on whose work they were engaged they behaved like wily courtiers, and almost every day I was reminded of Shakespeare's Polonius.

"I fancy it is going to rain," the man whose house was being painted would say, looking at the sky.

"It is, there is not a doubt it is," the painters would agree.

"I don't think it is a rain-cloud, though. Perhaps it won't rain after all."

"No, it won't, your honour! I am sure it won't."

But their attitude to their patrons behind their backs was usually one of irony, and when they saw, for instance, a gentleman sitting in the verandah reading a newspaper, they would observe:

"He reads the paper, but I daresay he has nothing to eat."

I never went home to see my own people. When I came back from work I often found waiting for me little notes, brief and anxious, in which my sister wrote to me about my father; that he had been particularly preoccupied at dinner and had eaten nothing, or that he had been giddy and staggering, or that he had locked himself in his room and had not come out for a long time. Such items of news troubled me; I could not sleep, and at times even walked up and down Great Dvoryansky Street at night by our house, looking in at the dark windows and trying to guess whether everything was well at home. On Sundays my sister came to see me, but came in secret, as though it were not to see me but our nurse. And if she came in to see me she was very pale, with tear-stained eyes, and she began crying at once.

"Our father will never live through this," she would say. "If anything should happen to him—God grant it may not—your conscience will torment you all your life. It's awful, Misail; for our mother's sake I beseech you: reform your ways."

"My darling sister," I would say, "how can I reform my ways if I am convinced that I am acting in accordance with my conscience? Do understand!"

"I know you are acting on your conscience, but perhaps it could be done differently, somehow, so as not to wound anybody."

"Ah, holy Saints!" the old woman sighed through the door. "Your life is ruined! There will be trouble, my dears, there will be trouble!"

## VI

One Sunday Dr. Blagovo turned up unexpectedly. He was wearing a military tunic over a silk shirt and high boots of patent leather.

"I have come to see you," he began, shaking my hand heartily like a student. "I am hearing about you every day, and I have been meaning to come and have a heart-to-heart talk, as they say. The boredom in the town is awful, there is not a living soul, no one to say a word to. It's hot, Holy Mother," he went on, taking off his tunic and sitting in his silk shirt. "My dear fellow, let me talk to you."

I was dull myself, and had for a long time been craving for the society of someone not a house painter. I was genuinely glad to see him.

"I'll begin by saying," he said, sitting down on my bed, "that I sympathize with you from the bottom of my heart, and deeply respect the life you are leading. They don't understand you here in the town, and, indeed, there is no one to understand, seeing that, as you know, they are all, with very few exceptions, regular Gogolesque pig faces here. But I saw what you were at once that time at the picnic. You are a noble soul, an honest, high-minded man! I respect you, and feel it a great honour to shake hands with you!" he went on enthusiastically. "To have made such a complete and violent change of life as you have done, you must have passed through a complicated spiritual crisis, and to continue this manner of life now, and to keep up to the high standard of your convictions continually, must be a strain on your mind and heart from day to day. Now to begin our talk, tell me, don't you consider that if you had spent your strength of will, this strained activity, all these powers on something else, for instance, on gradually becoming a great scientist, or artist, your life would have been broader and deeper and would have been more productive?"

We talked, and when we got upon manual labour I expressed this idea: that what is wanted is that the strong should not enslave the weak, that the minority should not be a parasite on the majority, nor a vampire for ever sucking its vital sap; that is, all, without exception, strong and weak, rich and poor, should take part equally in the struggle for existence, each one on his own account, and that there was no better means for equalizing things in that way than manual labour, in the form of universal service, compulsory for all.

"Then do you think everyone without exception ought to engage in manual labour?" asked the doctor.

"Yes."

"And don't you think that if everyone, including the best men, the thinkers and great scientists, taking part in the struggle for existence, each on his own account, are going to waste their time breaking stones and painting roofs, may not that threaten a grave danger to progress?"

"Where is the danger?" I asked. "Why, progress is in deeds of love, in fulfilling the moral law; if you don't enslave anyone, if you don't oppress anyone, what further progress do you want?"

"But, excuse me," Blagovo suddenly fired up, rising to his feet. "But, excuse me! If a snail in its shell busies itself over perfecting its own personality and muddles about with the moral law, do you call that progress?"

"Why muddles?" I said, offended. "If you don't force your neighbour to feed and clothe you, to transport you from place to place and defend you from your enemies, surely in the midst of a life entirely resting on slavery, that is progress, isn't it? To my mind it is the most important progress, and perhaps the only one possible and necessary for man."

"The limits of universal world progress are in infinity, and to talk of some 'possible' progress limited by our needs and temporary theories is, excuse my saying so, positively strange."

"If the limits of progress are in infinity as you say, it follows that its aims are not definite," I said. "To live without knowing definitely what you are living for!"

"So be it! But that 'not knowing' is not so dull as your 'knowing.' I am going up a ladder which is called progress, civilization, culture; I go on and up without knowing definitely where I am going, but really it is worth living for the sake of that delightful ladder; while you know what you are living for, you live for the sake of some people's not enslaving others, that the artist and the man who rubs his paints may dine equally well. But you know that's the petty, bourgeois, kitchen, grey side of life, and surely it is revolting to live for that alone? If some insects do enslave others, bother them, let them devour each other! We need not think about them. You know they will die and decay just the same, however zealously you rescue them from slavery. We must think of that great millennium which awaits humanity in the remote future."

Blagovo argued warmly with me, but at the same time one could see he was troubled by some irrelevant idea.

"I suppose your sister is not coming?" he said, looking at his watch. "She was at our house yesterday, and said she would be seeing you to-day. You keep saying slavery, slavery . . ." he went on. "But you know that is a special question, and all such questions are solved by humanity gradually."

We began talking of doing things gradually. I said that "the question of doing good or evil every one settles for himself, without waiting till humanity settles it by the way of gradual development. Moreover, this gradual process has more than one aspect. Side by side with the gradual development of human ideas the gradual growth of ideas of another order is observed. Serfdom is no more, but the capitalist system is growing. And in the very heyday of emancipating ideas, just as in the days of Baty, the majority feeds, clothes, and defends the minority while remaining hungry, inadequately clad, and defenceless. Such an order of things can be made to fit in finely with any tendencies and currents of thought you like, because the art of enslaving is also gradually being cultivated. We no longer flog our servants in the stable, but we give to slavery refined forms, at least, we succeed in finding a justification for it in each particular case. Ideas are ideas with us, but if now, at the end of the nineteenth century, it were possible to lay the burden of the most unpleasant of our physiological functions upon the working class, we should certainly do so, and afterwards, of course, justify ourselves by saying that if the best people, the thinkers and great scientists, were to waste their precious time on these functions, progress might be menaced with great danger."

But at this point my sister arrived. Seeing the doctor she was fluttered and troubled, and began saying immediately that it was time for her to go home to her father.

"Kleopatra Alexyevna," said Blagovo earnestly, pressing both hands to his heart, "what will happen to your father if you spend half an hour or so with your brother and me?"

He was frank, and knew how to communicate his liveliness to others. After a moment's thought, my sister laughed, and all at once became suddenly gay as she had been at the picnic. We went out into the country, and lying in the grass went on with our talk, and looked towards the town where all the windows facing west were like glittering gold because the sun was setting.

After that, whenever my sister was coming to see me Blagovo turned up too, and they always greeted each other as though their meeting in my room was accidental. My sister listened while the doctor and I argued, and at such times her expression was joyfully enthusiastic, full of tenderness and curiosity, and it seemed to me that a new world she had never dreamed of before, and which she was now striving to fathom, was gradually opening before her eyes. When the doctor was not there she was quiet and sad, and now if she sometimes shed tears as she sat on my bed it was for reasons of which she did not speak.

In August Radish ordered us to be ready to go to the railway-line. Two days before we were "banished" from the town my father came to see me. He sat down and in a leisurely way, without looking at me, wiped his red face, then took out of his pocket our town *Messenger*, and deliberately, with emphasis on each word, read out the news that the son of the branch manager of the State Bank, a young man of my age, had been appointed head of a Department in the Exchequer.

"And now look at you," he said, folding up the newspaper, "a beggar, in rags, good for nothing! Even working-class people and peasants obtain education in order to become men, while you, a Poloznev, with ancestors of rank and distinction, aspire to the gutter! But I have not come here to talk to you; I have washed my hands of you—" he added in a stifled voice, getting up. "I have come to find out where your sister is, you worthless fellow. She left home after dinner, and here it is nearly eight and she is not back. She has taken to going out frequently without telling me; she is less dutiful—and I see in it your evil and degrading influence. Where is she?"

In his hand he had the umbrella I knew so well, and I was already flustered and drew myself up like a schoolboy, expecting my father to begin hitting me with it, but he noticed my glance at the umbrella and most likely that restrained him.

"Live as you please!" he said. "I shall not give you my blessing!"

"Holy Saints!" my nurse muttered behind the door. "You poor, unlucky child! Ah, my heart bodes ill!"

I worked on the railway-line. It rained without stopping all August; it was damp and cold; they had not carried the corn in the fields, and on big farms where the wheat had been cut by machines it lay not in sheaves but in heaps, and I remember how those luckless heaps of wheat turned blacker every day and the grain was sprouting in them. It was hard to work; the pouring rain spoiled everything we managed to do. We were not allowed to live or to sleep in the railway buildings, and we took refuge in the damp and filthy mud huts in which the navvies had lived during the summer, and I could not sleep at night for the cold and the woodlice crawling on my face and hands. And when we worked near the bridges the navvies used to come in the evenings in a gang, simply in order to beat the painters—it was a form of sport to them. They used to beat us, to steal our brushes. And to annoy us and rouse us to fight they used to spoil our work; they would, for instance, smear over the signal boxes with green paint. To complete our troubles, Radish took to paying us very irregularly. All the painting work on the line was given out to a contractor; he gave it out to another; and this subcontractor gave it to Radish after subtracting twenty per cent. for himself. The job was not a profitable one in itself, and the rain made it worse; time was wasted; we could not work while Radish was obliged to pay the fellows by the day. The hungry painters almost came to beating him, called him a cheat, a blood-sucker, a Judas, while he, poor fellow, sighed, lifted up his hand to Heaven in despair, and was continually going to Madame Tcheprakov for money.

## VII

Autumn came on, rainy, dark, and muddy. The season of unemployment set in, and I used to sit at home out of work for three days at a stretch, or did various little jobs, not in the painting line. For instance, I wheeled earth, earning about fourpence a day by it. Dr. Blagovo had gone away to Petersburg. My sister had given up coming to see me. Radish was laid up at home ill, expecting death from day to day.

And my mood was autumnal too. Perhaps because, having become a workman, I saw our town life only from the seamy side, it was my lot almost every day to make discoveries which reduced me almost to despair. Those of my fellow-citizens, about whom I had no opinion before, or who had externally appeared perfectly decent, turned out now to be base, cruel people, capable of any dirty action. We common people were deceived, cheated, and kept waiting for hours together in the cold entry or the kitchen; we were insulted and treated with the utmost rudeness. In the autumn I papered the reading-room and two other rooms at the club; I was paid a penny three-farthings the piece, but had to sign a receipt at the rate of twopence halfpenny, and when I refused to do so, a gentleman of benevolent appearance in gold-rimmed spectacles, who must have been one of the club committee, said to me:

"If you say much more, you blackguard, I'll pound your face into a jelly!"

And when the flunkey whispered to him what I was, the son of Poloznev the architect, he became embarrassed, turned crimson, but immediately recovered himself and said: "Devil take him."

In the shops they palmed off on us workmen putrid meat, musty flour, and tea that had been used and dried again; the police hustled us in church, the assistants and nurses in the hospital plundered us, and if we were too poor to give them a bribe they revenged themselves by bringing us food in dirty vessels. In the post-office the pettiest official considered he had a right to treat us like animals, and to shout with coarse insolence: "You wait!" "Where are you shoving to?" Even the housedogs were unfriendly to us, and fell upon us with peculiar viciousness. But the thing that struck me most of all in my new position was the complete lack of justice, what is defined by the peasants in the words: "They have forgotten God." Rarely did a day pass without swindling. We were swindled by the merchants who sold us oil, by the contractors and the workmen and the people who employed us. I need not say that there could never be a question of our rights, and we always had to ask for the money we earned as though it were a charity, and to stand waiting for it at the back door, cap in hand.

I was papering a room at the club next to the reading-room; in the evening, when I was just getting ready to go, the daughter of

Dolzhikov, the engineer, walked into the room with a bundle of books under her arm.

I bowed to her.

"Oh, how do you do!" she said, recognizing me at once, and holding out her hand. "I'm very glad to see you."

She smiled and looked with curiosity and wonder at my smock, my pail of paste, the paper stretched on the floor; I was embarrassed, and she, too, felt awkward.

"You must excuse my looking at you like this," she said. "I have been told so much about you. Especially by Dr. Blagovo; he is simply in love with you. And I have made the acquaintance of your sister too; a sweet, dear girl, but I can never persuade her that there is nothing awful about your adopting the simple life. On the contrary, you have become the most interesting man in the town."

She looked again at the pail of paste and the wallpaper, and went on:

"I asked Dr. Blagovo to make me better acquainted with you, but apparently he forgot, or had not time. Anyway, we are acquainted all the same, and if you would come and see me quite simply I should be extremely indebted to you. I so long to have a talk. I am a simple person," she added, holding out her hand to me, "and I hope that you will feel no constraint with me. My father is not here, he is in Petersburg."

She went off into the reading-room, rustling her skirts, while I went home, and for a long time could not get to sleep.

That cheerless autumn some kind soul, evidently wishing to alleviate my existence, sent me from time to time tea and lemons, or biscuits, or roast game. Karpovna told me that they were always brought by a soldier, and from whom they came she did not know; and the soldier used to enquire whether I was well, and whether I dined every day, and whether I had warm clothing. When the frosts began I was presented in the same way in my absence with a soft knitted scarf brought by the soldier. There was a faint elusive smell of scent about it, and I guessed who my good fairy was. The scarf smelt of lilies-of-the-valley, the favourite scent of Anyuta Blagovo.

Towards winter there was more work and it was more cheerful. Radish recovered, and we worked together in the cemetery church, where we were putting the ground-work on the ikon-stand before gilding. It was a clean, quiet job, and, as our fellows used to say, profitable. One could get through a lot of work in a day, and the time passed quickly, imperceptibly. There was no swearing, no laughter, no loud talk. The place itself compelled one to quietness and decent behaviour, and disposed one to quiet, serious thoughts. Absorbed in our work we stood or sat motionless like statues; there was a deathly silence in keeping with the cemetery, so that if a tool fell, or a flame spluttered in the lamp, the noise of such sounds rang out abrupt and resonant, and made us look round. After a long silence we would hear a buzzing like the swarming of bees: it was the requiem of a baby being chanted slowly in subdued voices in the porch; or an artist, painting a dove with stars round it on a cupola would begin softly whistling, and recollecting himself with a start would at once relapse into silence; or Radish, answering his thoughts, would say with a sigh: "Anything is possible! Anything is possible!" or a slow disconsolate bell would begin ringing over our heads, and the painters would observe that it must be for the funeral of some wealthy person. . . .

My days I spent in this stillness in the twilight of the church, and in the long evenings I played billiards or went to the theatre in the gallery wearing the new trousers I had bought out of my own earnings. Concerts and performances had already begun at the Azhogins'; Radish used to paint the scenes alone now. He used to tell me the plot of the plays and describe the *tableaux vivants* which he witnessed. I listened to him with envy. I felt greatly drawn to the rehearsals, but I could not bring myself to go to the Azhogins'.

A week before Christmas Dr. Blagovo arrived. And again we argued and played billiards in the evenings. When he played he used to take off his coat and unbutton his shirt over his chest, and for some reason tried altogether to assume the air of a desperate rake. He did not drink much, but made a great uproar about it, and had a special faculty for getting through twenty roubles in an evening at such a poor cheap tavern as the *Volga*.

My sister began coming to see me again; they both expressed surprise every time on seeing each other, but from her joyful, guilty face it was evident that these meetings were not accidental. One evening, when we were playing billiards, the doctor said to me:

"I say, why don't you go and see Miss Dolzhikov? You don't know Mariya Viktorovna; she is a clever creature, a charmer, a simple, good-natured soul."

I described how her father had received me in the spring.

"Nonsense!" laughed the doctor, "the engineer's one thing and she's another. Really, my dear fellow, you mustn't be nasty to her; go and see her sometimes. For instance, let's go and see her tomorrow evening. What do you say?"

He persuaded me. The next evening I put on my new serge trousers, and in some agitation I set off to Miss Dolzhikov's. The footman did not seem so haughty and terrible, nor the furniture so gorgeous, as on that morning when I had come to ask a favour. Mariya Viktorovna was expecting me, and she received me like an old acquaintance, shaking hands with me in a friendly way. She was wearing a grey cloth dress with full sleeves, and had her hair done in the style which we used to call "dogs' ears," when it came into fashion in the town a year before. The hair was combed down over the ears, and this made Mariya Viktorovna's face look broader, and she seemed to me this time very much like her father, whose face was broad and red, with something in its expression like a sledge-driver. She was handsome and elegant, but not youthful looking; she looked thirty, though in reality she was not more than twenty-five.

"Dear Doctor, how grateful I am to you," she said, making me sit down. "If it hadn't been for him you wouldn't have come to see me. I am bored to death! My father has gone away and left me alone, and I don't know what to do with myself in this town."

Then she began asking me where I was working now, how much I earned, where I lived.

"Do you spend on yourself nothing but what you earn?" she asked.

"No."

"Happy man!" she sighed. "All the evil in life, it seems to me, comes from idleness, boredom, and spiritual emptiness, and all this is inevitable when one is accustomed to living at other people's expense. Don't think I am showing off, I tell you truthfully: it is not interesting or pleasant to be rich. 'Make to yourselves friends of the mammon of unrighteousness' is said, because there is not and cannot be a mammon that's righteous."

She looked round at the furniture with a grave, cold expression, as though she wanted to count it over, and went on:

"Comfort and luxury have a magical power; little by little they draw into their clutches even strong-willed people. At one time father and I lived simply, not in a rich style, but now you see how! It is something monstrous," she said, shrugging her shoulders; "we spend up to twenty thousand a year! In the provinces!"

"One comes to look at comfort and luxury as the invariable privilege of capital and education," I said, "and it seems to me that the comforts of life may be combined with any sort of labour, even the hardest and dirtiest. Your father is rich, and yet he says himself that it has been his lot to be a mechanic and an oiler."

She smiled and shook her head doubtfully: "My father sometimes eats bread dipped in kvass," she said. "It's a fancy, a whim!"

At that moment there was a ring and she got up.

"The rich and well-educated ought to work like everyone else," she said, "and if there is comfort it ought to be equal for all. There ought not to be any privileges. But that's enough philosophizing. Tell me something amusing. Tell me about the painters. What are they like? Funny?"

The doctor came in; I began telling them about the painters, but, being unaccustomed to talking, I was constrained, and described them like an ethnologist, gravely and tediously. The doctor, too, told us some anecdotes of working men: he staggered about, shed tears, dropped on his knees, and, even, mimicking a drunkard, lay on the floor; it was as good as a play, and Mariya Viktorovna laughed till she cried as she looked at him. Then he played on the piano and sang in his thin, pleasant tenor, while Mariya Viktorovna stood by and picked out what he was to sing, and corrected him when he made a mistake.

"I've heard that you sing, too?" I enquired.

"Sing, too!" cried the doctor in horror. "She sings exquisitely, a perfect artist, and you talk of her 'singing too'! What an idea!"

"I did study in earnest at one time," she said, answering my question, "but now I have given it up."

Sitting on a low stool she told us of her life in Petersburg, and mimicked some celebrated singers, imitating their voice and manner of singing. She made a sketch of the doctor in her album, then of me; she did not draw well, but both the portraits were like us. She laughed, and was full of mischief and charming grimaces, and this suited her better than talking about the mammon of unrighteousness, and it seemed to me that she had been talking just before about wealth and luxury, not in earnest, but in imitation of someone. She was a superb comic actress. I mentally compared her with our young ladies, and even the handsome, dignified Anyuta Blagovo could not stand comparison with her; the difference was immense, like the difference between a beautiful, cultivated rose and a wild briar.

We had supper together, the three of us. The doctor and Mariya Viktorovna drank red wine, champagne, and coffee with brandy in it; they clinked glasses and drank to friendship, to enlightenment, to progress, to liberty, and they did not get drunk but only flushed, and were continually, for no reason, laughing till they cried. So as not to be tiresome I drank claret too.

"Talented, richly endowed natures," said Miss Dolzhikov, "know how to live, and go their own way; mediocre people, like myself for instance, know nothing and can do nothing of themselves; there is nothing left for them but to discern some deep social movement, and to float where they are carried by it."

"How can one discern what doesn't exist?" asked the doctor.

"We think so because we don't see it."

"Is that so? The social movements are the invention of the new literature. There are none among us."

An argument began.

"There are no deep social movements among us and never have been," the doctor declared loudly. "There is no end to what the new literature has invented! It has invented intellectual workers in the country, and you may search through all our villages and find at the most some lout in a reefer jacket or a black frock-coat who will make four mistakes in spelling a word of three letters. Cultured life has not yet begun among us. There's the same savagery, the same uniform boorishness, the same triviality, as five hundred years ago. Movements, currents there have been, but it has all been petty, paltry, bent upon vulgar and mercenary interests—and one cannot see anything important in them. If you think you have discerned a deep social movement, and in following it you devote yourself to tasks in the modern taste, such as the emancipation of insects from slavery or abstinence from beef rissoles, I congratulate you, Madam. We must study, and study, and study and we must wait a bit with our deep social movements; we are not mature enough for them yet; and to tell the truth, we don't know anything about them."

"You don't know anything about them, but I do," said Mariya Viktorovna. "Goodness, how tiresome you are to-day!"

"Our duty is to study and to study, to try to accumulate as much knowledge as possible, for genuine social movements arise where there is knowledge; and the happiness of mankind in the future lies only in knowledge. I drink to science!"

"There is no doubt about one thing: one must organize one's life somehow differently," said Mariya Viktorovna, after a moment's silence and thought. "Life, such as it has been hitherto, is not worth having. Don't let us talk about it."

As we came away from her the cathedral clock struck two.

"Did you like her?" asked the doctor; "she's nice, isn't she?"

On Christmas day we dined with Mariya Viktorovna, and all through the holidays we went to see her almost every day. There was never anyone there but ourselves, and she was right when she said that she had no friends in the town but the doctor and me. We spent our time for the most part in conversation; sometimes the doctor brought some book or magazine and read aloud to us. In reality he was the first well-educated man I had met in my life: I cannot judge whether he knew a great deal, but he always displayed his knowledge as though he wanted other people to share it. When he talked about anything relating to medicine he was not like any one of the doctors in our town, but made a fresh, peculiar impression upon me, and I fancied that if he liked he might have become a real man of science. And he was perhaps the only person who had a real influence upon me at that time. Seeing him, and reading the books he gave me, I began little by little to feel a thirst for the knowledge which would have given significance to my cheerless labour. It seemed strange to me, for instance, that I had not known till then that the whole world was made up of sixty elements, I had not known what oil was, what paints were, and that I could have got on without knowing these things. My acquaintance with the doctor elevated me morally too. I was continually arguing with him and, though I usually remained of my own opinion, yet, thanks to him, I began to perceive that everything was not clear to me, and I began trying to work out as far as I could definite convictions in myself, that the dictates of conscience might be definite, and that there might be nothing vague in my mind. Yet, though he was the most cultivated and best man in the town, he was nevertheless far from perfection. In his manners, in his habit of turning every conversation into an argument, in his pleasant tenor, even in his friendliness, there was something coarse, like a divinity student, and when he took off his coat and sat in his silk shirt, or flung a tip to a waiter in the restaurant, I always fancied that culture might be all very well, but the Tatar was fermenting in him still.

At Epiphany he went back to Petersburg. He went off in the morning, and after dinner my sister came in. Without taking off her fur coat and her cap she sat down in silence, very pale, and kept her eyes fixed on the same spot. She was chilled by the frost and one could see that she was upset by it.

"You must have caught cold," I said.

Her eyes filled with tears; she got up and went out to Karpovna without saying a word to me, as though I had hurt her feelings. And a little later I heard her saying, in a tone of bitter reproach:

"Nurse, what have I been living for till now? What? Tell me, haven't I wasted my youth? All the best years of my life to know nothing but keeping accounts, pouring out tea, counting the halfpence, entertaining visitors, and thinking there was nothing better in the world! Nurse, do understand, I have the cravings of a human being, and I want to live, and they have turned me into something like a housekeeper. It's horrible, horrible!"

She flung her keys towards the door, and they fell with a jingle into my room. They were the keys of the sideboard, of the kitchen cupboard, of the cellar, and of the tea-caddy, the keys which my mother used to carry.

"Oh, merciful heavens!" cried the old woman in horror. "Holy Saints above!"

Before going home my sister came into my room to pick up the keys, and said:

"You must forgive me. Something queer has happened to me lately."

## VIII

On returning home late one evening from Mariya Viktorovna's I found waiting in my room a young police inspector in a new uniform; he was sitting at my table, looking through my books.

"At last," he said, getting up and stretching himself. "This is the third time I have been to you. The Governor commands you to present yourself before him at nine o'clock in the morning. Without fail."

He took from me a signed statement that I would act upon his Excellency's command, and went away. This late visit of the police inspector and unexpected invitation to the Governor's had an overwhelmingly oppressive effect upon me. From my earliest childhood I have felt terror-stricken in the presence of gendarmes, policemen, and law court officials, and now I was tormented by uneasiness, as though I were really guilty in some way. And I could not get to sleep. My nurse and Prokofy were also upset and could not sleep. My nurse had earache too; she moaned, and several times began crying with pain. Hearing that I was awake, Prokofy came into my room with a lamp and sat down at the table.

"You ought to have a drink of pepper cordial," he said, after a moment's thought. "If one does have a drink in this vale of tears it does no harm. And if Mamma were to pour a little pepper cordial in her ear it would do her a lot of good."

Between two and three he was going to the slaughter-house for the meat. I knew I should not sleep till morning now, and to get through the time till nine o'clock I went with him. We walked with a lantern, while his boy Nikolka, aged thirteen, with blue patches on his cheeks from frostbites, a regular young brigand to judge by his expression, drove after us in the sledge, urging on the horse in a husky voice.

"I suppose they will punish you at the Governor's," Prokofy said to me on the way. "There are rules of the trade for governors, and rules for the higher clergy, and rules for the officers, and rules for the doctors, and every class has its rules. But you haven't kept to your rules, and you can't be allowed."

The slaughter-house was behind the cemetery, and till then I had only seen it in the distance. It consisted of three gloomy barns, surrounded by a grey fence, and when the wind blew from that quarter on hot days in summer, it brought a stifling stench from them. Now going into the yard in the dark I did not see the barns; I kept coming across horses and sledges, some empty, some loaded up with meat. Men were walking about with lanterns, swearing in a disgusting way. Prokofy and Nikolka swore just as revoltingly, and the air was in a continual uproar with swearing, coughing, and the neighing of horses.

There was a smell of dead bodies and of dung. It was thawing, the snow was changing into mud; and in the darkness it seemed to me that I was walking through pools of blood.

Having piled up the sledges full of meat we set off to the butcher's shop in the market. It began to get light. Cooks with baskets and elderly ladies in mantles came along one after another. Prokofy, with a chopper in his hand, in a white apron spattered with blood, swore fearful oaths, crossed himself at the church, shouted aloud for the whole market to hear, that he was giving away the meat at cost price and even at a loss to himself. He gave short weight and short change, the cooks saw that, but, deafened by his shouts, did not protest, and only called him a hangman. Brandishing and bringing down his terrible chopper he threw himself into picturesque attitudes, and each time uttered the sound "Geck" with a ferocious expression, and I was afraid he really would chop off somebody's head or hand.

I spent all the morning in the butcher's shop, and when at last I went to the Governor's, my overcoat smelt of meat and blood. My state of mind was as though I were being sent spear in hand to meet a bear. I remember the tall staircase with a striped carpet on it, and the young official, with shiny buttons, who mutely motioned me to the door with both hands, and ran to announce me. I went into a hall luxuriously but frigidly and tastelessly furnished, and the high, narrow mirrors in the spaces between the walls, and the bright yellow window curtains, struck the eye particularly unpleasantly. One could see that the governors were changed, but the furniture remained the same. Again the young official motioned me with both hands to the door, and I went up to a big green table at which a military general, with the Order of Vladimir on his breast, was standing.

"Mr. Poloznev, I have asked you to come," he began, holding a letter in his hand, and opening his mouth like a round "o," "I have asked you to come here to inform you of this. Your highly respected father has appealed by letter and by word of mouth to the Marshal of the Nobility begging him to summon you, and to lay before you the inconsistency of your behaviour with the rank of the nobility to which you have the honour to belong. His Excellency Alexandr Pavlovitch, justly supposing that your conduct might serve as a bad example, and considering that mere persuasion on his part would not be sufficient, but that official intervention in earnest was essential, presents me here in this letter with his views in regard to you, which I share."

He said this, quietly, respectfully, standing erect, as though I were his superior officer and looking at me with no trace of severity. His face looked worn and wizened, and was all wrinkles; there were bags under his eyes; his hair was dyed; and it was impossible to tell from his appearance how old he was—forty or sixty.

"I trust," he went on, "that you appreciate the delicacy of our honoured Alexandr Pavlovitch, who has addressed himself to me not officially, but privately. I, too, have asked you to come here unofficially, and I am speaking to you, not as a Governor, but from a sincere regard for your father. And so I beg you either to alter your line of conduct and return to duties in keeping with your rank, or to avoid setting a bad example, remove to another district where you are not known, and where you can follow any occupation you please. In the other case, I shall be forced to take extreme measures."

He stood for half a minute in silence, looking at me with his mouth open.

"Are you a vegetarian?" he asked.

"No, your Excellency, I eat meat."

He sat down and drew some papers towards him. I bowed and went out.

It was not worth while now to go to work before dinner. I went home to sleep, but could not sleep from an unpleasant, sickly feeling, induced by the slaughter house and my conversation with the Governor, and when the evening came I went, gloomy and out of sorts, to Mariya Viktorovna. I told her how I had been at the Governor's, while she stared at me in perplexity as though she did not believe it, then suddenly began laughing gaily, loudly, irrepressibly, as only good-natured laughter-loving people can.

"If only one could tell that in Petersburg!" she brought out, almost falling over with laughter, and propping herself against the table. "If one could tell that in Petersburg!"

## IX

Now we used to see each other often, sometimes twice a day. She used to come to the cemetery almost every day after dinner, and read the epitaphs on the crosses and tombstones while she waited for me. Sometimes she would come into the church, and, standing by me, would look on while I worked. The stillness, the naïve work of the painters and gilders, Radish's sage reflections, and the fact that I did not differ externally from the other workmen, and worked just as they did in my waistcoat with no socks on, and that I was addressed familiarly by them—all this was new to her and touched her. One day a workman, who was painting a dove on the ceiling, called out to me in her presence:

"Misail, hand me up the white paint."

I took him the white paint, and afterwards, when I let myself down by the frail scaffolding, she looked at me, touched to tears and smiling.

"What a dear you are!" she said.

I remembered from my childhood how a green parrot, belonging to one of the rich men of the town, had escaped from its cage, and how for quite a month afterwards the beautiful bird had haunted the town, flying from garden to garden, homeless and solitary. Mariya Viktorovna reminded me of that bird.

"There is positively nowhere for me to go now but the cemetery," she said to me with a laugh. "The town has become disgustingly dull. At the Azhogins' they are still reciting, singing, lisping. I have grown to detest them of late; your sister is an unsociable creature; Mademoiselle Blagovo hates me for some reason. I don't care for the theatre. Tell me where am I to go?"

When I went to see her I smelt of paint and turpentine, and my hands were stained—and she liked that; she wanted me to come to her in my ordinary working clothes; but in her drawing-room those clothes made me feel awkward. I felt embarrassed, as though I were in uniform, so I always put on my new serge trousers when I went to her. And she did not like that.

"You must own you are not quite at home in your new character," she said to me one day. "Your workman's dress does not feel natural to you; you are awkward in it. Tell me, isn't that because you haven't a firm conviction, and are not satisfied? The very kind of work you have chosen—your painting—surely it does not satisfy you, does it?" she asked, laughing. "I know paint makes things look nicer and last longer, but those things belong to rich people who live in towns, and after all they are luxuries. Besides, you have often said yourself that everybody ought to get his bread by the work of his own hands, yet you get money and not bread. Why shouldn't you keep to the literal sense of your words? You ought to be getting bread, that is, you ought to be ploughing, sowing, reaping, threshing, or doing something which has a direct connection with agriculture, for instance, looking after cows, digging, building huts of logs...."

She opened a pretty cupboard that stood near her writing-table, and said:

"I am saying all this to you because I want to let you into my secret. *Voilà!* This is my agricultural library. Here I have fields, kitchen garden and orchard, and cattleyard and beehives. I read them greedily, and have already learnt all the theory to the tiniest detail. My dream, my darling wish, is to go to our Dubetchnya as soon as March is here. It's marvellous there, exquisite, isn't it? The first year I shall have a look round and get into things, and the year after I shall begin to work properly myself, putting my back into it as they say. My father has promised to give me Dubetchnya and I shall do exactly what I like with it."

Flushed, excited to tears, and laughing, she dreamed aloud how she would live at Dubetchnya, and what an interesting life it would be! I envied her. March was near, the days were growing longer and longer, and on bright sunny days water dripped from the roofs at midday, and there was a fragrance of spring; I, too, longed for the country.

And when she said that she should move to Dubetchnya, I realized vividly that I should remain in the town alone, and I felt that I envied her with her cupboard of books and her agriculture. I knew nothing of work on the land, and did not like it, and I should have liked to have told her that work on the land was slavish toil, but I remembered that something similar had been said more than once by my father, and I held my tongue.

Lent began. Viktor Ivanitch, whose existence I had begun to forget, arrived from Petersburg. He arrived unexpectedly, without even a telegram to say he was coming. When I went in, as usual in the evening, he was walking about the drawing-room, telling some story with his face freshly washed and shaven, looking ten years younger: his daughter was kneeling on the floor, taking out of his trunks boxes, bottles, and books, and handing them to Pavel the footman. I involuntarily drew back a step when I saw the engineer, but he held out both hands to me and said, smiling, showing his strong white teeth that looked like a sledge-driver's:

"Here he is, here he is! Very glad to see you, Mr. House-painter! Masha has told me all about it; she has been singing your praises. I quite understand and approve," he went on, taking my arm. "To be a good workman is ever so much more honest and more sensible than wasting government paper and wearing a cockade on your head. I myself worked in Belgium with these very hands and then spent two years as a mechanic. . . ."

He was wearing a short reefer jacket and indoor slippers; he walked like a man with the gout, rolling slightly from side to side and rubbing his hands. Humming something he softly purred and hugged himself with satisfaction at being at home again at last, and able to have his beloved shower bath.

"There is no disputing," he said to me at supper, "there is no disputing; you are all nice and charming people, but for some reason, as soon as you take to manual labour, or go in for saving the peasants, in the long run it all comes to no more than being a dissenter. Aren't you a dissenter? Here you don't take vodka. What's the meaning of that if it is not being a dissenter?"

To satisfy him I drank some vodka and I drank some wine, too. We tasted the cheese, the sausage, the pâtés, the pickles, and the savouries of all sorts that the engineer had brought with him, and the wine that had come in his absence from abroad. The wine was first-rate. For some reason the engineer got wine and cigars from abroad without paying duty; the caviare and the dried sturgeon someone sent him for nothing; he did not pay rent for his flat as the owner of the house provided the kerosene for the line; and altogether he and his daughter produced on me the impression that all the best in the world was at their service, and provided for them for nothing.

I went on going to see them, but not with the same eagerness. The engineer made me feel constrained, and in his presence I did not feel free. I could not face his clear, guileless eyes, his reflections wearied and sickened me; I was sickened, too, by the memory that so lately I had been in the employment of this red-faced, well-fed man, and that he had been brutally rude to me. It is true that he put his arm round my waist, slapped me on the shoulder in a friendly way, approved my manner of life, but I felt that, as before, he despised my insignificance, and only put up with me to please his daughter, and I couldn't now laugh and talk as I liked, and I behaved unsociably and kept expecting that in another minute he would address me as Panteley as he did his footman Pavel. How my pride as a provincial and a working man was revolted. I, a proletarian, a house painter, went every day to rich people who were alien to me, and whom the whole town regarded as though they were foreigners, and every day I drank costly wines with them and ate unusual dainties—my conscience refused to be reconciled to it! On my way to the house I sullenly avoided meeting people, and looked at them from under my brows as though I really were a dissenter, and when I was going home from the engineer's I was ashamed of my well-fed condition.

Above all I was afraid of being carried away. Whether I was walking along the street, or working, or talking to the other fellows, I was all the time thinking of one thing only, of going in the evening to see Mariya Viktorovna and was picturing her voice, her laugh, her movements. When I was getting ready to go to her I always spent a long time before my nurse's warped looking-glass, as I fastened my tie; my serge trousers were detestable in my eyes, and I suffered torments, and at the same time despised myself for being so trivial. When she called to me out of the other room that she was not dressed and asked me to wait, I listened to her dressing; it agitated me, I felt as though the ground were giving way under my feet. And when I saw a woman's figure in the street, even at a distance, I invariably compared it. It seemed to me that all our girls and women were vulgar, that they were absurdly dressed, and did not know how to hold themselves; and these comparisons aroused a feeling of pride in me: Mariya Viktorovna was the best of them all! And I dreamed of her and myself at night.

One evening at supper with the engineer we ate a whole lobster As I was going home afterwards I remembered that the engineer twice called me "My dear fellow" at supper, and I reflected that they treated me very kindly in that house, as they might an unfortunate big dog who had been kicked out by its owners, that they were amusing themselves with me, and that when they were tired of me they would turn me out like a dog. I felt ashamed and wounded, wounded to the point of tears as though I had been insulted, and looking up at the sky I took a vow to put an end to all this.

The next day I did not go to the Dolzhikov's. Late in the evening, when it was quite dark and raining, I walked along Great Dvoryansky Street, looking up at the windows. Everyone was asleep at the Azhogins', and the only light was in one of the furthest windows. It was Madame Azhogin in her own room, sewing by the light of three candles, imagining that she was combating superstition. Our house was in darkness, but at the Dolzhikovs', on the contrary, the windows were lighted up, but one could distinguish nothing through the flowers and the curtains. I kept walking up and down the street; the cold March rain drenched me through. I heard my father come home from the club; he stood knocking at the gate. A minute later a light appeared at the window, and I saw my sister, who was hastening down with a lamp, while with the other hand she was twisting her thick hair together as she went. Then my father walked about the drawing-room, talking and rubbing his hands, while my sister sat in a low chair, thinking and not listening to what he said.

But then they went away; the light went out. . . . I glanced round at the engineer's, and there, too, all was darkness now. In the dark and the rain I felt hopelessly alone, abandoned to the whims of destiny; I felt that all my doings, my desires, and everything I had thought and said till then were trivial in comparison with my loneliness, in comparison with my present suffering, and the suffering that lay before me in the future. Alas, the thoughts and doings of living creatures are not nearly so significant as their sufferings! And without clearly realizing what I was doing, I pulled at the bell of the Dolzhikovs' gate, broke it, and ran along the street like some naughty boy, with a feeling of terror in my heart, expecting every moment that they would come out and recognize me. When I stopped at the end of the street to take breath I could hear nothing but the sound of the rain, and somewhere in the distance a watchman striking on a sheet of iron.

For a whole week I did not go to the Dolzhikovs'. My serge trousers were sold. There was nothing doing in the painting trade. I knew the pangs of hunger again, and earned from twopence to fourpence a day, where I could, by heavy and unpleasant work. Struggling up to my knees in the cold mud, straining my chest, I tried to stifle my memories, and, as it were, to punish myself for the cheeses and preserves with which I had been regaled at the engineer's. But all the same, as soon as I lay in bed, wet and hungry, my sinful imagination immediately began to paint exquisite, seductive pictures, and with amazement I acknowledged to myself that I was in love, passionately in love, and I fell into a sound, heavy sleep, feeling that hard labour only made my body stronger and younger.

One evening snow began falling most inappropriately, and the wind blew from the north as though winter had come back again. When I returned from work that evening I found Mariya Viktorovna in my room. She was sitting in her fur coat, and had both hands in her muff.

"Why don't you come to see me?" she asked, raising her clear, clever eyes, and I was utterly confused with delight and stood stiffly upright before her, as I used to stand facing my father when he was going to beat me; she looked into my face and I could see from her eyes that she understood why I was confused.

"Why don't you come to see me?" she repeated. "If you don't want to come, you see, I have come to you."

She got up and came close to me.

"Don't desert me," she said, and her eyes filled with tears. "I am alone, utterly alone."

She began crying; and, hiding her face in her muff, articulated:

"Alone! My life is hard, very hard, and in all the world I have no one but you. Don't desert me!"

Looking for a handkerchief to wipe her tears she smiled; we were silent for some time, then I put my arms round her and kissed her, scratching my cheek till it bled with her hatpin as I did it.

And we began talking to each other as though we had been on the closest terms for ages and ages.

## X

Two days later she sent me to Dubetchnya and I was unutterably delighted to go. As I walked towards the station and afterwards, as I was sitting in the train, I kept laughing from no apparent cause, and people looked at me as though I were drunk. Snow was falling, and there were still frosts in the mornings, but the roads were already dark-coloured and rooks hovered over them, cawing.

At first I had intended to fit up an abode for us two, Masha and me, in the lodge at the side opposite Madame Tcheprakov's lodge, but it appeared that the doves and the ducks had been living there for a long time, and it was impossible to clean it without destroying a great number of nests. There was nothing for it but to live in the comfortless rooms of the big house with the sunblinds. The peasants called the house the palace; there were more than twenty rooms in it, and the only furniture was a piano and a child's arm-chair lying in the attic. And if Masha had brought all her furniture from the town we should even then have been unable to get rid of the impression of immense emptiness and cold. I picked out three small rooms with windows looking into the garden, and worked from early morning till night, setting them to rights, putting in new panes, papering the walls, filling up the holes and chinks in the floors. It was easy, pleasant work. I was continually running to the river to see whether the ice were not going; I kept fancying that starlings were flying. And at night, thinking of Masha, I listened with an unutterably sweet feeling, with clutching delight to the noise of the rats and the wind droning and knocking above the ceiling. It seemed as though some old house spirit were coughing in the attic.

The snow was deep; a great deal had fallen even at the end of March, but it melted quickly, as though by magic, and the spring floods passed in a tumultuous rush, so that by the beginning of April the starlings were already noisy, and yellow butterflies were flying in the garden. It was exquisite weather. Every day, towards evening, I used to walk to the town to meet Masha, and what a delight it was to walk with bare feet along the gradually drying, still soft road. Halfway I used to sit down and look towards the town, not venturing to go near it. The sight of it troubled me. I kept wondering how the people I knew would behave to me when they heard of my love. What would my father say? What troubled me particularly was the thought that my life was more complicated, and that I had completely lost all power to set it right, and that, like a balloon, it was bearing me away, God knows whither. I no longer considered the problem how to earn my daily bread, how to live, but thought about—I really don't know what.

Masha used to come in a carriage; I used to get in with her, and we drove to Dubetchnya, feeling light-hearted and free. Or, after waiting till the sun had set, I would go back dissatisfied and dreary, wondering why Masha had not come; at the gate or in the garden I would be met by a sweet, unexpected apparition—it was she! It would turn out that she had come by rail, and had walked from the station. What a festival it was! In a simple woollen dress with a kerchief on her head, with a modest sunshade, but laced in, slender, in expensive foreign boots—it was a talented actress playing the part of a little workgirl. We looked round our domain and decided which should be her room, and which mine, where we would have our avenue, our kitchen garden, our beehives.

We already had hens, ducks, and geese, which we loved because they were ours. We had, all ready for sowing, oats, clover, timothy grass, buckwheat, and vegetable seeds, and we always looked at all these stores and discussed at length the crop we might get; and everything Masha said to me seemed extraordinarily clever, and fine. This was the happiest time of my life.

Soon after St. Thomas's week we were married at our parish church in the village of Kurilovka, two miles from Dubetchnya. Masha wanted everything to be done quietly; at her wish our "best men" were peasant lads, the sacristan sang alone, and we came back from the church in a small, jolting chaise which she drove herself. Our only guest from the town was my sister Kleopatra, to whom Masha sent a note three days before the wedding. My sister came in a white dress and wore gloves. During the wedding she cried quietly from joy and tenderness. Her expression was motherly and infinitely kind. She was intoxicated with our happiness, and smiled as though she were absorbing a sweet delirium, and looking at her during our wedding, I realized that for her there was nothing in the world higher than love, earthly love, and that she was dreaming of it secretly, timidly, but continually and passionately. She embraced and kissed Masha, and, not knowing how to express her rapture, said to her of me: "He is good! He is very good!"

Before she went away she changed into her ordinary dress, and drew me into the garden to talk to me alone.

"Father is very much hurt," she said, "that you have written nothing to him. You ought to have asked for his blessing. But in reality he is very much pleased. He says that this marriage will raise you in the eyes of all society, and that under the influence of Mariya Viktorovna you will begin to take a more serious view of life. We talk of nothing but you in the evenings now, and yesterday he actually used the expression: 'Our Misail.' That pleased me. It seems as though he had some plan in his mind, and I fancy he wants to set you an example of magnanimity and be the first to speak of reconciliation. It is very possible he may come here to see you in a day or two."

She hurriedly made the sign of the cross over me several times and said:

"Well, God be with you. Be happy. Anyuta Blagovo is a very clever girl; she says about your marriage that God is sending you a fresh ordeal. To be sure—married life does not bring only joy but suffering too. That's bound to be so."

Masha and I walked a couple of miles to see her on her way; we walked back slowly and in silence, as though we were resting. Masha held my hand, my heart felt light, and I had no inclination to talk about love; we had become closer and more akin now that we were married, and we felt that nothing now could separate us.

"Your sister is a nice creature," said Masha, "but it seems as though she had been tormented for years. Your father must be a terrible man."

I began telling her how my sister and I had been brought up, and what a senseless torture our childhood had really been. When she heard how my father had so lately beaten me, she shuddered and drew closer to me.

"Don't tell me any more," she said. "It's horrible!"

Now she never left me. We lived together in the three rooms in the big house, and in the evenings we bolted the door which led to the empty part of the house, as though someone were living there whom we did not know, and were afraid of. I got up early, at dawn, and immediately set to work of some sort. I mended the carts, made paths in the garden, dug the flower beds, painted the roof of the house. When the time came to sow the oats I tried to plough the ground over again, to harrow and to sow, and I did it all conscientiously, keeping up with our labourer; I was worn out, the rain and the cold wind made my face and feet burn for hours afterwards. I dreamed of ploughed land at night. But field labour did not attract me. I did not understand farming, and I did not care for it; it was perhaps because my forefathers had not been tillers of the soil, and the very blood that flowed in my veins was purely of the city. I loved nature tenderly; I loved the fields and meadows and kitchen gardens, but the peasant who turned up the soil with his plough and urged on his pitiful horse, wet and tattered, with his craning neck, was to me the expression of coarse, savage, ugly force, and every time I looked at his uncouth movements I involuntarily began thinking of the legendary life of the remote past, before men knew the use of fire. The fierce bull that ran with the peasants' herd, and the horses, when they dashed about the village, stamping their hoofs, moved me to fear, and everything rather big, strong, and angry, whether it was the ram with its horns, the gander, or the yard-dog, seemed to me the expression of the same coarse, savage force. This mood was particularly strong in me in bad weather, when heavy clouds were hanging over the black ploughed land. Above all, when I was ploughing or sowing, and two or three people stood looking how I was doing it, I had not the feeling that this work was inevitable and obligatory, and it seemed to me that I was amusing myself. I preferred doing something in the yard, and there was nothing I liked so much as painting the roof.

I used to walk through the garden and the meadow to our mill. It was let to a peasant of Kurilovka called Stepan, a handsome, dark fellow with a thick black beard, who looked very strong. He did not like the miller's work, and looked upon it as dreary and unprofitable, and only lived at the mill in order not to live at home. He was a leather-worker, and was always surrounded by a pleasant smell of tar and leather. He was not fond of talking, he was listless and sluggish, and was always sitting in the doorway or on the river bank, humming "oo-loo-loo." His wife and mother-in-law, both white-faced, languid, and meek, used sometimes to come from Kurilovka to see him; they made low bows to him and addressed him formally, "Stepan Petrovitch," while he went on sitting on the river bank, softly humming "oo-loo-loo," without responding by word or movement to their bows. One hour and then a second would pass in silence. His mother-in-law and wife, after whispering together, would get up and gaze at him for some time, expecting him to look round; then they would make a low bow, and in sugary, chanting voices, say:

"Good-bye, Stepan Petrovitch!"

And they would go away. After that Stepan, picking up the parcel they had left, containing cracknels or a shirt, would heave a sigh and say, winking in their direction:

"The female sex!"

The mill with two sets of millstones worked day and night. I used to help Stepan; I liked the work, and when he went off I was glad to stay and take his place.

## XI

After bright warm weather came a spell of wet; all May it rained and was cold. The sound of the millwheels and of the rain disposed one to indolence and slumber. The floor trembled, there was a smell of flour, and that, too, induced drowsiness. My wife in a short fur-lined jacket, and in men's high golosh boots, would make her appearance twice a day, and she always said the same thing:

"And this is called summer! Worse than it was in October!"

We used to have tea and make the porridge together, or we would sit for hours at a stretch without speaking, waiting for the rain to stop. Once, when Stepan had gone off to the fair, Masha stayed all night at the mill. When we got up we could not tell what time it was, as the rainclouds covered the whole sky; but sleepy cocks were crowing at Dubetchnya, and landrails were calling in the meadows; it was still very, very early. . . . My wife and I went down to the millpond and drew out the net which Stepan had thrown in over night in our presence. A big pike was struggling in it, and a cray-fish was twisting about, clawing upwards with its pincers.

"Let them go," said Masha. "Let them be happy too."

Because we got up so early and afterwards did nothing, that day seemed very long, the longest day in my life. Towards evening Stepan came back and I went home.

"Your father came to-day," said Masha.

"Where is he?" I asked.

"He has gone away. I would not see him."

Seeing that I remained standing and silent, that I was sorry for my father, she said:

"One must be consistent. I would not see him, and sent word to him not to trouble to come and see us again."

A minute later I was out at the gate and walking to the town to explain things to my father. It was muddy, slippery, cold. For the first time since my marriage I felt suddenly sad, and in my brain exhausted by that long, grey day, there was stirring the thought that perhaps I was not living as I ought. I was worn out; little by little I was overcome by despondency and indolence, I did not want to move or think, and after going on a little I gave it up with a wave of my hand and turned back.

The engineer in a leather overcoat with a hood was standing in the middle of the yard.

"Where's the furniture? There used to be lovely furniture in the Empire style: there used to be pictures, there used to be vases, while now you could play ball in it! I bought the place with the furniture. The devil take her!"

Moisey, a thin pock-marked fellow of twenty-five, with insolent little eyes, who was in the service of the general's widow, stood near him crumpling up his cap in his hands; one of his cheeks was bigger than the other, as though he had lain too long on it.

"Your honour was graciously pleased to buy the place without the furniture," he brought out irresolutely; "I remember."

"Hold your tongue!" shouted the engineer; he turned crimson and shook with anger . . . and the echo in the garden loudly repeated his shout.

## XII

When I was doing anything in the garden or the yard, Moisey would stand beside me, and folding his arms behind his back he would stand lazily and impudently staring at me with his little eyes. And this irritated me to such a degree that I threw up my work and went away.

From Stepan we heard that Moisey was Madame Tcheprakov's lover. I noticed that when people came to her to borrow money they addressed themselves first to Moisey, and once I saw a peasant, black from head to foot—he must have been a coalheaver—bow down at Moisey's feet. Sometimes, after a little whispering, he gave out money himself, without consulting his mistress, from which I concluded that he did a little business on his own account.

He used to shoot in our garden under our windows, carried off victuals from our cellar, borrowed our horses without asking permission, and we were indignant and began to feel as though Dubetchnya were not ours, and Masha would say, turning pale:

"Can we really have to go on living with these reptiles another eighteen months?"

Madame Tcheprakov's son, Ivan, was serving as a guard on our railway-line. He had grown much thinner and feebler during the winter, so that a single glass was enough to make him drunk, and he shivered out of the sunshine. He wore the guard's uniform with aversion and was ashamed of it, but considered his post a good one, as he could steal the candles and sell them. My new position excited in him a mixed feeling of wonder, envy, and a vague hope that something of the same sort might happen to him. He used to watch Masha with ecstatic eyes, ask me what I had for dinner now, and his lean and ugly face wore a sad and sweetish expression, and he moved his fingers as though he were feeling my happiness with them.

"Listen, Better-than-nothing," he said fussily, relighting his cigarette at every instant; there was always a litter where he stood, for he wasted dozens of matches, lighting one cigarette. "Listen, my life now is the nastiest possible. The worst of it is any subaltern can shout: 'Hi, there, guard!' I have overheard all sorts of things in the train, my boy, and do you know, I have learned that life's a beastly thing! My mother has been the ruin of me! A doctor in the train told me that if parents are immoral, their children are drunkards or criminals. Think of that!"

Once he came into the yard, staggering; his eyes gazed about blankly, his breathing was laboured; he laughed and cried and babbled as though in a high fever, and the only words I could catch in his muddled talk were, "My mother! Where's my mother?" which he uttered with a wail like a child who has lost his mother in a crowd. I led him into our garden and laid him down under a tree, and Masha and I took turns to sit by him all that day and all night. He was very sick, and Masha looked with aversion at his pale, wet face, and said:

"Is it possible these reptiles will go on living another year and a half in our yard? It's awful! it's awful!"

And how many mortifications the peasants caused us! How many bitter disappointments in those early days in the spring months, when we so longed to be happy. My wife built a school. I drew a plan of a school for sixty boys, and the Zemstvo Board approved of it, but advised us to build the school at Kurilovka the big village which was only two miles from us. Moreover, the school at Kurilovka in which children—from four villages, our Dubetchnya being one of the number—were taught, was old and too small, and the floor was scarcely safe to walk upon. At the end of March at Masha's wish, she was appointed guardian of the Kurilovka school, and at the beginning of April we three times summoned the village assembly, and tried to persuade the peasants that their school was old and overcrowded, and that it was essential to build a new one. A member of the Zemstvo Board and the Inspector of Peasant Schools came, and they, too, tried to persuade them. After each meeting the peasants surrounded us, begging for a bucket of vodka; we were hot in the crowd; we were soon exhausted, and returned home dissatisfied and a little ill at ease. In the end the peasants set apart a plot of ground for the school, and were obliged to bring all the building material from the town with their own horses. And the very first Sunday after the spring corn was sown carts set off from Kurilovka and Dubetchnya to fetch bricks for the foundations. They set off as soon as it was light, and came back late in the evening; the peasants were drunk, and said they were worn out.

As ill-luck would have it, the rain and the cold persisted all through May. The road was in an awful state: it was deep in mud. The carts usually drove into our yard when they came back from the town— and what a horrible ordeal it was. A potbellied horse would appear at the gate, setting its front legs wide apart; it would stumble forward before coming into the yard; a beam, nine yards long, wet and slimy-looking, crept in on a waggon. Beside it, muffled up against the rain, strode a peasant with the skirts of his coat tucked up in his belt, not looking where he was going, but stepping through the puddles. Another cart would appear with boards, then a third with a beam, a fourth . . . and the space before our house was gradually crowded up with horses, beams, and planks. Men and women, with their heads muffled and their skirts tucked up, would stare angrily at our windows, make an uproar, and clamour for the mistress to come out to them; coarse oaths were audible. Meanwhile Moisey stood at one side, and we fancied he was enjoying our discomfiture.

"We are not going to cart any more," the peasants would shout. "We are worn out! Let her go and get the stuff herself."

Masha, pale and flustered, expecting every minute that they would break into the house, would send them out a half-pail of vodka; after that the noise would subside and the long beams, one after another, would crawl slowly out of the yard.

When I was setting off to see the building my wife was worried and said:

"The peasants are spiteful; I only hope they won't do you a mischief. Wait a minute, I'll come with you."

We drove to Kurilovka together, and there the carpenters asked us for a drink. The framework of the house was ready. It was time to lay the foundation, but the masons had not come; this caused delay, and the carpenters complained. And when at last the masons did come, it appeared that there was no sand; it had been somehow overlooked that it would be needed. Taking advantage of our helpless position, the peasants demanded thirty kopecks for each cartload, though the distance from the building to the river where they got the sand was less than a quarter of a mile, and more than five hundred cartloads were found to be necessary. There was no end to the misunderstandings, swearing, and importunity; my wife was indignant, and the foreman of the masons, Tit Petrov, an old man of seventy, took her by the arm, and said:

"You look here! You look here! You only bring me the sand; I set ten men on at once, and in two days it will be done! You look here!"

But they brought the sand and two days passed, and four, and a week, and instead of the promised foundations there was still a yawning hole.

"It's enough to drive one out of one's senses," said my wife, in distress. "What people! What people!"

In the midst of these disorderly doings the engineer arrived; he brought with him parcels of wine and savouries, and after a prolonged meal lay down for a nap in the verandah and snored so loudly that the labourers shook their heads and said: "Well!"

Masha was not pleased at his coming, she did not trust him, though at the same time she asked his advice. When, after sleeping too long after dinner, he got up in a bad humour and said unpleasant things about our management of the place, or expressed regret that he had bought Dubetchnya, which had already been a loss to him, poor Masha's face wore an expression of misery. She would complain to him, and he would yawn and say that the peasants ought to be flogged.

He called our marriage and our life a farce, and said it was a caprice, a whim.

"She has done something of the sort before," he said about Masha. "She once fancied herself a great opera singer and left me; I was looking for her for two months, and, my dear soul, I spent a thousand roubles on telegrams alone."

He no longer called me a dissenter or Mr. Painter, and did not as in the past express approval of my living like a workman, but said:

"You are a strange person! You are not a normal person! I won't venture to prophesy, but you will come to a bad end!"

And Masha slept badly at night, and was always sitting at our bedroom window thinking. There was no laughter at supper now, no charming grimaces. I was wretched, and when it rained, every drop that fell seemed to pierce my heart, like small shot, and I felt ready to fall on my knees before Masha and apologize for the weather. When the peasants made a noise in the yard I felt guilty also. For hours at a time I sat still in one place, thinking of nothing but what a splendid person Masha was, what a wonderful person. I loved her passionately, and I was fascinated by everything she did, everything she said. She had a bent for quiet, studious pursuits; she was fond of reading for hours together, of studying. Although her knowledge of farming was only from books she surprised us all by what she knew; and every piece of advice she gave was of value; not one was ever thrown away; and, with all that, what nobility, what taste, what graciousness, that graciousness which is only found in well-educated people.

To this woman, with her sound, practical intelligence, the disorderly surroundings with petty cares and sordid anxieties in which we were living now were an agony: I saw that and could not sleep at night; my brain worked feverishly and I had a lump in my throat. I rushed about not knowing what to do.

I galloped to the town and brought Masha books, newspapers, sweets, flowers; with Stepan I caught fish, wading for hours up to my neck in the cold water in the rain to catch eel-pout to vary our fare; I demeaned myself to beg the peasants not to make a noise; I plied them with vodka, bought them off, made all sorts of promises. And how many other foolish things I did!

At last the rain ceased, the earth dried. One would get up at four o'clock in the morning; one would go out into the garden—where there was dew sparkling on the flowers, the twitter of birds, the hum of insects, not one cloud in the sky; and the garden, the meadows, and the river were so lovely, yet there were memories of the peasants, of their carts, of the engineer. Masha and I drove out together in the racing droshky to the fields to look at the oats. She used to drive, I sat behind; her shoulders were raised and the wind played with her hair.

"Keep to the right!" she shouted to those she met.

"You are like a sledge-driver," I said to her one day.

"Maybe! Why, my grandfather, the engineer's father, was a sledge-driver. Didn't you know that?" she asked, turning to me, and at once she mimicked the way sledge-drivers shout and sing.

"And thank God for that," I thought as I listened to her. "Thank God."

And again memories of the peasants, of the carts, of the engineer. . . .

## XIII

Dr. Blagovo arrived on his bicycle. My sister began coming often. Again there were conversations about manual labour, about progress, about a mysterious millennium awaiting mankind in the remote future. The doctor did not like our farmwork, because it interfered with arguments, and said that ploughing, reaping, grazing calves were unworthy of a free man, and all these coarse forms of the struggle for existence men would in time relegate to animals and machines, while they would devote themselves exclusively to scientific investigation. My sister kept begging them to let her go home earlier, and if she stayed on till late in the evening, or spent the night with us, there would be no end to the agitation.

"Good Heavens, what a baby you are still!" said Masha reproachfully. "It is positively absurd."

"Yes, it is absurd," my sister agreed, "I know it's absurd; but what is to be done if I haven't the strength to get over it? I keep feeling as though I were doing wrong."

At haymaking I ached all over from the unaccustomed labour; in the evening, sitting on the verandah and talking with the others, I suddenly dropped asleep, and they laughed aloud at me. They waked me up and made me sit down to supper; I was overpowered with drowsiness and I saw the lights, the faces, and the plates as it were in a dream, heard the voices, but did not understand them. And getting up early in the morning, I took up the scythe at once, or went to the building and worked hard all day.

When I remained at home on holidays I noticed that my sister and Masha were concealing something from me, and even seemed to be avoiding me. My wife was tender to me as before, but she had thoughts of her own apart, which she did not share with me. There was no doubt that her exasperation with the peasants was growing, the life was becoming more and more distasteful to her, and yet she did not complain to me. She talked to the doctor now more readily than she did to me, and I did not understand why it was so.

It was the custom in our province at haymaking and harvest time for the labourers to come to the manor house in the evening and be regaled with vodka; even young girls drank a glass. We did not keep up this practice; the mowers and the peasant women stood about in our yard till late in the evening expecting vodka, and then departed abusing us. And all the time Masha frowned grimly and said nothing, or murmured to the doctor with exasperation: "Savages! Petchenyegs!"

In the country newcomers are met ungraciously, almost with hostility, as they are at school. And we were received in this way. At first we were looked upon as stupid, silly people, who had bought an estate simply because we did not know what to do with our money. We were laughed at. The peasants grazed their cattle in our wood and even in our garden; they drove away our cows and horses to the village, and then demanded money for the damage done by them. They came in whole companies into our yard, and loudly clamoured that at the mowing we had cut some piece of land that did not belong to us; and as we did not yet know the boundaries of our estate very accurately, we took their word for it and paid damages. Afterwards it turned out that there had been no mistake at the mowing. They barked the lime-trees in our wood. One of the Dubetchnya peasants, a regular shark, who did a trade in vodka without a licence, bribed our labourers, and in collaboration with them cheated us in a most treacherous way. They took the new wheels off our carts and replaced them with old ones, stole our ploughing harness and actually sold them to us, and so on. But what was most mortifying of all was what happened at the building; the peasant women stole by night boards, bricks, tiles, pieces of iron. The village elder with witnesses made a search in their huts; the village meeting fined them two roubles each, and afterwards this money was spent on drink by the whole commune.

When Masha heard about this, she would say to the doctor or my sister indignantly:

"What beasts! It's awful! awful!"

And I heard her more than once express regret that she had ever taken it into her head to build the school.

"You must understand," the doctor tried to persuade her, "that if you build this school and do good in general, it's not for the sake of the peasants, but in the name of culture, in the name of the future; and the worse the peasants are the more reason for building the school. Understand that!"

But there was a lack of conviction in his voice, and it seemed to me that both he and Masha hated the peasants.

Masha often went to the mill, taking my sister with her, and they both said, laughing, that they went to have a look at Stepan, he was so handsome. Stepan, it appeared, was torpid and taciturn only with men; in feminine society his manners were free and easy, and he talked incessantly. One day, going down to the river to bathe, I accidentally overheard a conversation. Masha and Kleopatra, both in white dresses, were sitting on the bank in the spreading shade of a willow, and Stepan was standing by them with his hands behind his back, and was saying:

"Are peasants men? They are not men, but, asking your pardon, wild beasts, impostors. What life has a peasant? Nothing but eating and drinking; all he cares for is victuals to be cheaper and swilling liquor at the tavern like a fool; and there's no conversation, no manners, no formality, nothing but ignorance! He lives in filth, his wife lives in filth, and his children live in filth. What he stands up in, he lies down to sleep in; he picks the potatoes out of the soup with his fingers; he drinks kvass with a cockroach in it, and doesn't bother to blow it away!"

"It's their poverty, of course," my sister put in.

"Poverty? There is want to be sure, there's different sorts of want, Madam. If a man is in prison, or let us say blind or crippled, that really is trouble I wouldn't wish anyone, but if a man's free and has all his senses, if he has his eyes and his hands and his strength and God, what more does he want? It's cockering themselves, and it's ignorance, Madam, it's not poverty. If you, let us suppose, good gentlefolk, by your education, wish out of kindness to help him he will drink away your money in his low way; or, what's worse, he will open a drinkshop, and with your money start robbing the people. You say poverty, but does the rich peasant live better? He, too, asking your pardon, lives like a swine: coarse, loud-mouthed, cudgel-headed, broader than he is long, fat, red-faced mug, I'd like to swing my fist and send him flying, the scoundrel. There's Larion, another rich one at Dubetchnya, and I bet he strips the bark off your trees as much as any poor one; and he is a foul-mouthed fellow; his children are the same, and when he has had a drop too much he'll topple with his nose in a puddle and sleep there. They are all a worthless lot, Madam. If you live in a village with them it is like hell. It has stuck in my teeth, that village has, and thank the Lord, the King of Heaven, I've plenty to eat and clothes to wear, I served out my time in the dragoons, I was village elder for three years, and now I am a free Cossack, I live where I like. I don't want to live in the village, and no one has the right to force me. They say—my wife. They say you are bound to live in your cottage with your wife. But why so? I am not her hired man."

"Tell me, Stepan, did you marry for love?" asked Masha.

"Love among us in the village!" answered Stepan, and he gave a laugh. "Properly speaking, Madam, if you care to know, this is my second marriage. I am not a Kurilovka man, I am from Zalegoshtcho, but afterwards I was taken into Kurilovka when I married. You see my father did not want to divide the land among us. There were five of us brothers. I took my leave and went to another village to live with my wife's family, but my first wife died when she was young."

"What did she die of?"

"Of foolishness. She used to cry and cry and cry for no reason, and so she pined away. She was always drinking some sort of herbs to make her better looking, and I suppose she damaged her inside. And my second wife is a Kurilovka woman too, there is nothing in her. She's a village woman, a peasant woman, and nothing more. I was taken in when they plighted me to her. I thought she was young and fair-skinned, and that they lived in a clean way. Her mother was just like a Flagellant and she drank coffee, and the chief thing, to be sure, they were clean in their ways. So I married her, and next day we sat down to dinner; I bade my mother-in-law give me a spoon, and she gives me a spoon, and I see her wipe it out with her finger. So much for you, thought I; nice sort of cleanliness yours is. I lived a year with them and then I went away. I might have married a girl from the town," he went on after a pause. "They say a wife is a helpmate to her husband. What do I want with a helpmate? I help myself; I'd rather she talked to me, and not clack, clack, clack, but circumstantially, feelingly. What is life without good conversation?"

Stepan suddenly paused, and at once there was the sound of his dreary, monotonous "oo-loo-loo-loo." This meant that he had seen me.

Masha used often to go to the mill, and evidently found pleasure in her conversations with Stepan. Stepan abused the peasants with such sincerity and conviction, and she was attracted to him. Every time she came back from the mill the feeble-minded peasant, who looked after the garden, shouted at her:

"Wench Palashka! Hulla, wench Palashka!" and he would bark like a dog: "Ga! Ga!"

And she would stop and look at him attentively, as though in that idiot's barking she found an answer to her thoughts, and probably he attracted her in the same way as Stepan's abuse. At home some piece of news would await her, such, for instance, as that the geese from the village had ruined our cabbage in the garden, or that Larion had stolen the reins; and shrugging her shoulders, she would say with a laugh:

"What do you expect of these people?"

She was indignant, and there was rancour in her heart, and meanwhile I was growing used to the peasants, and I felt more and more drawn to them. For the most part they were nervous, irritable, downtrodden people; they were people whose imagination had been stifled, ignorant, with a poor, dingy outlook on life, whose thoughts were ever the same—of the grey earth, of grey days, of black bread, people who cheated, but like birds hiding nothing but their head behind the tree—people who could not count. They would not come to mow for us for twenty roubles, but they came for half a pail of vodka, though for twenty roubles they could have bought four pails. There really was filth and drunkenness and foolishness and deceit, but with all that one yet felt that the life of the peasants rested on a firm, sound foundation. However uncouth a wild animal the peasant following the plough seemed, and however he might stupefy himself with vodka, still, looking at him more closely, one felt that there was in him what was needed, something very important, which was lacking in Masha and in the doctor, for instance, and that was that he believed the chief thing on earth was truth and justice, and that his salvation, and that of the whole people, was only to be found in truth and justice, and so more than anything in the world he loved just dealing. I told my wife she saw the spots on the glass, but not the glass itself; she said nothing in reply, or hummed like Stepan "oo-loo-loo-loo." When this good-hearted and clever woman turned pale with indignation, and with a quiver in her voice spoke to the doctor of the drunkenness and dishonesty, it perplexed me, and I was struck by the shortness of her memory. How could she forget that her father the engineer drank too, and drank heavily, and that the money with which Dubetchnya had been bought had been acquired by a whole series of shameless, impudent dishonesties? How could she forget it?

## XIV

My sister, too, was leading a life of her own which she carefully hid from me. She was often whispering with Masha. When I went up to her she seemed to shrink into herself, and there was a guilty, imploring look in her eyes; evidently there was something going on in her heart of which she was afraid or ashamed. So as to avoid meeting me in the garden, or being left alone with me, she always kept close to Masha, and I rarely had an opportunity of talking to her except at dinner.

One evening I was walking quietly through the garden on my way back from the building. It was beginning to get dark. Without noticing me, or hearing my step, my sister was walking near a spreading old apple-tree, absolutely noiselessly as though she were a phantom. She was dressed in black, and was walking rapidly backwards and forwards on the same track, looking at the ground. An apple fell from the tree; she started at the sound, stood still and pressed her hands to her temples. At that moment I went up to her.

In a rush of tender affection which suddenly flooded my heart, with tears in my eyes, suddenly remembering my mother and our childhood, I put my arm round her shoulders and kissed her.

"What is the matter?" I asked her. "You are unhappy; I have seen it for a long time. Tell me what's wrong?"

"I am frightened," she said, trembling.

"What is it?" I insisted. "For God's sake, be open!"

"I will, I will be open; I will tell you the whole truth. To hide it from you is so hard, so agonizing. Misail, I love . . ." she went on in a whisper, "I love him . . . I love him. . . . I am happy, but why am I so frightened?"

There was the sound of footsteps; between the trees appeared Dr. Blagovo in his silk shirt with his high top boots. Evidently they had arranged to meet near the apple-tree. Seeing him, she rushed impulsively towards him with a cry of pain as though he were being taken from her.

"Vladimir! Vladimir!"

She clung to him and looked greedily into his face, and only then I noticed how pale and thin she had become of late. It was particularly noticeable from her lace collar which I had known for so long, and which now hung more loosely than ever before about her thin, long neck. The doctor was disconcerted, but at once recovered himself, and, stroking her hair, said:

"There, there. . . . Why so nervous? You see, I'm here."

We were silent, looking with embarrassment at each other, then we walked on, the three of us together, and I heard the doctor say to me:

"Civilized life has not yet begun among us. Old men console themselves by making out that if there is nothing now, there was something in the forties or the sixties; that's the old: you and I are young; our brains have not yet been touched by *marasmus senilis*; we cannot comfort ourselves with such illusions. The beginning of Russia was in 862, but the beginning of civilized Russia has not come yet."

But I did not grasp the meaning of these reflections. It was somehow strange, I could not believe it, that my sister was in love, that she was walking and holding the arm of a stranger and looking tenderly at him. My sister, this nervous, frightened, crushed, fettered creature, loved a man who was married and had children! I felt sorry for something, but what exactly I don't know; the presence of the doctor was for some reason distasteful to me now, and I could not imagine what would come of this love of theirs.

XV

Masha and I drove to Kurilovka to the dedication of the school.

"Autumn, autumn, autumn, . . ." said Masha softly, looking away. "Summer is over. There are no birds and nothing is green but the willows."

Yes, summer was over. There were fine, warm days, but it was fresh in the morning, and the shepherds went out in their sheepskins already; and in our garden the dew did not dry off the asters all day long. There were plaintive sounds all the time, and one could not make out whether they came from the shutters creaking on their rusty hinges, or from the flying cranes—and one's heart felt light, and one was eager for life.

"The summer is over," said Masha. "Now you and I can balance our accounts. We have done a lot of work, a lot of thinking; we are the better for it—all honour and glory to us—we have succeeded in self-improvement; but have our successes had any perceptible influence on the life around us, have they brought any benefit to anyone whatever? No. Ignorance, physical uncleanliness, drunkenness, an appallingly high infant mortality, everything remains as it was, and no one is the better for your having ploughed and sown, and my having wasted money and read books. Obviously we have been working only for ourselves and have had advanced ideas only for ourselves." Such reasonings perplexed me, and I did not know what to think.

"We have been sincere from beginning to end," said I, "and if anyone is sincere he is right."

"Who disputes it? We were right, but we haven't succeeded in properly accomplishing what we were right in. To begin with, our external methods themselves—aren't they mistaken? You want to be of use to men, but by the very fact of your buying an estate, from the very start you cut yourself off from any possibility of doing anything useful for them. Then if you work, dress, eat like a peasant you sanctify, as it were, by your authority, their heavy, clumsy dress, their horrible huts, their stupid beards. . . . On the other hand, if we suppose that you work for long, long years, your whole life, that in the end some practical results are obtained, yet what are they, your results, what can they do against such elemental forces as wholesale ignorance, hunger, cold, degeneration? A drop in the ocean! Other methods of struggle are needed, strong, bold, rapid! If one really wants to be of use one must get out of the narrow circle of ordinary social work, and try to act direct upon the mass! What is wanted, first of all, is a loud, energetic propaganda. Why is it that art—music, for instance—is so living, so popular, and in reality so powerful? Because the musician or the singer affects thousands at once.

Precious, precious art!" she went on, looking dreamily at the sky. "Art gives us wings and carries us far, far away! Anyone who is sick of filth, of petty, mercenary interests, anyone who is revolted, wounded, and indignant, can find peace and satisfaction only in the beautiful."

When we drove into Kurilovka the weather was bright and joyous. Somewhere they were threshing; there was a smell of rye straw. A mountain ash was bright red behind the hurdle fences, and all the trees wherever one looked were ruddy or golden. They were ringing the bells, they were carrying the ikons to the school, and we could hear them sing: "Holy Mother, our Defender," and how limpid the air was, and how high the doves were flying.

The service was being held in the classroom. Then the peasants of Kurilovka brought Masha the ikon, and the peasants of Dubetchnya offered her a big loaf and a gilt salt cellar. And Masha broke into sobs.

"If anything has been said that shouldn't have been or anything done not to your liking, forgive us," said an old man, and he bowed down to her and to me.

As we drove home Masha kept looking round at the school; the green roof, which I had painted, and which was glistening in the sun, remained in sight for a long while. And I felt that the look Masha turned upon it now was one of farewell.

### XVI

In the evening she got ready to go to the town. Of late she had taken to going often to the town and staying the night there. In her absence I could not work, my hands felt weak and limp; our huge courtyard seemed a dreary, repulsive, empty hole. The garden was full of angry noises, and without her the house, the trees, the horses were no longer "ours."

I did not go out of the house, but went on sitting at her table beside her bookshelf with the books on land work, those old favourites no longer wanted and looking at me now so shamefacedly. For whole hours together, while it struck seven, eight, nine, while the autumn night, black as soot, came on outside, I kept examining her old glove, or the pen with which she always wrote, or her little scissors. I did nothing, and realized clearly that all I had done before, ploughing, mowing, chopping, had only been because she wished it. And if she had sent me to clean a deep well, where I had to stand up to my waist in deep water, I should have crawled into the well without considering whether it was necessary or not. And now when she was not near, Dubetchnya, with its ruins, its untidiness, its banging shutters, with its thieves by day and by night, seemed to me a chaos in which any work would be useless. Besides, what had I to work for here, why anxiety and thought about the future, if I felt that the earth was giving way under my feet, that I had played my part in Dubetchnya, and that the fate of the books on farming was awaiting me too? Oh, what misery it was at night, in hours of solitude, when I was listening every minute in alarm, as though I were expecting someone to shout that it was time for me to go away! I did not grieve for Dubetchnya. I grieved for my love which, too, was threatened with its autumn. What an immense happiness it is to love and be loved, and how awful to feel that one is slipping down from that high pinnacle!

Masha returned from the town towards the evening of the next day. She was displeased with something, but she concealed it, and only said, why was it all the window frames had been put in for the winter it was enough to suffocate one. I took out two frames. We were not hungry, but we sat down to supper.

"Go and wash your hands," said my wife; "you smell of putty."

She had brought some new illustrated papers from the town, and we looked at them together after supper. There were supplements with fashion plates and patterns. Masha looked through them casually, and was putting them aside to examine them properly later on; but one dress, with a flat skirt as full as a bell and large sleeves, interested her, and she looked at it for a minute gravely and attentively.

"That's not bad," she said.

"Yes, that dress would suit you beautifully," I said, "beautifully."

And looking with emotion at the dress, admiring that patch of grey simply because she liked it, I went on tenderly:

"A charming, exquisite dress! Splendid, glorious, Masha! My precious Masha!"

And tears dropped on the fashion plate.

"Splendid Masha . . ." I muttered; "sweet, precious Masha. . . ."

She went to bed, while I sat another hour looking at the illustrations.

"It's a pity you took out the window frames," she said from the bedroom, "I am afraid it may be cold. Oh, dear, what a draught there is!"

I read something out of the column of odds and ends, a receipt for making cheap ink, and an account of the biggest diamond in the world. I came again upon the fashion plate of the dress she liked, and I imagined her at a ball, with a fan, bare shoulders, brilliant, splendid, with a full understanding of painting, music, literature, and how small and how brief my part seemed!

Our meeting, our marriage, had been only one of the episodes of which there would be many more in the life of this vital, richly gifted woman. All the best in the world, as I have said already, was at her service, and she received it absolutely for nothing, and even ideas and the intellectual movement in vogue served simply for her recreation, giving variety to her life, and I was only the sledge-driver who drove her from one entertainment to another. Now she did not need me. She would take flight, and I should be alone.

And as though in response to my thought, there came a despairing scream from the garden.

"He-e-elp!"

It was a shrill, womanish voice, and as though to mimic it the wind whistled in the chimney on the same shrill note. Half a minute passed, and again through the noise of the wind, but coming, it seemed, from the other end of the yard:

"He-e-elp!"

"Misail, do you hear?" my wife asked me softly. "Do you hear?"

She came out from the bedroom in her nightgown, with her hair down, and listened, looking at the dark window.

"Someone is being murdered," she said. "That is the last straw."

I took my gun and went out. It was very dark outside, the wind was high, and it was difficult to stand. I went to the gate and listened, the trees roared, the wind whistled and, probably at the feeble-minded peasant's, a dog howled lazily. Outside the gates the darkness was absolute, not a light on the railway-line. And near the lodge, which a year before had been the office, suddenly sounded a smothered scream:

"He-e-elp!"

"Who's there?" I called.

There were two people struggling. One was thrusting the other out, while the other was resisting, and both were breathing heavily.

"Leave go," said one, and I recognized Ivan Tcheprakov; it was he who was shrieking in a shrill, womanish voice: "Let go, you damned brute, or I'll bite your hand off."

The other I recognized as Moisey. I separated them, and as I did so I could not resist hitting Moisey two blows in the face. He fell down, then got up again, and I hit him once more.

"He tried to kill me," he muttered. "He was trying to get at his mamma's chest. . . . I want to lock him up in the lodge for security."

Tcheprakov was drunk and did not recognize me; he kept drawing deep breaths, as though he were just going to shout "help" again.

I left them and went back to the house; my wife was lying on her bed; she had dressed. I told her what had happened in the yard, and did not conceal the fact that I had hit Moisey.

"It's terrible to live in the country," she said.

"And what a long night it is. Oh dear, if only it were over!"

"He-e-elp!" we heard again, a little later.

"I'll go and stop them," I said.

"No, let them bite each other's throats," she said with an expression of disgust.

She was looking up at the ceiling, listening, while I sat beside her, not daring to speak to her, feeling as though I were to blame for their shouting "help" in the yard and for the night's seeming so long.

We were silent, and I waited impatiently for a gleam of light at the window, and Masha looked all the time as though she had awakened from a trance and now was marvelling how she, so clever, and well-educated, so elegant, had come into this pitiful, provincial, empty hole among a crew of petty, insignificant people, and how she could have so far forgotten herself as ever to be attracted by one of these people, and for more than six months to have been his wife. It seemed to me that at that moment it did not matter to her whether it was I, or Moisey, or Tcheprakov; everything for her was merged in that savage drunken "help"—I and our marriage, and our work together, and the mud and slush of autumn, and when she sighed or moved into a more comfortable position I read in her face: "Oh, that morning would come quickly!"

In the morning she went away. I spent another three days at Dubetchnya expecting her, then I packed all our things in one room, locked it, and walked to the town. It was already evening when I rang at the engineer's, and the street lamps were burning in Great Dvoryansky Street. Pavel told me there was no one at home; Viktor Ivanitch had gone to Petersburg, and Mariya Viktorovna was probably at the rehearsal at the Azhogins'. I remember with what emotion I went on to the Azhogins', how my heart throbbed and fluttered as I mounted the stairs, and stood waiting a long while on the landing at the top, not daring to enter that temple of the muses! In the big room there were lighted candles everywhere, on a little table, on the piano, and on the stage, everywhere in threes; and the first performance was fixed for the thirteenth, and now the first rehearsal was on a Monday, an unlucky day. All part of the war against superstition! All the devotees of the scenic art were gathered together; the eldest, the middle, and the youngest sisters were walking about the stage, reading their parts in exercise books. Apart from all the rest stood Radish, motionless, with the side of his head pressed to the wall as he gazed with adoration at the stage, waiting for the rehearsal to begin. Everything as it used to be.

I was making my way to my hostess; I had to pay my respects to her, but suddenly everyone said "Hush!" and waved me to step quietly. There was a silence. The lid of the piano was raised; a lady sat down at it screwing up her short-sighted eyes at the music, and my Masha walked up to the piano, in a low-necked dress, looking beautiful, but with a special, new sort of beauty not in the least like the Masha who used to come and meet me in the spring at the mill. She sang: "Why do I love the radiant night?"

It was the first time during our whole acquaintance that I had heard her sing. She had a fine, mellow, powerful voice, and while she sang I felt as though I were eating a ripe, sweet, fragrant melon. She ended, the audience applauded, and she smiled, very much pleased, making play with her eyes, turning over the music, smoothing her skirts, like a bird that has at last broken out of its cage and preens its wings in freedom. Her hair was arranged over her ears, and she had an unpleasant, defiant expression in her face, as though she wanted to throw down a challenge to us all, or to shout to us as she did to her horses: "Hey, there, my beauties!"

And she must at that moment have been very much like her grandfather the sledge-driver.

"You here too?" she said, giving me her hand. "Did you hear me sing? Well, what did you think of it?" and without waiting for my answer she went on: "It's a very good thing you are here. I am going to-night to Petersburg for a short time. You'll let me go, won't you?"

At midnight I went with her to the station. She embraced me affectionately, probably feeling grateful to me for not asking unnecessary questions, and she promised to write to me, and I held her hands a long time, and kissed them, hardly able to restrain my tears and not uttering a word.

And when she had gone I stood watching the retreating lights, caressing her in imagination and softly murmuring:

"My darling Masha, glorious Masha. . . ."

I spent the night at Karpovna's, and next morning I was at work with Radish, re-covering the furniture of a rich merchant who was marrying his daughter to a doctor.

## XVII

My sister came after dinner on Sunday and had tea with me.

"I read a great deal now," she said, showing me the books which she had fetched from the public library on her way to me. "Thanks to your wife and to Vladimir, they have awakened me to self-realization. They have been my salvation; they have made me feel myself a human being. In old days I used to lie awake at night with worries of all sorts, thinking what a lot of sugar we had used in the week, or hoping the cucumbers would not be too salt. And now, too, I lie awake at night, but I have different thoughts. I am distressed that half my life has been passed in such a foolish, cowardly way. I despise my past; I am ashamed of it. And I look upon our father now as my enemy. Oh, how grateful I am to your wife! And Vladimir! He is such a wonderful person! They have opened my eyes!"

"That's bad that you don't sleep at night," I said.

"Do you think I am ill? Not at all. Vladimir sounded me, and said I was perfectly well. But health is not what matters, it is not so important. Tell me: am I right?"

She needed moral support, that was obvious. Masha had gone away. Dr. Blagovo was in Petersburg, and there was no one left in the town but me, to tell her she was right. She looked intently into my face, trying to read my secret thoughts, and if I were absorbed or silent in her presence she thought this was on her account, and was grieved. I always had to be on my guard, and when she asked me whether she was right I hastened to assure her that she was right, and that I had a deep respect for her.

"Do you know they have given me a part at the Azhogins'?" she went on. "I want to act on the stage, I want to live—in fact, I mean to drain the full cup. I have no talent, none, and the part is only ten lines, but still this is immeasurably finer and loftier than pouring out tea five times a day, and looking to see if the cook has eaten too much. Above all, let my father see I am capable of protest."

After tea she lay down on my bed, and lay for a little while with her eyes closed, looking very pale.

"What weakness," she said, getting up. "Vladimir says all city-bred women and girls are anæmic from doing nothing. What a clever man Vladimir is! He is right, absolutely right. We must work!"

Two days later she came to the Azhogins' with her manuscript for the rehearsal. She was wearing a black dress with a string of coral round her neck, and a brooch that in the distance was like a pastry puff, and in her ears earrings sparkling with brilliants. When I looked at her I felt uncomfortable. I was struck by her lack of taste. That she had very inappropriately put on earrings and brilliants, and that she was strangely dressed, was remarked by other people too; I saw smiles on people's faces, and heard someone say with a laugh: "Kleopatra of Egypt."

She was trying to assume society manners, to be unconstrained and at her ease, and so seemed artificial and strange. She had lost simplicity and sweetness.

"I told father just now that I was going to the rehearsal," she began, coming up to me, "and he shouted that he would not give me his blessing, and actually almost struck me. Only fancy, I don't know my part," she said, looking at her manuscript. "I am sure to make a mess of it. So be it, the die is cast," she went on in intense excitement. "The die is cast...."

It seemed to her that everyone was looking at her, and that all were amazed at the momentous step she had taken, that everyone was expecting something special of her, and it would have been impossible to convince her that no one was paying attention to people so petty and insignificant as she and I were.

She had nothing to do till the third act, and her part, that of a visitor, a provincial crony, consisted only in standing at the door as though listening, and then delivering a brief monologue. In the interval before her appearance, an hour and a half at least, while they were moving about on the stage reading their parts, drinking tea and arguing, she did not leave my side, and was all the time muttering her part and nervously crumpling up the manuscript. And imagining that everyone was looking at her and waiting for her appearance, with a trembling hand she smoothed back her hair and said to me:

"I shall certainly make a mess of it. . . . What a load on my heart, if only you knew! I feel frightened, as though I were just going to be led to execution."

At last her turn came.

"Kleopatra Alexyevna, it's your cue!" said the stage manager.

She came forward into the middle of the stage with an expression of horror on her face, looking ugly and angular, and for half a minute stood as though in a trance, perfectly motionless, and only her big earrings shook in her ears.

"The first time you can read it," said someone.

It was clear to me that she was trembling, and trembling so much that she could not speak, and could not unfold her manuscript, and that she was incapable of acting her part; and I was already on the point of going to her and saying something, when she suddenly dropped on her knees in the middle of the stage and broke into loud sobs.

All was commotion and hubbub. I alone stood still, leaning against the side scene, overwhelmed by what had happened, not understanding and not knowing what to do. I saw them lift her up and lead her away. I saw Anyuta Blagovo come up to me; I had not seen her in the room before, and she seemed to have sprung out of the earth. She was wearing her hat and veil, and, as always, had an air of having come only for a moment.

"I told her not to take a part," she said angrily, jerking out each word abruptly and turning crimson. "It's insanity! You ought to have prevented her!"

Madame Azhogin, in a short jacket with short sleeves, with cigarette ash on her breast, looking thin and flat, came rapidly towards me.

"My dear, this is terrible," she brought out, wringing her hands, and, as her habit was, looking intently into my face. "This is terrible! Your sister is in a condition. . . . She is with child. Take her away, I implore you. . . ."

She was breathless with agitation, while on one side stood her three daughters, exactly like her, thin and flat, huddling together in a scared way. They were alarmed, overwhelmed, as though a convict had been caught in their house. What a disgrace, how dreadful! And yet this estimable family had spent its life waging war on superstition; evidently they imagined that all the superstition and error of humanity was limited to the three candles, the thirteenth of the month, and to the unluckiness of Monday!

"I beg you. . . I beg," repeated Madame Azhogin, pursing up her lips in the shape of a heart on the syllable "you." "I beg you to take her home."

## XVIII

A little later my sister and I were walking along the street. I covered her with the skirts of my coat; we hastened, choosing back streets where there were no street lamps, avoiding passers-by; it was as though we were running away. She was no longer crying, but looked at me with dry eyes. To Karpovna's, where I took her, it was only twenty minutes' walk, and, strange to say, in that short time we succeeded in thinking of our whole life; we talked over everything, considered our position, reflected. . . .

We decided we could not go on living in this town, and that when I had earned a little money we would move to some other place. In some houses everyone was asleep, in others they were playing cards; we hated these houses; we were afraid of them. We talked of the fanaticism, the coarseness of feeling, the insignificance of these respectable families, these amateurs of dramatic art whom we had so alarmed, and I kept asking in what way these stupid, cruel, lazy, and dishonest people were superior to the drunken and superstitious peasants of Kurilovka, or in what way they were better than animals, who in the same way are thrown into a panic when some incident disturbs the monotony of their life limited by their instincts. What would have happened to my sister now if she had been left to live at home?

What moral agonies would she have experienced, talking with my father, meeting every day with acquaintances? I imagined this to myself, and at once there came into my mind people, all people I knew, who had been slowly done to death by their nearest relations. I remembered the tortured dogs, driven mad, the live sparrows plucked naked by boys and flung into the water, and a long, long series of obscure lingering miseries which I had looked on continually from early childhood in that town; and I could not understand what these sixty thousand people lived for, what they read the gospel for, why they prayed, why they read books and magazines. What good had they gained from all that had been said and written hitherto if they were still possessed by the same spiritual darkness and hatred of liberty, as they were a hundred and three hundred years ago? A master carpenter spends his whole life building houses in the town, and always, to the day of his death, calls a "gallery" a "galdery." So these sixty thousand people have been reading and hearing of truth, of justice, of mercy, of freedom for generations, and yet from morning till night, till the day of their death, they are lying, and tormenting each other, and they fear liberty and hate it as a deadly foe.

"And so my fate is decided," said my sister, as we arrived home. "After what has happened I cannot go back *there*. Heavens, how good that is! My heart feels lighter."

She went to bed at once. Tears were glittering on her eyelashes, but her expression was happy; she fell into a sound sweet sleep, and one could see that her heart was lighter and that she was resting. It was a long, long time since she had slept like that.

And so we began our life together. She was always singing and saying that her life was very happy, and the books I brought her from the public library I took back unread, as now she could not read; she wanted to do nothing but dream and talk of the future, mending my linen, or helping Karpovna near the stove; she was always singing, or talking of her Vladimir, of his cleverness, of his charming manners, of his kindness, of his extraordinary learning, and I assented to all she said, though by now I disliked her doctor. She wanted to work, to lead an independent life on her own account, and she used to say that she would become a school-teacher or a doctor's assistant as soon as her health would permit her, and would herself do the scrubbing and the washing. Already she was passionately devoted to her child; he was not yet born, but she knew already the colour of his eyes, what his hands would be like, and how he would laugh. She was fond of talking about education, and as her Vladimir was the best man in the world, all her discussion of education could be summed up in the question how to make the boy as fascinating as his father. There was no end to her talk, and everything she said made her intensely joyful. Sometimes I was delighted, too, though I could not have said why.

I suppose her dreaminess infected me. I, too, gave up reading, and did nothing but dream. In the evenings, in spite of my fatigue, I walked up and down the room, with my hands in my pockets, talking of Masha.

"What do you think?" I would ask of my sister. "When will she come back? I think she'll come back at Christmas, not later; what has she to do there?"

"As she doesn't write to you, it's evident she will come back very soon."

"That's true," I assented, though I knew perfectly well that Masha would not return to our town.

I missed her fearfully, and could no longer deceive myself, and tried to get other people to deceive me. My sister was expecting her doctor, and I—Masha; and both of us talked incessantly, laughed, and did not notice that we were preventing Karpovna from sleeping. She lay on the stove and kept muttering:

"The samovar hummed this morning, it did hum! Oh, it bodes no good, my dears, it bodes no good!"

No one ever came to see us but the postman, who brought my sister letters from the doctor, and Prokofy, who sometimes came in to see us in the evening, and after looking at my sister without speaking went away, and when he was in the kitchen said:

"Every class ought to remember its rules, and anyone, who is so proud that he won't understand that, will find it a vale of tears."

He was very fond of the phrase "a vale of tears." One day—it was in Christmas week, when I was walking by the bazaar—he called me into the butcher's shop, and not shaking hands with me, announced that he had to speak to me about something very important. His face was red from the frost and vodka; near him, behind the counter, stood Nikolka, with the expression of a brigand, holding a bloodstained knife in his hand.

"I desire to express my word to you," Prokofy began. "This incident cannot continue, because, as you understand yourself that for such a vale, people will say nothing good of you or of us. Mamma, through pity, cannot say something unpleasant to you, that your sister should move into another lodging on account of her condition, but I won't have it any more, because I can't approve of her behaviour."

I understood him, and I went out of the shop. The same day my sister and I moved to Radish's. We had no money for a cab, and we walked on foot; I carried a parcel of our belongings on my back; my sister had nothing in her hands, but she gasped for breath and coughed, and kept asking whether we should get there soon.

XIX

At last a letter came from Masha.

"Dear, good M. A." (she wrote), "our kind, gentle 'angel' as the old painter calls you, farewell; I am going with my father to America for the exhibition. In a few days I shall see the ocean—so far from Dubetchnya, it's dreadful to think! It's far and unfathomable as the sky, and I long to be there in freedom. I am triumphant, I am mad, and you see how incoherent my letter is. Dear, good one, give me my freedom, make haste to break the thread, which still holds, binding you and me together. My meeting and knowing you was a ray from heaven that lighted up my existence; but my becoming your wife was a mistake, you understand that, and I am oppressed now by the consciousness of the mistake, and I beseech you, on my knees, my generous friend, quickly, quickly, before I start for the ocean, telegraph that you consent to correct our common mistake, to remove the solitary stone from my wings, and my father, who will undertake all the arrangements, promised me not to burden you too much with formalities. And so I am free to fly whither I will? Yes?

"Be happy, and God bless you; forgive me, a sinner.

"I am well, I am wasting money, doing all sorts of silly things, and I thank God every minute that such a bad woman as I has no children. I sing and have success, but it's not an infatuation; no, it's my haven, my cell to which I go for peace. King David had a ring with an inscription on it: 'All things pass.' When one is sad those words make one cheerful, and when one is cheerful it makes one sad. I have got myself a ring like that with Hebrew letters on it, and this talisman keeps me from infatuations. All things pass, life will pass, one wants nothing. Or at least one wants nothing but the sense of freedom, for when anyone is free, he wants nothing, nothing, nothing. Break the thread. A warm hug to you and your sister. Forgive and forget your M."

My sister used to lie down in one room, and Radish, who had been ill again and was now better, in another. Just at the moment when I received this letter my sister went softly into the painter's room, sat down beside him and began reading aloud. She read to him every day, Ostrovsky or Gogol, and he listened, staring at one point, not laughing, but shaking his head and muttering to himself from time to time:

"Anything may happen! Anything may happen!"

If anything ugly or unseemly were depicted in the play he would say as though vindictively, thrusting his finger into the book:

"There it is, lying! That's what it does, lying does."

The plays fascinated him, both from their subjects and their moral, and from their skilful, complex construction, and he marvelled at "him," never calling the author by his name. How neatly *he* has put it all together.

This time my sister read softly only one page, and could read no more: her voice would not last out. Radish took her hand and, moving his parched lips, said, hardly audibly, in a husky voice:

"The soul of a righteous man is white and smooth as chalk, but the soul of a sinful man is like pumice stone. The soul of a righteous man is like clear oil, but the soul of a sinful man is gas tar. We must labour, we must sorrow, we must suffer sickness," he went on, "and he who does not labour and sorrow will not gain the Kingdom of Heaven. Woe, woe to them that are well fed, woe to the mighty, woe to the rich, woe to the moneylenders! Not for them is the Kingdom of Heaven. Lice eat grass, rust eats iron. . ."

"And lying the soul," my sister added laughing. I read the letter through once more. At that moment there walked into the kitchen a soldier who had been bringing us twice a week parcels of tea, French bread and game, which smelt of scent, from some unknown giver. I had no work. I had had to sit at home idle for whole days together, and probably whoever sent us the French bread knew that we were in want.

I heard my sister talking to the soldier and laughing gaily. Then, lying down, she ate some French bread and said to me:

"When you wouldn't go into the service, but became a house painter, Anyuta Blagovo and I knew from the beginning that you were right, but we were frightened to say so aloud. Tell me what force is it that hinders us from saying what one thinks? Take Anyuta Blagovo now, for instance. She loves you, she adores you, she knows you are right, she loves me too, like a sister, and knows that I am right, and I daresay in her soul envies me, but some force prevents her from coming to see us, she shuns us, she is afraid."

My sister crossed her arms over her breast, and said passionately:

"How she loves you, if only you knew! She has confessed her love to no one but me, and then very secretly in the dark. She led me into a dark avenue in the garden, and began whispering how precious you were to her. You will see, she'll never marry, because she loves you. Are you sorry for her?"

"Yes."

"It's she who has sent the bread. She is absurd really, what is the use of being so secret? I used to be absurd and foolish, but now I have got away from that and am afraid of nobody. I think and say aloud what I like, and am happy. When I lived at home I hadn't a conception of happiness, and now I wouldn't change with a queen."

Dr. Blagovo arrived. He had taken his doctor's degree, and was now staying in our town with his father; he was taking a rest, and said that he would soon go back to Petersburg again. He wanted to study anti-toxins against typhus, and, I believe, cholera; he wanted to go abroad to perfect his training, and then to be appointed a professor. He had already left the army service, and wore a roomy serge reefer jacket, very full trousers, and magnificent neckties. My sister was in ecstasies over his scarfpin, his studs, and the red silk handkerchief which he wore, I suppose from foppishness, sticking out of the breast pocket of his jacket. One day, having nothing to do, she and I counted up all the suits we remembered him wearing, and came to the conclusion that he had at least ten. It was clear that he still loved my sister as before, but he never once even in jest spoke of taking her with him to Petersburg or abroad, and I could not picture to myself clearly what would become of her if she remained alive and what would become of her child. She did nothing but dream endlessly, and never thought seriously of the future; she said he might go where he liked, and might abandon her even, so long as he was happy himself; that what had been was enough for her.

As a rule he used to sound her very carefully on his arrival, and used to insist on her taking milk and drops in his presence. It was the same on this occasion. He sounded her and made her drink a glass of milk, and there was a smell of creosote in our room afterwards.

"That's a good girl," he said, taking the glass from her. "You mustn't talk too much now; you've taken to chattering like a magpie of late. Please hold your tongue."

She laughed. Then he came into Radish's room where I was sitting and affectionately slapped me on the shoulder.

"Well, how goes it, old man?" he said, bending down to the invalid.

"Your honour," said Radish, moving his lips slowly, "your honour, I venture to submit. . . . We all walk in the fear of God, we all have to die. . . . Permit me to tell you the truth. . . . Your honour, the Kingdom of Heaven will not be for you!"

"There's no help for it," the doctor said jestingly; "there must be somebody in hell, you know."

And all at once something happened with my consciousness; as though I were in a dream, as though I were standing on a winter night in the slaughterhouse yard, and Prokofy beside me, smelling of pepper cordial; I made an effort to control myself, and rubbed my eyes, and at once it seemed to me that I was going along the road to the interview with the Governor. Nothing of the sort had happened to me before, or has happened to me since, and these strange memories that were like dreams, I ascribed to overexhaustion of my nerves. I lived through the scene at the slaughterhouse, and the interview with the Governor, and at the same time was dimly aware that it was not real.

When I came to myself I saw that I was no longer in the house, but in the street, and was standing with the doctor near a lamp-post.

"It's sad, it's sad," he was saying, and tears were trickling down his cheeks. "She is in good spirits, she's always laughing and hopeful, but her position's hopeless, dear boy. Your Radish hates me, and is always trying to make me feel that I have treated her badly. He is right from his standpoint, but I have my point of view too; and I shall never regret all that has happened. One must love; we ought all to love—oughtn't we? There would be no life without love; anyone who fears and avoids love is not free."

Little by little he passed to other subjects, began talking of science, of his dissertation which had been liked in Petersburg. He was carried away by his subject, and no longer thought of my sister, nor of his grief, nor of me. Life was of absorbing interest to him. She has America and her ring with the inscription on it, I thought, while this fellow has his doctor's degree and a professor's chair to look forward to, and only my sister and I are left with the old things.

When I said good-bye to him, I went up to the lamp-post and read the letter once more. And I remembered, I remembered vividly how that spring morning she had come to me at the mill, lain down and covered herself with her jacket—she wanted to be like a simple peasant woman. And how, another time—it was in the morning also—we drew the net out of the water, and heavy drops of rain fell upon us from the riverside willows, and we laughed.

It was dark in our house in Great Dvoryansky Street. I got over the fence and, as I used to do in the old days, went by the back way to the kitchen to borrow a lantern. There was no one in the kitchen. The samovar hissed near the stove, waiting for my father. "Who pours out my father's tea now?" I thought. Taking the lantern I went out to the shed, built myself up a bed of old newspapers and lay down. The hooks on the walls looked forbidding, as they used to of old, and their shadows flickered. It was cold. I felt that my sister would come in in a minute, and bring me supper, but at once I remembered that she was ill and was lying at Radish's, and it seemed to me strange that I should have climbed over the fence and be lying here in this unheated shed. My mind was in a maze, and I saw all sorts of absurd things.

There was a ring. A ring familiar from childhood: first the wire rustled against the wall, then a short plaintive ring in the kitchen. It was my father come back from the club. I got up and went into the kitchen. Axinya the cook clasped her hands on seeing me, and for some reason burst into tears.

"My own!" she said softly. "My precious! O Lord!"

And she began crumpling up her apron in her agitation. In the window there were standing jars of berries in vodka. I poured myself out a teacupful and greedily drank it off, for I was intensely thirsty. Axinya had quite recently scrubbed the table and benches, and there was that smell in the kitchen which is found in bright, snug kitchens kept by tidy cooks. And that smell and the chirp of the cricket used to lure us as children into the kitchen, and put us in the mood for hearing fairy tales and playing at "Kings" . . .

"Where's Kleopatra?" Axinya asked softly, in a fluster, holding her breath; "and where is your cap, my dear? Your wife, you say, has gone to Petersburg?"

She had been our servant in our mother's time, and used once to give Kleopatra and me our baths, and to her we were still children who had to be talked to for their good. For a quarter of an hour or so she laid before me all the reflections which she had with the sagacity of an old servant been accumulating in the stillness of that kitchen, all the time since we had seen each other. She said that the doctor could be forced to marry Kleopatra; he only needed to be thoroughly frightened; and that if an appeal were promptly written the bishop would annul the first marriage; that it would be a good thing for me to sell Dubetchnya without my wife's knowledge, and put the money in the bank in my own name; that if my sister and I were to bow down at my father's feet and ask him properly, he might perhaps forgive us; that we ought to have a service sung to the Queen of Heaven. . . .

"Come, go along, my dear, and speak to him," she said, when she heard my father's cough. "Go along, speak to him; bow down, your head won't drop off."

I went in. My father was sitting at the table sketching a plan of a summer villa, with Gothic windows, and with a fat turret like a fireman's watch tower—something peculiarly stiff and tasteless. Going into the study I stood still where I could see this drawing. I did not know why I had gone in to my father, but I remember that when I saw his lean face, his red neck, and his shadow on the wall, I wanted to throw myself on his neck, and as Axinya had told me, bow down at his feet; but the sight of the summer villa with the Gothic windows, and the fat turret, restrained me.

"Good evening," I said.

He glanced at me, and at once dropped his eyes on his drawing.

"What do you want?" he asked, after waiting a little.

"I have come to tell you my sister's very ill. She can't live very long," I added in a hollow voice.

"Well," sighed my father, taking off his spectacles, and laying them on the table. "What thou sowest that shalt thou reap. What thou sowest," he repeated, getting up from the table, "that shalt thou reap. I ask you to remember how you came to me two years ago, and on this very spot I begged you, I besought you to give up your errors; I reminded you of your duty, of your honour, of what you owed to your forefathers whose traditions we ought to preserve as sacred. Did you obey me? You scorned my counsels, and obstinately persisted in clinging to your false ideals; worse still you drew your sister into the path of error with you, and led her to lose her moral principles and sense of shame. Now you are both in a bad way. Well, as thou sowest, so shalt thou reap!"

As he said this he walked up and down the room. He probably imagined that I had come to him to confess my wrong doings, and he probably expected that I should begin begging him to forgive my sister and me. I was cold, I was shivering as though I were in a fever, and spoke with difficulty in a husky voice.

"And I beg you, too, to remember," I said, "on this very spot I besought you to understand me, to reflect, to decide with me how and for what we should live, and in answer you began talking about our forefathers, about my grandfather who wrote poems. One tells you now that your only daughter is hopelessly ill, and you go on again about your forefathers, your traditions. . . . And such frivolity in your old age, when death is close at hand, and you haven't more than five or ten years left!"

"What have you come here for?" my father asked sternly, evidently offended at my reproaching him for his frivolity.

"I don't know. I love you, I am unutterably sorry that we are so far apart—so you see I have come. I love you still, but my sister has broken with you completely. She does not forgive you, and will never forgive you now. Your very name arouses her aversion for the past, for life."

"And who is to blame for it?" cried my father. "It's your fault, you scoundrel!"

"Well, suppose it is my fault?" I said. "I admit I have been to blame in many things, but why is it that this life of yours, which you think binding upon us, too—why is it so dreary, so barren? How is it that in not one of these houses you have been building for the last thirty years has there been anyone from whom I might have learnt how to live, so as not to be to blame? There is not one honest man in the whole town! These houses of yours are nests of damnation, where mothers and daughters are made away with, where children are tortured. . . . My poor mother!" I went on in despair. "My poor sister! One has to stupefy oneself with vodka, with cards, with scandal; one must become a scoundrel, a hypocrite, or go on drawing plans for years and years, so as not to notice all the horrors that lie hidden in these houses. Our town has existed for hundreds of years, and all that time it has not produced one man of service to our country—not one. You have stifled in the germ everything in the least living and bright. It's a town of shopkeepers, publicans, counting-house clerks, canting hypocrites; it's a useless, unnecessary town, which not one soul would regret if it suddenly sank through the earth."

"I don't want to listen to you, you scoundrel!" said my father, and he took up his ruler from the table. "You are drunk. Don't dare come and see your father in such a state! I tell you for the last time, and you can repeat it to your depraved sister, that you'll get nothing from me, either of you. I have torn my disobedient children out of my heart, and if they suffer for their disobedience and obstinacy I do not pity them. You can go whence you came. It has pleased God to chastise me with you, but I will bear the trial with resignation, and, like Job, I will find consolation in my sufferings and in unremitting labour. You must not cross my threshold till you have mended your ways. I am a just man, all I tell you is for your benefit, and if you desire your own good you ought to remember all your life what I say and have said to you...."

I waved my hand in despair and went away. I don't remember what happened afterwards, that night and next day.

I am told that I walked about the streets bareheaded, staggering, and singing aloud, while a crowd of boys ran after me, shouting:

"Better-than-nothing!"

## XX

If I wanted to order a ring for myself, the inscription I should choose would be: "Nothing passes away." I believe that nothing passes away without leaving a trace, and that every step we take, however small, has significance for our present and our future existence.

What I have been through has not been for nothing. My great troubles, my patience, have touched people's hearts, and now they don't call me "Better-than-nothing," they don't laugh at me, and when I walk by the shops they don't throw water over me. They have grown used to my being a workman, and see nothing strange in my carrying a pail of paint and putting in windows, though I am of noble rank; on the contrary, people are glad to give me orders, and I am now considered a first-rate workman, and the best foreman after Radish, who, though he has regained his health, and though, as before, he paints the cupola on the belfry without scaffolding, has no longer the force to control the workmen; instead of him I now run about the town looking for work, I engage the workmen and pay them, borrow money at a high rate of interest, and now that I myself am a contractor, I understand how it is that one may have to waste three days racing about the town in search of tilers on account of some twopenny-halfpenny job. People are civil to me, they address me politely, and in the houses where I work, they offer me tea, and send to enquire whether I wouldn't like dinner. Children and young girls often come and look at me with curiosity and compassion.

One day I was working in the Governor's garden, painting an arbour there to look like marble. The Governor, walking in the garden, came up to the arbour and, having nothing to do, entered into conversation with me, and I reminded him how he had once summoned me to an interview with him. He looked into my face intently for a minute, then made his mouth like a round "O," flung up his hands, and said: "I don't remember!"

I have grown older, have become silent, stern, and austere, I rarely laugh, and I am told that I have grown like Radish, and that like him I bore the workmen by my useless exhortations.

Mariya Viktorovna, my former wife, is living now abroad, while her father is constructing a railway somewhere in the eastern provinces, and is buying estates there. Dr. Blagovo is also abroad. Dubetchnya has passed again into the possession of Madame Tcheprakov, who has bought it after forcing the engineer to knock the price down twenty per cent. Moisey goes about now in a bowler hat; he often drives into the town in a racing droshky on business of some sort, and stops near the bank. They say he has already bought up a mortgaged estate, and is constantly making enquiries at the bank about Dubetchnya, which he means to buy too. Poor Ivan Tcheprakov was for a long while out of work, staggering about the town and drinking. I tried to get him into our work, and for a time he painted roofs and put in window-panes in our company, and even got to like it, and stole oil, asked for tips, and drank like a regular painter. But he soon got sick of the work, and went back to Dubetchnya, and afterwards the workmen confessed to me that he had tried to persuade them to join him one night and murder Moisey and rob Madame Tcheprakov.

My father has greatly aged; he is very bent, and in the evenings walks up and down near his house. I never go to see him.

During an epidemic of cholera Prokofy doctored some of the shopkeepers with pepper cordial and pitch, and took money for doing so, and, as I learned from the newspapers, was flogged for abusing the doctors as he sat in his shop. His shop boy Nikolka died of cholera. Karpovna is still alive and, as always, she loves and fears her Prokofy. When she sees me, she always shakes her head mournfully, and says with a sigh: "Your life is ruined."

On working days I am busy from morning till night. On holidays, in fine weather, I take my tiny niece (my sister reckoned on a boy, but the child is a girl) and walk in a leisurely way to the cemetery. There I stand or sit down, and stay a long time gazing at the grave that is so dear to me, and tell the child that her mother lies here.

Sometimes, by the graveside, I find Anyuta Blagovo. We greet each other and stand in silence, or talk of Kleopatra, of her child, of how sad life is in this world; then, going out of the cemetery we walk along in silence and she slackens her pace on purpose to walk beside me a little longer. The little girl, joyous and happy, pulls at her hand, laughing and screwing up her eyes in the bright sunlight, and we stand still and join in caressing the dear child.

When we reach the town Anyuta Blagovo, agitated and flushing crimson, says good-bye to me and walks on alone, austere and respectable. . . . And no one who met her could, looking at her, imagine that she had just been walking beside me and even caressing the child.

## AT A COUNTRY HOUSE

PAVEL ILYITCH RASHEVITCH walked up and down, stepping softly on the floor covered with little Russian plaids, and casting a long shadow on the wall and ceiling while his guest, Meier, the deputy examining magistrate, sat on the sofa with one leg drawn up under him smoking and listening. The clock already pointed to eleven, and there were sounds of the table being laid in the room next to the study.

"Say what you like," Rashevitch was saying, "from the standpoint of fraternity, equality, and the rest of it, Mitka, the swineherd, is perhaps a man the same as Goethe and Frederick the Great; but take your stand on a scientific basis, have the courage to look facts in the face, and it will be obvious to you that blue blood is not a mere prejudice, that it is not a feminine invention. Blue blood, my dear fellow, has an historical justification, and to refuse to recognize it is, to my thinking, as strange as to refuse to recognize the antlers on a stag. One must reckon with facts! You are a law student and have confined your attention to the humane studies, and you can still flatter yourself with illusions of equality, fraternity, and so on; I am an incorrigible Darwinian, and for me words such as lineage, aristocracy, noble blood, are not empty sounds."

Rashevitch was roused and spoke with feeling. His eyes sparkled, his pince-nez would not stay on his nose, he kept nervously shrugging his shoulders and blinking, and at the word "Darwinian" he looked jauntily in the looking-glass and combed his grey beard with both hands. He was wearing a very short and shabby reefer jacket and narrow trousers; the rapidity of his movements, his jaunty air, and his abbreviated jacket all seemed out of keeping with him, and his big comely head, with long hair suggestive of a bishop or a veteran poet, seemed to have been fixed on to the body of a tall, lanky, affected youth. When he stood with his legs wide apart, his long shadow looked like a pair of scissors.

He was fond of talking, and he always fancied that he was saying something new and original. In the presence of Meier he was conscious of an unusual flow of spirits and rush of ideas. He found the examining magistrate sympathetic, and was stimulated by his youth, his health, his good manners, his dignity, and, above all, by his cordial attitude to himself and his family. Rashevitch was not a favourite with his acquaintances; as a rule they fought shy of him, and, as he knew, declared that he had driven his wife into her grave with his talking, and they called him, behind his back, a spiteful creature and a toad. Meier, a man new to the district and unprejudiced, visited him often and readily and had even been known to say that Rashevitch and his daughters were the only people in the district with whom he felt as much at home as with his own people. Rashevitch liked him too, because he was a young man who might be a good match for his elder daughter, Genya.

And now, enjoying his ideas and the sound of his own voice, and looking with pleasure at the plump but well-proportioned, neatly cropped, correct Meier, Rashevitch dreamed of how he would arrange his daughter's marriage with a good man, and then how all his worries over the estate would pass to his son-in-law. Hateful worries! The interest owing to the bank had not been paid for the last two quarters, and fines and arrears of all sorts had mounted up to more than two thousand.

"To my mind there can be no doubt," Rashevitch went on, growing more and more enthusiastic, "that if a Richard Coeur-de-Lion, or Frederick Barbarossa, for instance, is brave and noble those qualities will pass by heredity to his son, together with the convolutions and bumps of the brain, and if that courage and nobility of soul are preserved in the son by means of education and exercise, and if he marries a princess who is also noble and brave, those qualities will be transmitted to his grandson, and so on, until they become a generic characteristic and pass organically into the flesh and blood. Thanks to a strict sexual selection, to the fact that high-born families have instinctively guarded themselves against marriage with their inferiors, and young men of high rank have not married just anybody, lofty, spiritual qualities have been transmitted from generation to generation in their full purity, have been preserved, and as time goes on have, through exercise, become more exalted and lofty. For the fact that there is good in humanity we are indebted to nature, to the normal, natural, consistent order of things, which has throughout the ages scrupulously segregated blue blood from plebeian. Yes, my dear boy, no low lout, no cook's son has given us literature, science, art, law, conceptions of honour and duty . . . . For all these things mankind is indebted exclusively to the aristocracy, and from that point of view, the point of view of natural history, an inferior Sobakevitch by the very fact of his blue blood is superior and more useful than the very best merchant, even though the latter may have built fifteen museums. Say what you like! And when I refuse to shake hands with a low lout or a cook's son, or to let him sit down to table with me, by that very act I am safeguarding what is the best thing on earth, and am carrying out one of Mother Nature's finest designs for leading us up to perfection. . ."

Rashevitch stood still, combing his beard with both hands; his shadow, too, stood still on the wall, looking like a pair of scissors.

"Take Mother-Russia now," he went on, thrusting his hands in his pockets and standing first on his heels and then on his toes. "Who are her best people? Take our first-rate painters, writers, composers . . . . Who are they? They were all of aristocratic origin. Pushkin, Lermontov, Turgenev, Gontcharov, Tolstoy, they were not sexton's children."

"Gontcharov was a merchant," said Meier.

"Well, the exception only proves the rule. Besides, Gontcharov's genius is quite open to dispute. But let us drop names and turn to facts. What would you say, my good sir, for instance, to this eloquent fact: when one of the mob forces his way where he has not been permitted before, into society, into the world of learning, of literature, into the Zemstvo or the law courts, observe, Nature herself, first of all, champions the higher rights of humanity, and is the first to wage war on the rabble. As soon as the plebeian forces himself into a place he is not fit for he begins to ail, to go into consumption, to go out of his mind, and to degenerate, and nowhere do we find so many puny, neurotic wrecks, consumptives, and starvelings of all sorts as among these darlings. They die like flies in autumn. If it were not for this providential degeneration there would not have been a stone left standing of our civilization, the rabble would have demolished everything. Tell me, if you please, what has the inroad of the barbarians given us so far? What has the rabble brought with it?" Rashevitch assumed a mysterious, frightened expression, and went on: "Never has literature and learning been at such low ebb among us as now. The men of to-day, my good sir, have neither ideas nor ideals, and all their sayings and doings are permeated by one spirit—to get all they can and to strip someone to his last thread. All these men of to-day who give themselves out as honest and progressive people can be bought at a rouble a piece, and the distinguishing mark of the 'intellectual' of to-day is that you have to keep strict watch over your pocket when you talk to him, or else he will run off with your purse." Rashevitch winked and burst out laughing. "Upon my soul, he will!" he said, in a thin, gleeful voice. "And morals! What of their morals?" Rashevitch looked round towards the door. "No one is surprised nowadays when a wife robs and leaves her husband. What's that, a trifle! Nowadays, my dear boy, a chit of a girl of twelve is scheming to get a lover, and all these amateur theatricals and literary evenings are only invented to make it easier to get a rich merchant to take a girl on as his mistress. . . . Mothers sell their daughters, and people make no bones about asking a husband at what price he sells his wife, and one can haggle over the bargain, you know, my dear. . . ."

Meier, who had been sitting motionless and silent all the time, suddenly got up from the sofa and looked at his watch.

"I beg your pardon, Pavel Ilyitch," he said, "it is time for me to be going."

But Pavel Ilyitch, who had not finished his remarks, put his arm round him and, forcibly reseating him on the sofa, vowed that he would not let him go without supper. And again Meier sat and listened, but he looked at Rashevitch with perplexity and uneasiness, as though he were only now beginning to understand him. Patches of red came into his face. And when at last a maidservant came in to tell them that the young ladies asked them to go to supper, he gave a sigh of relief and was the first to walk out of the study.

At the table in the next room were Rashevitch's daughters, Genya and Iraida, girls of four-and-twenty and two-and-twenty respectively, both very pale, with black eyes, and exactly the same height. Genya had her hair down, and Iraida had hers done up high on her head. Before eating anything they each drank a wineglassful of bitter liqueur, with an air as though they had drunk it by accident for the first time in their lives and both were overcome with confusion and burst out laughing.

"Don't be naughty, girls," said Rashevitch.

Genya and Iraida talked French with each other, and Russian with their father and their visitor. Interrupting one another, and mixing up French words with Russian, they began rapidly describing how just at this time in August, in previous years, they had set off to the boarding school and what fun it had been. Now there was nowhere to go, and they had to stay at their home in the country, summer and winter without change. Such dreariness!

"Don't be naughty, girls," Rashevitch said again.

He wanted to be talking himself. If other people talked in his presence, he suffered from a feeling like jealousy.

"So that's how it is, my dear boy," he began, looking affectionately at Meier. "In the simplicity and goodness of our hearts, and from fear of being suspected of being behind the times, we fraternize with, excuse me, all sorts of riff-raff, we preach fraternity and equality with money-lenders and innkeepers; but if we would only think, we should see how criminal that good-nature is. We have brought things to such a pass, that the fate of civilization is hanging on a hair. My dear fellow, what our forefathers gained in the course of ages will be to-morrow, if not to-day, outraged and destroyed by these modern Huns. . . ."

After supper they all went into the drawing-room. Genya and Iraida lighted the candles on the piano, got out their music. . . . But their father still went on talking, and there was no telling when he would leave off. They looked with misery and vexation at their egoist-father, to whom the pleasure of chattering and displaying his intelligence was evidently more precious and important than his daughters' happiness. Meier, the only young man who ever came to their house, came—they knew—for the sake of their charming, feminine society, but the irrepressible old man had taken possession of him, and would not let him move a step away.

"Just as the knights of the west repelled the invasions of the Mongols, so we, before it is too late, ought to unite and strike together against our foe," Rashevitch went on in the tone of a preacher, holding up his right hand. "May I appear to the riff-raff not as Pavel Ilyitch, but as a mighty, menacing Richard Coeur-de-Lion. Let us give up sloppy sentimentality; enough of it! Let us all make a compact, that as soon as a plebeian comes near us we fling some careless phrase straight in his ugly face: 'Paws off! Go back to your kennel, you cur!' straight in his ugly face," Rashevitch went on gleefully, flicking his crooked finger in front of him. "In his ugly face!"

"I can't do that," Meier brought out, turning away.

"Why not?" Rashevitch answered briskly, anticipating a prolonged and interesting argument. "Why not?"

"Because I am of the artisan class myself!"

As he said this Meier turned crimson, and his neck seemed to swell, and tears actually gleamed in his eyes.

"My father was a simple workman," he said, in a rough, jerky voice, "but I see no harm in that."

Rashevitch was fearfully confused. Dumbfounded, as though he had been caught in the act of a crime, he gazed helplessly at Meier, and did not know what to say. Genya and Iraida flushed crimson, and bent over their music; they were ashamed of their tactless father. A minute passed in silence, and there was a feeling of unbearable discomfort, when all at once with a sort of painful stiffness and inappropriateness, there sounded in the air the words:

"Yes, I am of the artisan class, and I am proud of it!"

Thereupon Meier, stumbling awkwardly among the furniture, took his leave, and walked rapidly into the hall, though his carriage was not yet at the door.

"You'll have a dark drive to-night," Rashevitch muttered, following him. "The moon does not rise till late to-night."

They stood together on the steps in the dark, and waited for the horses to be brought. It was cool.

"There's a falling star," said Meier, wrapping himself in his overcoat.

"There are a great many in August."

When the horses were at the door, Rashevitch gazed intently at the sky, and said with a sigh:

"A phenomenon worthy of the pen of Flammarion. . . ."

After seeing his visitor off, he walked up and down the garden, gesticulating in the darkness, reluctant to believe that such a queer, stupid misunderstanding had only just occurred. He was ashamed and vexed with himself. In the first place it had been extremely incautious and tactless on his part to raise the damnable subject of blue blood, without finding out beforehand what his visitor's position was. Something of the same sort had happened to him before; he had, on one occasion in a railway carriage, begun abusing the Germans, and it had afterwards appeared that all the persons he had been conversing with were German. In the second place he felt that Meier would never come and see him again. These intellectuals who have risen from the people are morbidly sensitive, obstinate and slow to forgive.

"It's bad, it's bad," muttered Rashevitch, spitting; he had a feeling of discomfort and loathing as though he had eaten soap. "Ah, it's bad!"

He could see from the garden, through the drawing-room window, Genya by the piano, very pale, and looking scared, with her hair down. She was talking very, very rapidly. . . . Iraida was walking up and down the room, lost in thought; but now she, too, began talking rapidly with her face full of indignation. They were both talking at once. Rashevitch could not hear a word, but he guessed what they were talking about. Genya was probably complaining that her father drove away every decent person from the house with his talk, and to-day he had driven away from them their one acquaintance, perhaps a suitor, and now the poor young man would not have one place in the whole district where he could find rest for his soul. And judging by the despairing way in which she threw up her arms, Iraida was talking probably on the subject of their dreary existence, their wasted youth. . . .

When he reached his own room, Rashevitch sat down on his bed and began to undress. He felt oppressed, and he was still haunted by the same feeling as though he had eaten soap. He was ashamed. As he undressed he looked at his long, sinewy, elderly legs, and remembered that in the district they called him the "toad," and after every long conversation he always felt ashamed. Somehow or other, by some fatality, it always happened that he began mildly, amicably, with good intentions, calling himself an old student, an idealist, a Quixote, but without being himself aware of it, gradually passed into abuse and slander, and what was most surprising, with perfect sincerity criticized science, art and morals, though he had not read a book for the last twenty years, had been nowhere farther than their provincial town, and did not really know what was going on in the world. If he sat down to write anything, if it were only a letter of congratulation, there would somehow be abuse in the letter. And all this was strange, because in reality he was a man of feeling, given to tears. Could he be possessed by some devil which hated and slandered in him, apart from his own will?

"It's bad," he sighed, as he lay down under the quilt. "It's bad."

His daughters did not sleep either. There was a sound of laughter and screaming, as though someone was being pursued; it was Genya in hysterics. A little later Iraida was sobbing too. A maidservant ran barefoot up and down the passage several times. . . .

"What a business! Good Lord! . . ." muttered Rashevitch, sighing and tossing from side to side. "It's bad."

He had a nightmare. He dreamt he was standing naked, as tall as a giraffe, in the middle of the room, and saying, as he flicked his finger before him:

"In his ugly face! his ugly face! his ugly face!"

He woke up in a fright, and first of all remembered that a misunderstanding had happened in the evening, and that Meier would certainly not come again. He remembered, too, that he had to pay the interest at the bank, to find husbands for his daughters, that one must have food and drink, and close at hand were illness, old age, unpleasantnesses, that soon it would be winter, and that there was no wood. . . .

It was past nine o'clock in the morning. Rashevitch slowly dressed, drank his tea and ate two hunks of bread and butter. His daughters did not come down to breakfast; they did not want to meet him, and that wounded him. He lay down on his sofa in his study, then sat down to his table and began writing a letter to his daughters. His hand shook and his eyes smarted. He wrote that he was old, and no use to anyone and that nobody loved him, and he begged his daughters to forget him, and when he died to bury him in a plain, deal coffin without ceremony, or to send his body to Harkov to the dissecting theatre. He felt that every line he wrote reeked of malice and affectation, but he could not stop, and went on writing and writing.

"The toad!" he suddenly heard from the next room; it was the voice of his elder daughter, a voice with a hiss of indignation. "The toad!"

"The toad!" the younger one repeated like an echo. "The toad!"

## A FATHER

"I ADMIT I have had a drop. . . . You must excuse me. I went into a beer shop on the way here, and as it was so hot had a couple of bottles. It's hot, my boy."

Old Musatov took a nondescript rag out of his pocket and wiped his shaven, battered face with it.

"I have come only for a minute, Borenka, my angel," he went on, not looking at his son, "about something very important. Excuse me, perhaps I am hindering you. Haven't you ten roubles, my dear, you could let me have till Tuesday? You see, I ought to have paid for my lodging yesterday, and money, you see! . . . None! Not to save my life!"

Young Musatov went out without a word, and began whispering the other side of the door with the landlady of the summer villa and his colleagues who had taken the villa with him. Three minutes later he came back, and without a word gave his father a ten-rouble note. The latter thrust it carelessly into his pocket without looking at it, and said:

"*Merci.* Well, how are you getting on? It's a long time since we met."

"Yes, a long time, not since Easter."

"Half a dozen times I have been meaning to come to you, but I've never had time. First one thing, then another. . . . It's simply awful! I am talking nonsense though. . . . All that's nonsense. Don't you believe me, Borenka. I said I would pay you back the ten roubles on Tuesday, don't believe that either. Don't believe a word I say. I have nothing to do at all, it's simply laziness, drunkenness, and I am ashamed to be seen in such clothes in the street. You must excuse me, Borenka. Here I have sent the girl to you three times for money and written you piteous letters. Thanks for the money, but don't believe the letters; I was telling fibs. I am ashamed to rob you, my angel; I know that you can scarcely make both ends meet yourself, and feed on locusts, but my impudence is too much for me. I am such a specimen of impudence—fit for a show! . . . You must excuse me, Borenka. I tell you the truth, because I can't see your angel face without emotion."

A minute passed in silence. The old man heaved a deep sigh and said:

"You might treat me to a glass of beer perhaps."

His son went out without a word, and again there was a sound of whispering the other side of the door. When a little later the beer was brought in, the old man seemed to revive at the sight of the bottles and abruptly changed his tone.

"I was at the races the other day, my boy," he began telling him, assuming a scared expression. "We were a party of three, and we pooled three roubles on Frisky. And, thanks to that Frisky, we got thirty-two roubles each for our rouble. I can't get on without the races, my boy. It's a gentlemanly diversion. My virago always gives me a dressing over the races, but I go. I love it, and that's all about it."

Boris, a fair-haired young man with a melancholy immobile face, was walking slowly up and down, listening in silence. When the old man stopped to clear his throat, he went up to him and said:

"I bought myself a pair of boots the other day, father, which turn out to be too tight for me. Won't you take them? I'll let you have them cheap."

"If you like," said the old man with a grimace, "only for the price you gave for them, without any cheapening."

"Very well, I'll let you have them on credit."

The son groped under the bed and produced the new boots. The father took off his clumsy, rusty, evidently second-hand boots and began trying on the new ones.

"A perfect fit," he said. "Right, let me keep them. And on Tuesday, when I get my pension, I'll send you the money for them. That's not true, though," he went on, suddenly falling into the same tearful tone again. "And it was a lie about the races, too, and a lie about the pension. And you are deceiving me, Borenka. . . . I feel your generous tactfulness. I see through you! Your boots were too small, because your heart is too big. Ah, Borenka, Borenka! I understand it all and feel it!"

"Have you moved into new lodgings?" his son interrupted, to change the conversation.

"Yes, my boy. I move every month. My virago can't stay long in the same place with her temper."

"I went to your lodgings, I meant to ask you to stay here with me. In your state of health it would do you good to be in the fresh air."

"No," said the old man, with a wave of his hand, "the woman wouldn't let me, and I shouldn't care to myself. A hundred times you have tried to drag me out of the pit, and I have tried myself, but nothing came of it. Give it up. I must stick in my filthy hole. This minute, here I am sitting, looking at your angel face, yet something is drawing me home to my hole. Such is my fate. You can't draw a dung-beetle to a rose. But it's time I was going, my boy. It's getting dark."

"Wait a minute then, I'll come with you. I have to go to town to-day myself."

Both put on their overcoats and went out. When a little while afterwards they were driving in a cab, it was already dark, and lights began to gleam in the windows.

"I've robbed you, Borenka!" the father muttered. "Poor children, poor children! It must be a dreadful trouble to have such a father! Borenka, my angel, I cannot lie when I see your face. You must excuse me. . . . What my depravity has come to, my God. Here I have just been robbing you, and put you to shame with my drunken state; I am robbing your brothers, too, and put them to shame, and you should have seen me yesterday! I won't conceal it, Borenka. Some neighbours, a wretched crew, came to see my virago; I got drunk, too, with them, and I blackguarded you poor children for all I was worth. I abused you, and complained that you had abandoned me. I wanted, you see, to touch the drunken hussies' hearts, and pose as an unhappy father. It's my way, you know, when I want to screen my vices I throw all the blame on my innocent children. I can't tell lies and hide things from you, Borenka. I came to see you as proud as a peacock, but when I saw your gentleness and kind heart, my tongue clave to the roof of my mouth, and it upset my conscience completely."

"Hush, father, let's talk of something else."

"Mother of God, what children I have," the old man went on, not heeding his son. "What wealth God has bestowed on me. Such children ought not to have had a black sheep like me for a father, but a real man with soul and feeling! I am not worthy of you!"

The old man took off his cap with a button at the top and crossed himself several times.

"Thanks be to Thee, O Lord!" he said with a sigh, looking from side to side as though seeking for an ikon. "Remarkable, exceptional children! I have three sons, and they are all like one. Sober, steady, hard-working, and what brains! Cabman, what brains! Grigory alone has brains enough for ten. He speaks French, he speaks German, and talks better than any of your lawyers—one is never tired of listening. My children, my children, I can't believe that you are mine! I can't believe it! You are a martyr, my Borenka, I am ruining you, and I shall go on ruining you. . . . You give to me endlessly, though you know your money is thrown away. The other day I sent you a pitiful letter, I described how ill I was, but you know I was lying, I wanted the money for rum. And you give to me because you are afraid to wound me by refusing. I know all that, and feel it. Grisha's a martyr, too. On Thursday I went to his office, drunk, filthy, ragged, reeking of vodka like a cellar . . . I went straight up, such a figure, I pestered him with nasty talk, while his colleagues and superiors and petitioners were standing round. I have disgraced him for life. And he wasn't the least confused, only turned a bit pale, but smiled and came up to me as though there were nothing the matter, even introduced me to his colleagues. Then he took me all the way home, and not a word of reproach. I rob him worse than you. Take your brother Sasha now, he's a martyr too! He married, as you know, a colonel's daughter of an aristocratic circle, and got a dowry with her. . . . You would think he would have nothing to do with me. No, brother, after his wedding he came with his young wife and paid me the first visit . . . in my hole. . . . Upon my soul!"

The old man gave a sob and then began laughing.

"And at that moment, as luck would have it, we were eating grated radish with kvass and frying fish, and there was a stink enough in the flat to make the devil sick. I was lying down—I'd had a drop—my virago bounced out at the young people with her face crimson. . . . It was a disgrace in fact. But Sasha rose superior to it all."

"Yes, our Sasha is a good fellow," said Boris.

"The most splendid fellow! You are all pure gold, you and Grisha and Sasha and Sonya. I worry you, torment you, disgrace you, rob you, and all my life I have not heard one word of reproach from you, you have never given me one cross look. It would be all very well if I had been a decent father to you—but as it is! You have had nothing from me but harm. I am a bad, dissipated man. . . . Now, thank God, I am quieter and I have no strength of will, but in old days when you were little I had determination, will. Whatever I said or did I always thought it was right. Sometimes I'd come home from the club at night, drunk and ill-humoured, and scold at your poor mother for spending money. The whole night I would be railing at her, and think it the right thing too; you would get up in the morning and go to school, while I'd still be venting my temper upon her. Heavens! I did torture her, poor martyr! When you came back from school and I was asleep you didn't dare to have dinner till I got up. At dinner again there would be a flare up. I daresay you remember. I wish no one such a father; God sent me to you for a trial. Yes, for a trial! Hold out, children, to the end! Honour thy father and thy days shall be long. Perhaps for your noble conduct God will grant you long life. Cabman, stop!"

The old man jumped out of the cab and ran into a tavern. Half an hour later he came back, cleared his throat in a drunken way, and sat down beside his son.

"Where's Sonya now?" he asked. "Still at boarding-school?"

"No, she left in May, and is living now with Sasha's mother-in-law."

"There!" said the old man in surprise. "She is a jolly good girl! So she is following her brother's example. . . . Ah, Borenka, she has no mother, no one to rejoice over her! I say, Borenka, does she . . . does she know how I am living? Eh?"

Boris made no answer. Five minutes passed in profound silence. The old man gave a sob, wiped his face with a rag and said:

"I love her, Borenka! She is my only daughter, you know, and in one's old age there is no comfort like a daughter. Could I see her, Borenka?"

"Of course, when you like."

"Really? And she won't mind?"

"Of course not, she has been trying to find you so as to see you."

"Upon my soul! What children! Cabman, eh? Arrange it, Borenka darling! She is a young lady now, *delicatesse, consommé*, and all the rest of it in a refined way, and I don't want to show myself to her in such an abject state. I'll tell you how we'll contrive to work it. For three days I will keep away from spirits, to get my filthy, drunken phiz into better order. Then I'll come to you, and you shall lend me for the time some suit of yours; I'll shave and have my hair cut, then you go and bring her to your flat. Will you?"

"Very well."

"Cabman, stop!"

The old man sprang out of the cab again and ran into a tavern. While Boris was driving with him to his lodging he jumped out twice again, while his son sat silent and waited patiently for him. When, after dismissing the cab, they made their way across a long, filthy yard to the "virago's" lodging, the old man put on an utterly shamefaced and guilty air, and began timidly clearing his throat and clicking with his lips.

"Borenka," he said in an ingratiating voice, "if my virago begins saying anything, don't take any notice . . . and behave to her, you know, affably. She is ignorant and impudent, but she's a good baggage. There is a good, warm heart beating in her bosom!"

The long yard ended, and Boris found himself in a dark entry. The swing door creaked, there was a smell of cooking and a smoking samovar. There was a sound of harsh voices. Passing through the passage into the kitchen Boris could see nothing but thick smoke, a line with washing on it, and the chimney of the samovar through a crack of which golden sparks were dropping.

"And here is my cell," said the old man, stooping down and going into a little room with a low-pitched ceiling, and an atmosphere unbearably stifling from the proximity of the kitchen.

Here three women were sitting at the table regaling themselves. Seeing the visitors, they exchanged glances and left off eating.

"Well, did you get it?" one of them, apparently the "virago" herself, asked abruptly.

"Yes, yes," muttered the old man. "Well, Boris, pray sit down. Everything is plain here, young man . . . we live in a simple way."

He bustled about in an aimless way. He felt ashamed before his son, and at the same time apparently he wanted to keep up before the women his dignity as cock of the walk, and as a forsaken, unhappy father.

"Yes, young man, we live simply with no nonsense," he went on muttering. "We are simple people, young man. . . . We are not like you, we don't want to keep up a show before people. No! . . . Shall we have a drink of vodka?"

One of the women (she was ashamed to drink before a stranger) heaved a sigh and said:

"Well, I'll have another drink on account of the mushrooms. . . . They are such mushrooms, they make you drink even if you don't want to. Ivan Gerasimitch, offer the young gentleman, perhaps he will have a drink!"

The last word she pronounced in a mincing drawl.

"Have a drink, young man!" said the father, not looking at his son. "We have no wine or liqueurs, my boy, we live in a plain way."

"He doesn't like our ways," sighed the "virago." "Never mind, never mind, he'll have a drink."

Not to offend his father by refusing, Boris took a wineglass and drank in silence. When they brought in the samovar, to satisfy the old man, he drank two cups of disgusting tea in silence, with a melancholy face. Without a word he listened to the virago dropping hints about there being in this world cruel, heartless children who abandon their parents.

"I know what you are thinking now!" said the old man, after drinking more and passing into his habitual state of drunken excitement. "You think I have let myself sink into the mire, that I am to be pitied, but to my thinking, this simple life is much more normal than your life, . . . I don't need anybody, and . . . and I don't intend to eat humble pie. . . . I can't endure a wretched boy's looking at me with compassion."

After tea he cleaned a herring and sprinkled it with onion, with such feeling, that tears of emotion stood in his eyes. He began talking again about the races and his winnings, about some Panama hat for which he had paid sixteen roubles the day before. He told lies with the same relish with which he ate herring and drank. His son sat on in silence for an hour, and began to say good-bye.

"I don't venture to keep you," the old man said, haughtily. "You must excuse me, young man, for not living as you would like!"

He ruffled up his feathers, snorted with dignity, and winked at the women.

"Good-bye, young man," he said, seeing his son into the entry. "Attendez."

In the entry, where it was dark, he suddenly pressed his face against the young man's sleeve and gave a sob.

"I should like to have a look at Sonitchka," he whispered. "Arrange it, Borenka, my angel. I'll shave, I'll put on your suit . . . I'll put on a straight face . . . I'll hold my tongue while she is there. Yes, yes, I will hold my tongue!"

He looked round timidly towards the door, through which the women's voices were heard, checked his sobs, and said aloud:

"Good-bye, young man! Attendez."

## ON THE ROAD

*"Upon the breast of a gigantic crag, A golden cloudlet rested for one night."*

LERMONTOV.

IN the room which the tavern keeper, the Cossack Semyon Tchistopluy, called the "travellers' room," that is kept exclusively for travellers, a tall, broad-shouldered man of forty was sitting at the big unpainted table. He was asleep with his elbows on the table and his head leaning on his fist. An end of tallow candle, stuck into an old pomatum pot, lighted up his light brown beard, his thick, broad nose, his sunburnt cheeks, and the thick, black eyebrows overhanging his closed eyes. . . . The nose and the cheeks and the eyebrows, all the features, each taken separately, were coarse and heavy, like the furniture and the stove in the "travellers' room," but taken all together they gave the effect of something harmonious and even beautiful. Such is the lucky star, as it is called, of the Russian face: the coarser and harsher its features the softer and more good-natured it looks. The man was dressed in a gentleman's reefer jacket, shabby, but bound with wide new braid, a plush waistcoat, and full black trousers thrust into big high boots.

On one of the benches, which stood in a continuous row along the wall, a girl of eight, in a brown dress and long black stockings, lay asleep on a coat lined with fox. Her face was pale, her hair was flaxen, her shoulders were narrow, her whole body was thin and frail, but her nose stood out as thick and ugly a lump as the man's. She was sound asleep, and unconscious that her semi-circular comb had fallen off her head and was cutting her cheek.

The "travellers' room" had a festive appearance. The air was full of the smell of freshly scrubbed floors, there were no rags hanging as usual on the line that ran diagonally across the room, and a little lamp was burning in the corner over the table, casting a patch of red light on the ikon of St. George the Victorious. From the ikon stretched on each side of the corner a row of cheap oleographs, which maintained a strict and careful gradation in the transition from the sacred to the profane. In the dim light of the candle end and the red ikon lamp the pictures looked like one continuous stripe, covered with blurs of black. When the tiled stove, trying to sing in unison with the weather, drew in the air with a howl, while the logs, as though waking up, burst into bright flame and hissed angrily, red patches began dancing on the log walls, and over the head of the sleeping man could be seen first the Elder Seraphim, then the Shah Nasir-ed-Din, then a fat, brown baby with goggle eyes, whispering in the ear of a young girl with an extraordinarily blank, and indifferent face. . . .

Outside a storm was raging. Something frantic and wrathful, but profoundly unhappy, seemed to be flinging itself about the tavern with the ferocity of a wild beast and trying to break in. Banging at the doors, knocking at the windows and on the roof, scratching at the walls, it alternately threatened and besought, then subsided for a brief interval, and then with a gleeful, treacherous howl burst into the chimney, but the wood flared up, and the fire, like a chained dog, flew wrathfully to meet its foe, a battle began, and after it—sobs, shrieks, howls of wrath. In all of this there was the sound of angry misery and unsatisfied hate, and the mortified impatience of something accustomed to triumph.

Bewitched by this wild, inhuman music the "travellers' room" seemed spellbound for ever, but all at once the door creaked and the potboy, in a new print shirt, came in. Limping on one leg, and blinking his sleepy eyes, he snuffed the candle with his fingers, put some more wood on the fire and went out. At once from the church, which was three hundred paces from the tavern, the clock struck midnight. The wind played with the chimes as with the snowflakes; chasing the sounds of the clock it whirled them round and round over a vast space, so that some strokes were cut short or drawn out in long, vibrating notes, while others were completely lost in the general uproar. One stroke sounded as distinctly in the room as though it had chimed just under the window. The child, sleeping on the fox-skin, started and raised her head. For a minute she stared blankly at the dark window, at Nasir-ed-Din over whom a crimson glow from the fire flickered at that moment, then she turned her eyes upon the sleeping man.

"Daddy," she said.

But the man did not move. The little girl knitted her brow angrily, lay down, and curled up her legs. Someone in the tavern gave a loud, prolonged yawn. Soon afterwards there was the squeak of the swing door and the sound of indistinct voices. Someone came in, shaking the snow off, and stamping in felt boots which made a muffled thud.

"What is it?" a woman's voice asked languidly.

"Mademoiselle Ilovaisky has come, . . . ." answered a bass voice.

Again there was the squeak of the swing door. Then came the roar of the wind rushing in. Someone, probably the lame boy, ran to the door leading to the "travellers' room," coughed deferentially, and lifted the latch.

"This way, lady, please," said a woman's voice in dulcet tones. "It's clean in here, my beauty. . . ."

The door was opened wide and a peasant with a beard appeared in the doorway, in the long coat of a coachman, plastered all over with snow from head to foot, and carrying a big trunk on his shoulder. He was followed into the room by a feminine figure, scarcely half his height, with no face and no arms, muffled and wrapped up like a bundle and also covered with snow. A damp chill, as from a cellar, seemed to come to the child from the coachman and the bundle, and the fire and the candles flickered.

"What nonsense!" said the bundle angrily, "We could go perfectly well. We have only nine more miles to go, mostly by the forest, and we should not get lost. . . ."

"As for getting lost, we shouldn't, but the horses can't go on, lady!" answered the coachman. "And it is Thy Will, O Lord! As though I had done it on purpose!"

"God knows where you have brought me. . . . Well, be quiet. . . . There are people asleep here, it seems. You can go. . . ."

The coachman put the portmanteau on the floor, and as he did so, a great lump of snow fell off his shoulders. He gave a sniff and went out.

Then the little girl saw two little hands come out from the middle of the bundle, stretch upwards and begin angrily disentangling the network of shawls, kerchiefs, and scarves. First a big shawl fell on the ground, then a hood, then a white knitted kerchief. After freeing her head, the traveller took off her pelisse and at once shrank to half the size. Now she was in a long, grey coat with big buttons and bulging pockets. From one pocket she pulled out a paper parcel, from the other a bunch of big, heavy keys, which she put down so carelessly that the sleeping man started and opened his eyes. For some time he looked blankly round him as though he didn't know where he was, then he shook his head, went to the corner and sat down.... The newcomer took off her great coat, which made her shrink to half her size again, she took off her big felt boots, and sat down, too.

By now she no longer resembled a bundle: she was a thin little brunette of twenty, as slim as a snake, with a long white face and curly hair. Her nose was long and sharp, her chin, too, was long and sharp, her eyelashes were long, the corners of her mouth were sharp, and, thanks to this general sharpness, the expression of her face was biting. Swathed in a closely fitting black dress with a mass of lace at her neck and sleeves, with sharp elbows and long pink fingers, she recalled the portraits of mediæval English ladies. The grave concentration of her face increased this likeness.

The lady looked round at the room, glanced sideways at the man and the little girl, shrugged her shoulders, and moved to the window. The dark windows were shaking from the damp west wind. Big flakes of snow glistening in their whiteness, lay on the window frame, but at once disappeared, borne away by the wind. The savage music grew louder and louder....

After a long silence the little girl suddenly turned over, and said angrily, emphasizing each word:

"Oh, goodness, goodness, how unhappy I am! Unhappier than anyone!"

The man got up and moved with little steps to the child with a guilty air, which was utterly out of keeping with his huge figure and big beard.

"You are not asleep, dearie?" he said, in an apologetic voice. "What do you want?"

"I don't want anything, my shoulder aches! You are a wicked man, Daddy, and God will punish you! You'll see He will punish you."

"My darling, I know your shoulder aches, but what can I do, dearie?" said the man, in the tone in which men who have been drinking excuse themselves to their stern spouses. "It's the journey has made your shoulder ache, Sasha. To-morrow we shall get there and rest, and the pain will go away...."

"To-morrow, to-morrow.... Every day you say to-morrow. We shall be going on another twenty days."

"But we shall arrive to-morrow, dearie, on your father's word of honour. I never tell a lie, but if we are detained by the snowstorm it is not my fault."

"I can't bear any more, I can't, I can't!"

Sasha jerked her leg abruptly and filled the room with an unpleasant wailing. Her father made a despairing gesture, and looked hopelessly towards the young lady. The latter shrugged her shoulders, and hesitatingly went up to Sasha.

"Listen, my dear," she said, "it is no use crying. It's really naughty; if your shoulder aches it can't be helped."

"You see, Madam," said the man quickly, as though defending himself, "we have not slept for two nights, and have been travelling in a revolting conveyance. Well, of course, it is natural she should be ill and miserable, ... and then, you know, we had a drunken driver, our portmanteau has been stolen ... the snowstorm all the time, but what's the use of crying, Madam? I am exhausted, though, by sleeping in a sitting position, and I feel as though I were drunk. Oh, dear! Sasha, and I feel sick as it is, and then you cry!"

The man shook his head, and with a gesture of despair sat down.

"Of course you mustn't cry," said the young lady. "It's only little babies cry. If you are ill, dear, you must undress and go to sleep.... Let us take off your things!"

When the child had been undressed and pacified a silence reigned again. The young lady seated herself at the window, and looked round wonderingly at the room of the inn, at the ikon, at the stove. . . . Apparently the room and the little girl with the thick nose, in her short boy's nightgown, and the child's father, all seemed strange to her. This strange man was sitting in a corner; he kept looking about him helplessly, as though he were drunk, and rubbing his face with the palm of his hand. He sat silent, blinking, and judging from his guilty-looking figure it was difficult to imagine that he would soon begin to speak. Yet he was the first to begin. Stroking his knees, he gave a cough, laughed, and said:

"It's a comedy, it really is. . . . I look and I cannot believe my eyes: for what devilry has destiny driven us to this accursed inn? What did she want to show by it? Life sometimes performs such *'salto mortale,'* one can only stare and blink in amazement. Have you come from far, Madam?"

"No, not from far," answered the young lady. "I am going from our estate, fifteen miles from here, to our farm, to my father and brother. My name is Ilovaisky, and the farm is called Ilovaiskoe. It's nine miles away. What unpleasant weather!"

"It couldn't be worse."

The lame boy came in and stuck a new candle in the pomatum pot.

"You might bring us the samovar, boy," said the man, addressing him.

"Who drinks tea now?" laughed the boy. "It is a sin to drink tea before mass. . . ."

"Never mind boy, you won't burn in hell if we do. . . ."

Over the tea the new acquaintances got into conversation.

Mlle. Ilovaisky learned that her companion was called Grigory Petrovitch Liharev, that he was the brother of the Liharev who was Marshal of Nobility in one of the neighbouring districts, and he himself had once been a landowner, but had "run through everything in his time." Liharev learned that her name was Marya Mihailovna, that her father had a huge estate, but that she was the only one to look after it as her father and brother looked at life through their fingers, were irresponsible, and were too fond of harriers.

"My father and brother are all alone at the farm," she told him, brandishing her fingers (she had the habit of moving her fingers before her pointed face as she talked, and after every sentence moistened her lips with her sharp little tongue). "They, I mean men, are an irresponsible lot, and don't stir a finger for themselves. I can fancy there will be no one to give them a meal after the fast! We have no mother, and we have such servants that they can't lay the tablecloth properly when I am away. You can imagine their condition now! They will be left with nothing to break their fast, while I have to stay here all night. How strange it all is."

She shrugged her shoulders, took a sip from her cup, and said:

"There are festivals that have a special fragrance: at Easter, Trinity and Christmas there is a peculiar scent in the air. Even unbelievers are fond of those festivals. My brother, for instance, argues that there is no God, but he is the first to hurry to Matins at Easter."

Liharev raised his eyes to Mlle. Ilovaisky and laughed.

"They argue that there is no God," she went on, laughing too, "but why is it, tell me, all the celebrated writers, the learned men, clever people generally, in fact, believe towards the end of their life?"

"If a man does not know how to believe when he is young, Madam, he won't believe in his old age if he is ever so much of a writer."

Judging from Liharev's cough he had a bass voice, but, probably from being afraid to speak aloud, or from exaggerated shyness, he spoke in a tenor. After a brief pause he heaved a sign and said:

"The way I look at it is that faith is a faculty of the spirit. It is just the same as a talent, one must be born with it. So far as I can judge by myself, by the people I have seen in my time, and by all that is done around us, this faculty is present in Russians in its highest degree. Russian life presents us with an uninterrupted succession of convictions and aspirations, and if you care to know, it has not yet the faintest notion of lack of faith or scepticism. If a Russian does not believe in God, it means he believes in something else."

Liharev took a cup of tea from Mlle. Ilovaisky, drank off half in one gulp, and went on:

"I will tell you about myself. Nature has implanted in my breast an extraordinary faculty for belief. Whisper it not to the night, but half my life I was in the ranks of the Atheists and Nihilists, but there was not one hour in my life in which I ceased to believe. All talents, as a rule, show themselves in early childhood, and so my faculty showed itself when I could still walk upright under the table. My mother liked her children to eat a great deal, and when she gave me food she used to say: 'Eat! Soup is the great thing in life!' I believed, and ate the soup ten times a day, ate like a shark, ate till I was disgusted and stupefied. My nurse used to tell me fairy tales, and I believed in house-spirits, in wood-elves, and in goblins of all kinds. I used sometimes to steal corrosive sublimate from my father, sprinkle it on cakes, and carry them up to the attic that the house-spirits, you see, might eat them and be killed. And when I was taught to read and understand what I read, then there was a fine to-do. I ran away to America and went off to join the brigands, and wanted to go into a monastery, and hired boys to torture me for being a Christian. And note that my faith was always active, never dead. If I was running away to America I was not alone, but seduced someone else, as great a fool as I was, to go with me, and was delighted when I was nearly frozen outside the town gates and when I was thrashed; if I went to join the brigands I always came back with my face battered. A most restless childhood, I assure you! And when they sent me to the high school and pelted me with all sorts of truths—that is, that the earth goes round the sun, or that white light is not white, but is made up of seven colours—my poor little head began to go round! Everything was thrown into a whirl in me: Navin who made the sun stand still, and my mother who in the name of the Prophet Elijah disapproved of lightning conductors, and my father who was indifferent to the truths I had learned. My enlightenment inspired me. I wandered about the house and stables like one possessed, preaching my truths, was horrified by ignorance, glowed with hatred for anyone who saw in white light nothing but white light. . . . But all that's nonsense and childishness. Serious, so to speak, manly enthusiasms began only at the university. You have, no doubt, Madam, taken your degree somewhere?"

"I studied at Novotcherkask at the Don Institute."

"Then you have not been to a university? So you don't know what science means. All the sciences in the world have the same passport, without which they regard themselves as meaningless . . . the striving towards truth! Every one of them, even pharmacology, has for its aim not utility, not the alleviation of life, but truth. It's remarkable! When you set to work to study any science, what strikes you first of all is its beginning. I assure you there is nothing more attractive and grander, nothing is so staggering, nothing takes a man's breath away like the beginning of any science. From the first five or six lectures you are soaring on wings of the brightest hopes, you already seem to yourself to be welcoming truth with open arms. And I gave myself up to science, heart and soul, passionately, as to the woman one loves. I was its slave; I found it the sun of my existence, and asked for no other. I studied day and night without rest, ruined myself over books, wept when before my eyes men exploited science for their own personal ends. But my enthusiasm did not last long. The trouble is that every science has a beginning but not an end, like a recurring decimal. Zoology has discovered 35,000 kinds of insects, chemistry reckons 60 elements. If in time tens of noughts can be written after these figures, Zoology and chemistry will be just as far from their end as now, and all contemporary scientific work consists in increasing these numbers. I saw through this trick when I discovered the 35,001-st and felt no satisfaction. Well, I had no time to suffer from disillusionment, as I was soon possessed by a new faith. I plunged into Nihilism, with its manifestoes, its 'black divisions,' and all the rest of it. I 'went to the people,' worked in factories, worked as an oiler, as a barge hauler. Afterwards, when wandering over Russia, I had a taste of Russian life, I turned into a fervent devotee of that life. I loved the Russian people with poignant intensity; I loved their God and believed in Him, and in their language, their creative genius. . . . And so on, and so on. . . . I have been a Slavophile in my time, I used to pester Aksakov with letters, and I was a Ukrainophile, and an archæologist, and a collector of specimens of peasant art. . . . I was enthusiastic over ideas, people, events, places . . . my enthusiasm was endless! Five years ago I was working for the abolition of private property; my last creed was non-resistance to evil."

Sasha gave an abrupt sigh and began moving. Liharev got up and went to her.

"Won't you have some tea, dearie?" he asked tenderly.

"Drink it yourself," the child answered rudely. Liharev was disconcerted, and went back to the table with a guilty step.

"Then you have had a lively time," said Mlle. Ilovaisky; "you have something to remember."

"Well, yes, it's all very lively when one sits over tea and chatters to a kind listener, but you should ask what that liveliness has cost me! What price have I paid for the variety of my life? You see, Madam, I have not held my convictions like a German doctor of philosophy, *zierlichmännerlich*, I have not lived in solitude, but every conviction I have had has bound my back to the yoke, has torn my body to pieces. Judge, for yourself. I was wealthy like my brothers, but now I am a beggar. In the delirium of my enthusiasm I smashed up my own fortune and my wife's—a heap of other people's money. Now I am forty-two, old age is close upon me, and I am homeless, like a dog that has dropped behind its waggon at night. All my life I have not known what peace meant, my soul has been in continual agitation, distressed even by its hopes . . . I have been wearied out with heavy irregular work, have endured privation, have five times been in prison, have dragged myself across the provinces of Archangel and of Tobolsk . . . it's painful to think of it! I have lived, but in my fever I have not even been conscious of the process of life itself. Would you believe it, I don't remember a single spring, I never noticed how my wife loved me, how my children were born. What more can I tell you? I have been a misfortune to all who have loved me. . . . My mother has worn mourning for me all these fifteen years, while my proud brothers, who have had to wince, to blush, to bow their heads, to waste their money on my account, have come in the end to hate me like poison."

Liharev got up and sat down again.

"If I were simply unhappy I should thank God," he went on without looking at his listener. "My personal unhappiness sinks into the background when I remember how often in my enthusiasms I have been absurd, far from the truth, unjust, cruel, dangerous! How often

I have hated and despised those whom I ought to have loved, and *vice versa*, I have changed a thousand times. One day I believe, fall down and worship, the next I flee like a coward from the gods and friends of yesterday, and swallow in silence the 'scoundrel!' they hurl after me. God alone has seen how often I have wept and bitten my pillow in shame for my enthusiasms. Never once in my life have I intentionally lied or done evil, but my conscience is not clear! I cannot even boast, Madam, that I have no one's life upon my conscience, for my wife died before my eyes, worn out by my reckless activity. Yes, my wife! I tell you they have two ways of treating women nowadays. Some measure women's skulls to prove woman is inferior to man, pick out her defects to mock at her, to look original in her eyes, and to justify their sensuality. Others do their utmost to raise women to their level, that is, force them to learn by heart the 35,000 species, to speak and write the same foolish things as they speak and write themselves."

Liharev's face darkened.

"I tell you that woman has been and always will be the slave of man," he said in a bass voice, striking his fist on the table. "She is the soft, tender wax which a man always moulds into anything he likes. . . . . My God! for the sake of some trumpery masculine enthusiasm she will cut off her hair, abandon her family, die among strangers! . . . among the ideas for which she has sacrificed herself there is not a single feminine one. . . . . An unquestioning, devoted slave! I have not measured skulls, but I say this from hard, bitter experience: the proudest, most independent women, if I have succeeded in communicating to them my enthusiasm, have followed me without criticism, without question, and done anything I chose; I have turned a nun into a Nihilist who, as I heard afterwards, shot a gendarme; my wife never left me for a minute in my wanderings, and like a weathercock changed her faith in step with my changing enthusiasms."

Liharev jumped up and walked up and down the room.

"A noble, sublime slavery!" he said, clasping his hands. "It is just in it that the highest meaning of woman's life lies! Of all the fearful medley of thoughts and impressions accumulated in my brain from my association with women my memory, like a filter, has retained no ideas, no clever saying, no philosophy, nothing but that extraordinary, resignation to fate, that wonderful mercifulness, forgiveness of everything."

Liharev clenched his fists, stared at a fixed point, and with a sort of passionate intensity, as though he were savouring each word as he uttered it, hissed through his clenched teeth:

"That . . . that great-hearted fortitude, faithfulness unto death, poetry of the heart. . . . The meaning of life lies in just that unrepining martyrdom, in the tears which would soften a stone, in the boundless, all-forgiving love which brings light and warmth into the chaos of life. . . ."

Mlle. Ilovaisky got up slowly, took a step towards Liharev, and fixed her eyes upon his face. From the tears that glittered on his eyelashes, from his quivering, passionate voice, from the flush on his cheeks, it was clear to her that women were not a chance, not a simple subject of conversation. They were the object of his new enthusiasm, or, as he said himself, his new faith! For the first time in her life she saw a man carried away, fervently believing. With his gesticulations, with his flashing eyes he seemed to her mad, frantic, but there was a feeling of such beauty in the fire of his eyes, in his words, in all the movements of his huge body, that without noticing what she was doing she stood facing him as though rooted to the spot, and gazed into his face with delight.

"Take my mother," he said, stretching out his hand to her with an imploring expression on his face, "I poisoned her existence, according to her ideas disgraced the name of Liharev, did her as much harm as the most malignant enemy, and what do you think? My brothers give her little sums for holy bread and church services, and outraging her religious feelings, she saves that money and sends it in secret to her erring Grigory. This trifle alone elevates and ennobles the soul far more than all the theories, all the clever sayings and the 35,000 species. I can give you thousands of instances. Take you, even, for instance! With tempest and darkness outside you are going to your father and your brother to cheer them with your affection in the holiday, though very likely they have forgotten and are not thinking of you. And, wait a bit, and you will love a man and follow him to the North Pole. You would, wouldn't you?"

"Yes, if I loved him."

"There, you see," cried Liharev delighted, and he even stamped with his foot. "Oh dear! How glad I am that I have met you! Fate is kind to me, I am always meeting splendid people. Not a day passes but one makes acquaintance with somebody one would give one's soul for. There are ever so many more good people than bad in this world. Here, see, for instance, how openly and from our hearts we have been talking as though we had known each other a hundred years. Sometimes, I assure you, one restrains oneself for ten years and holds one's tongue, is reserved with one's friends and one's wife, and meets some cadet in a train and babbles one's whole soul out to him. It is the first time I have the honour of seeing you, and yet I have confessed to you as I have never confessed in my life. Why is it?"

Rubbing his hands and smiling good-humouredly Liharev walked up and down the room, and fell to talking about women again. Meanwhile they began ringing for matins.

"Goodness," wailed Sasha. "He won't let me sleep with his talking!"

"Oh, yes!" said Liharev, startled. "I am sorry, darling, sleep, sleep.... I have two boys besides her," he whispered. "They are living with their uncle, Madam, but this one can't exist a day without her father. She's wretched, she complains, but she sticks to me like a fly to honey. I have been chattering too much, Madam, and it would do you no harm to sleep. Wouldn't you like me to make up a bed for you?"

Without waiting for permission he shook the wet pelisse, stretched it on a bench, fur side upwards, collected various shawls and scarves, put the overcoat folded up into a roll for a pillow, and all this he did in silence with a look of devout reverence, as though he were not handling a woman's rags, but the fragments of holy vessels. There was something apologetic, embarrassed about his whole figure, as though in the presence of a weak creature he felt ashamed of his height and strength....

When Mlle. Ilovaisky had lain down, he put out the candle and sat down on a stool by the stove.

"So, Madam," he whispered, lighting a fat cigarette and puffing the smoke into the stove. "Nature has put into the Russian an extraordinary faculty for belief, a searching intelligence, and the gift of speculation, but all that is reduced to ashes by irresponsibility, laziness, and dreamy frivolity. . . . Yes. . . ."

She gazed wonderingly into the darkness, and saw only a spot of red on the ikon and the flicker of the light of the stove on Liharev's face. The darkness, the chime of the bells, the roar of the storm, the lame boy, Sasha with her fretfulness, unhappy Liharev and his sayings— all this was mingled together, and seemed to grow into one huge impression, and God's world seemed to her fantastic, full of marvels and magical forces. All that she had heard was ringing in her ears, and human life presented itself to her as a beautiful poetic fairy-tale without an end.

The immense impression grew and grew, clouded consciousness, and turned into a sweet dream. She was asleep, though she saw the little ikon lamp and a big nose with the light playing on it.

She heard the sound of weeping.

"Daddy, darling," a child's voice was tenderly entreating, "let's go back to uncle! There is a Christmas-tree there! Styopa and Kolya are there!"

"My darling, what can I do?" a man's bass persuaded softly. "Understand me! Come, understand!"

And the man's weeping blended with the child's. This voice of human sorrow, in the midst of the howling of the storm, touched the girl's ear with such sweet human music that she could not bear the delight of it, and wept too. She was conscious afterwards of a big, black shadow coming softly up to her, picking up a shawl that had dropped on to the floor and carefully wrapping it round her feet.

Mlle. Ilovaisky was awakened by a strange uproar. She jumped up and looked about her in astonishment. The deep blue dawn was looking in at the window half-covered with snow. In the room there was a grey twilight, through which the stove and the sleeping child and Nasir-ed-Din stood out distinctly. The stove and the lamp were both out. Through the wide-open door she could see the big tavern room with a counter and chairs. A man, with a stupid, gipsy face and astonished eyes, was standing in the middle of the room in a puddle of melting snow, holding a big red star on a stick. He was surrounded by a group of boys, motionless as statues, and plastered over with snow. The light shone through the red paper of the star, throwing a glow of red on their wet faces. The crowd was shouting in disorder, and from its uproar Mlle. Ilovaisky could make out only one couplet:

> "Hi, you Little Russian lad,
> Bring your sharp knife,
> We will kill the Jew, we will kill him,
> The son of tribulation. . ."

Liharev was standing near the counter, looking feelingly at the singers and tapping his feet in time. Seeing Mlle. Ilovaisky, he smiled all over his face and came up to her. She smiled too.

"A happy Christmas!" he said. "I saw you slept well."

She looked at him, said nothing, and went on smiling.

After the conversation in the night he seemed to her not tall and broad shouldered, but little, just as the biggest steamer seems to us a little thing when we hear that it has crossed the ocean.

"Well, it is time for me to set off," she said. "I must put on my things. Tell me where you are going now?"

"I? To the station of Klinushki, from there to Sergievo, and from Sergievo, with horses, thirty miles to the coal mines that belong to a horrid man, a general called Shashkovsky. My brothers have got me the post of superintendent there. . . . I am going to be a coal miner."

"Stay, I know those mines. Shashkovsky is my uncle, you know. But . . . what are you going there for?" asked Mlle. Ilovaisky, looking at Liharev in surprise.

"As superintendent. To superintend the coal mines."

"I don't understand!" she shrugged her shoulders. "You are going to the mines. But you know, it's the bare steppe, a desert, so dreary that you couldn't exist a day there! It's horrible coal, no one will buy it, and my uncle's a maniac, a despot, a bankrupt . . . . You won't get your salary!"

"No matter," said Liharev, unconcernedly, "I am thankful even for coal mines."

She shrugged her shoulders, and walked about the room in agitation.

"I don't understand, I don't understand," she said, moving her fingers before her face. "It's impossible, and . . . and irrational! You must understand that it's . . . it's worse than exile. It is a living tomb! O Heavens!" she said hotly, going up to Liharev and moving her fingers before his smiling face; her upper lip was quivering, and her sharp face turned pale, "Come, picture it, the bare steppe, solitude. There is no one to say a word to there, and you . . . are enthusiastic over women! Coal mines . . . and women!"

Mlle. Ilovaisky was suddenly ashamed of her heat and, turning away from Liharev, walked to the window.

"No, no, you can't go there," she said, moving her fingers rapidly over the pane.

Not only in her heart, but even in her spine she felt that behind her stood an infinitely unhappy man, lost and outcast, while he, as though he were unaware of his unhappiness, as though he had not shed tears in the night, was looking at her with a kindly smile. Better he should go on weeping! She walked up and down the room several times in agitation, then stopped short in a corner and sank into thought. Liharev was saying something, but she did not hear him. Turning her back on him she took out of her purse a money note, stood for a long time crumpling it in her hand, and looking round at Liharev, blushed and put it in her pocket.

The coachman's voice was heard through the door. With a stern, concentrated face she began putting on her things in silence. Liharev wrapped her up, chatting gaily, but every word he said lay on her heart like a weight. It is not cheering to hear the unhappy or the dying jest.

When the transformation of a live person into a shapeless bundle had been completed, Mlle. Ilovaisky looked for the last time round the "travellers' room," stood a moment in silence, and slowly walked out. Liharev went to see her off. . . .

Outside, God alone knows why, the winter was raging still. Whole clouds of big soft snowflakes were whirling restlessly over the earth, unable to find a resting-place. The horses, the sledge, the trees, a bull tied to a post, all were white and seemed soft and fluffy.

"Well, God help you," muttered Liharev, tucking her into the sledge. "Don't remember evil against me . . . ."

She was silent. When the sledge started, and had to go round a huge snowdrift, she looked back at Liharev with an expression as though she wanted to say something to him. He ran up to her, but she did not say a word to him, she only looked at him through her long eyelashes with little specks of snow on them.

Whether his finely intuitive soul were really able to read that look, or whether his imagination deceived him, it suddenly began to seem to him that with another touch or two that girl would have forgiven him his failures, his age, his desolate position, and would have followed him without question or reasonings. He stood a long while as though rooted to the spot, gazing at the tracks left by the sledge runners. The snowflakes greedily settled on his hair, his beard, his shoulders. . . . Soon the track of the runners had vanished, and he himself covered with snow, began to look like a white rock, but still his eyes kept seeking something in the clouds of snow.

## ROTHSCHILD'S FIDDLE

THE town was a little one, worse than a village, and it was inhabited by scarcely any but old people who died with an infrequency that was really annoying. In the hospital and in the prison fortress very few coffins were needed. In fact business was bad. If Yakov Ivanov had been an undertaker in the chief town of the province he would certainly have had a house of his own, and people would have addressed him as Yakov Matveyitch; here in this wretched little town people called him simply Yakov; his nickname in the street was for some reason Bronze, and he lived in a poor way like a humble peasant, in a little old hut in which there was only one room, and in this room he and Marfa, the stove, a double bed, the coffins, his bench, and all their belongings were crowded together.

Yakov made good, solid coffins. For peasants and working people he made them to fit himself, and this was never unsuccessful, for there were none taller and stronger than he, even in the prison, though he was seventy. For gentry and for women he made them to measure, and used an iron foot-rule for the purpose. He was very unwilling to take orders for children's coffins, and made them straight off without measurements, contemptuously, and when he was paid for the work he always said:

"I must confess I don't like trumpery jobs."

Apart from his trade, playing the fiddle brought him in a small income.

The Jews' orchestra conducted by Moisey Ilyitch Shahkes, the tinsmith, who took more than half their receipts for himself, played as a rule at weddings in the town. As Yakov played very well on the fiddle, especially Russian songs, Shahkes sometimes invited him to join the orchestra at a fee of half a rouble a day, in addition to tips from the visitors. When Bronze sat in the orchestra first of all his face became crimson and perspiring; it was hot, there was a suffocating smell of garlic, the fiddle squeaked, the double bass wheezed close to his right ear, while the flute wailed at his left, played by a gaunt, red-haired Jew who had a perfect network of red and blue veins all over his face, and who bore the name of the famous millionaire

Rothschild. And this accursed Jew contrived to play even the liveliest things plaintively. For no apparent reason Yakov little by little became possessed by hatred and contempt for the Jews, and especially for Rothschild; he began to pick quarrels with him, rail at him in unseemly language and once even tried to strike him, and Rothschild was offended and said, looking at him ferociously:

"If it were not that I respect you for your talent, I would have sent you flying out of the window."

Then he began to weep. And because of this Yakov was not often asked to play in the orchestra; he was only sent for in case of extreme necessity in the absence of one of the Jews.

Yakov was never in a good temper, as he was continually having to put up with terrible losses. For instance, it was a sin to work on Sundays or Saints' days, and Monday was an unlucky day, so that in the course of the year there were some two hundred days on which, whether he liked it or not, he had to sit with his hands folded. And only think, what a loss that meant. If anyone in the town had a wedding without music, or if Shahkes did not send for Yakov, that was a loss, too. The superintendent of the prison was ill for two years and was wasting away, and Yakov was impatiently waiting for him to die, but the superintendent went away to the chief town of the province to be doctored, and there took and died. There's a loss for you, ten roubles at least, as there would have been an expensive coffin to make, lined with brocade. The thought of his losses haunted Yakov, especially at night; he laid his fiddle on the bed beside him, and when all sorts of nonsensical ideas came into his mind he touched a string; the fiddle gave out a sound in the darkness, and he felt better.

On the sixth of May of the previous year Marfa had suddenly been taken ill. The old woman's breathing was laboured, she drank a great deal of water, and she staggered as she walked, yet she lighted the stove in the morning and even went herself to get water. Towards evening she lay down. Yakov played his fiddle all day; when it was quite dark he took the book in which he used every day to put down his losses, and, feeling dull, he began adding up the total for the year. It came to more than a thousand roubles. This so agitated him that he flung the reckoning beads down, and trampled them under his feet. Then he picked up the reckoning beads, and again spent a long time clicking with them and heaving deep, strained sighs. His face was crimson and wet with perspiration. He thought that if he had put that lost thousand roubles in the bank, the interest for a year would have been at least forty roubles, so that forty roubles was a loss too. In fact, wherever one turned there were losses and nothing else.

"Yakov!" Marfa called unexpectedly. "I am dying."

He looked round at his wife. Her face was rosy with fever, unusually bright and joyful-looking. Bronze, accustomed to seeing her face always pale, timid, and unhappy-looking, was bewildered. It looked as if she really were dying and were glad that she was going away for ever from that hut, from the coffins, and from Yakov. . . . And she gazed at the ceiling and moved her lips, and her expression was one of happiness, as though she saw death as her deliverer and were whispering with him.

It was daybreak; from the windows one could see the flush of dawn. Looking at the old woman, Yakov for some reason reflected that he had not once in his life been affectionate to her, had had no feeling for her, had never once thought to buy her a kerchief, or to bring her home some dainty from a wedding, but had done nothing but shout at her, scold her for his losses, shake his fists at her; it is true he had never actually beaten her, but he had frightened her, and at such times she had always been numb with terror. Why, he had forbidden her to drink tea because they spent too much without that, and she drank only hot water. And he understood why she had such a strange, joyful face now, and he was overcome with dread.

As soon as it was morning he borrowed a horse from a neighbour and took Marfa to the hospital. There were not many patients there, and so he had not long to wait, only three hours. To his great satisfaction the patients were not being received by the doctor, who was himself ill, but by the assistant, Maxim Nikolaitch, an old man of whom everyone in the town used to say that, though he drank and was quarrelsome, he knew more than the doctor.

"I wish you good-day," said Yakov, leading his old woman into the consulting room. "You must excuse us, Maxim Nikolaitch, we are always troubling you with our trumpery affairs. Here you see my better half is ailing, the partner of my life, as they say, excuse the expression...."

Knitting his grizzled brows and stroking his whiskers the assistant began to examine the old woman, and she sat on a stool, a wasted, bent figure with a sharp nose and open mouth, looking like a bird that wants to drink.

"H———m... Ah!..." the assistant said slowly, and he heaved a sigh. "Influenza and possibly fever. There's typhus in the town now. Well, the old woman has lived her life, thank God.... How old is she?"

"She'll be seventy in another year, Maxim Nikolaitch."

"Well, the old woman has lived her life, it's time to say good-bye."

"You are quite right in what you say, of course, Maxim Nikolaitch," said Yakov, smiling from politeness, "and we thank you feelingly for your kindness, but allow me to say every insect wants to live."

"To be sure," said the assistant, in a tone which suggested that it depended upon him whether the woman lived or died. "Well, then, my good fellow, put a cold compress on her head, and give her these powders twice a day, and so good-bye. Bonjour."

From the expression of his face Yakov saw that it was a bad case, and that no sort of powders would be any help; it was clear to him that Marfa would die very soon, if not to-day, to-morrow. He nudged the assistant's elbow, winked at him, and said in a low voice:

"If you would just cup her, Maxim Nikolaitch."

"I have no time, I have no time, my good fellow. Take your old woman and go in God's name. Goodbye."

"Be so gracious," Yakov besought him. "You know yourself that if, let us say, it were her stomach or her inside that were bad, then powders or drops, but you see she had got a chill! In a chill the first thing is to let blood, Maxim Nikolaitch."

But the assistant had already sent for the next patient, and a peasant woman came into the consulting room with a boy.

"Go along! go along," he said to Yakov, frowning. "It's no use to —"

"In that case put on leeches, anyway! Make us pray for you for ever."

The assistant flew into a rage and shouted:

"You speak to me again! You blockhead. . . ."

Yakov flew into a rage too, and he turned crimson all over, but he did not utter a word. He took Marfa on his arm and led her out of the room. Only when they were sitting in the cart he looked morosely and ironically at the hospital, and said:

"A nice set of artists they have settled here! No fear, but he would have cupped a rich man, but even a leech he grudges to the poor. The Herods!"

When they got home and went into the hut, Marfa stood for ten minutes holding on to the stove. It seemed to her that if she were to lie down Yakov would talk to her about his losses, and scold her for lying down and not wanting to work. Yakov looked at her drearily and thought that to-morrow was St. John the Divine's, and next day St. Nikolay the Wonder-worker's, and the day after that was Sunday, and then Monday, an unlucky day. For four days he would not be able to work, and most likely Marfa would die on one of those days; so he would have to make the coffin to-day. He picked up his iron rule, went up to the old woman and took her measure. Then she lay down, and he crossed himself and began making the coffin.

When the coffin was finished Bronze put on his spectacles and wrote in his book: "Marfa Ivanov's coffin, two roubles, forty kopecks."

And he heaved a sigh. The old woman lay all the time silent with her eyes closed. But in the evening, when it got dark, she suddenly called the old man.

"Do you remember, Yakov," she asked, looking at him joyfully. "Do you remember fifty years ago God gave us a little baby with flaxen hair? We used always to be sitting by the river then, singing songs . . . under the willows," and laughing bitterly, she added: "The baby girl died."

Yakov racked his memory, but could not remember the baby or the willows.

"It's your fancy," he said.

The priest arrived; he administered the sacrament and extreme unction. Then Marfa began muttering something unintelligible, and towards morning she died. Old women, neighbours, washed her, dressed her, and laid her in the coffin. To avoid paying the sacristan, Yakov read the psalms over the body himself, and they got nothing out of him for the grave, as the grave-digger was a crony of his. Four peasants carried the coffin to the graveyard, not for money, but from respect. The coffin was followed by old women, beggars, and a couple of crazy saints, and the people who met it crossed themselves piously. . . . And Yakov was very much pleased that it was so creditable, so decorous, and so cheap, and no offence to anyone. As he took his last leave of Marfa he touched the coffin and thought: "A good piece of work!"

But as he was going back from the cemetery he was overcome by acute depression. He didn't feel quite well: his breathing was laboured and feverish, his legs felt weak, and he had a craving for drink. And thoughts of all sorts forced themselves on his mind. He remembered again that all his life he had never felt for Marfa, had never been affectionate to her. The fifty-two years they had lived in the same hut had dragged on a long, long time, but it had somehow happened that in all that time he had never once thought of her, had paid no attention to her, as though she had been a cat or a dog. And yet, every day, she had lighted the stove, had cooked and baked, had gone for the water, had chopped the wood, had slept with him in the same bed, and when he came home drunk from the weddings always reverently hung his fiddle on the wall and put him to bed, and all this in silence, with a timid, anxious expression.

Rothschild, smiling and bowing, came to meet Yakov.

"I was looking for you, uncle," he said. "Moisey Ilyitch sends you his greetings and bids you come to him at once."

Yakov felt in no mood for this. He wanted to cry.

"Leave me alone," he said, and walked on.

"How can you," Rothschild said, fluttered, running on in front. "Moisey Ilyitch will be offended! He bade you come at once!"

Yakov was revolted at the Jew's gasping for breath and blinking, and having so many red freckles on his face. And it was disgusting to look at his green coat with black patches on it, and all his fragile, refined figure.

"Why are you pestering me, garlic?" shouted Yakov. "Don't persist!"

The Jew got angry and shouted too:

"Not so noisy, please, or I'll send you flying over the fence!"

"Get out of my sight!" roared Yakov, and rushed at him with his fists. "One can't live for you scabby Jews!"

Rothschild, half dead with terror, crouched down and waved his hands over his head, as though to ward off a blow; then he leapt up and ran away as fast as his legs could carry him: as he ran he gave little skips and kept clasping his hands, and Yakov could see how his long thin spine wriggled. Some boys, delighted at the incident, ran after him shouting "Jew! Jew!" Some dogs joined in the chase barking. Someone burst into a roar of laughter, then gave a whistle; the dogs barked with even more noise and unanimity. Then a dog must have bitten Rothschild, as a desperate, sickly scream was heard.

Yakov went for a walk on the grazing ground, then wandered on at random in the outskirts of the town, while the street boys shouted:

"Here's Bronze! Here's Bronze!"

He came to the river, where the curlews floated in the air uttering shrill cries and the ducks quacked. The sun was blazing hot, and there was a glitter from the water, so that it hurt the eyes to look at it. Yakov walked by a path along the bank and saw a plump, rosy-cheeked lady come out of the bathing-shed, and thought about her: "Ugh! you otter!"

Not far from the bathing-shed boys were catching crayfish with bits of meat; seeing him, they began shouting spitefully, "Bronze! Bronze!" And then he saw an old spreading willow-tree with a big hollow in it, and a crow's nest on it. . . . And suddenly there rose up vividly in Yakov's memory a baby with flaxen hair, and the willow-tree Marfa had spoken of. Why, that is it, the same willow-tree—green, still, and sorrowful. . . . How old it has grown, poor thing!

He sat down under it and began to recall the past. On the other bank, where now there was the water meadow, in those days there stood a big birchwood, and yonder on the bare hillside that could be seen on the horizon an old, old pine forest used to be a bluish patch in the distance. Big boats used to sail on the river. But now it was all smooth and unruffled, and on the other bank there stood now only one birch-tree, youthful and slender like a young lady, and there was nothing on the river but ducks and geese, and it didn't look as though there had ever been boats on it. It seemed as though even the geese were fewer than of old. Yakov shut his eyes, and in his imagination huge flocks of white geese soared, meeting one another.

He wondered how it had happened that for the last forty or fifty years of his life he had never once been to the river, or if he had been by it he had not paid attention to it. Why, it was a decent sized river, not a trumpery one; he might have gone in for fishing and sold the fish to merchants, officials, and the bar-keeper at the station, and then have put money in the bank; he might have sailed in a boat from one house to another, playing the fiddle, and people of all classes would have paid to hear him; he might have tried getting big boats afloat again—that would be better than making coffins; he might have bred geese, killed them and sent them in the winter to Moscow. Why, the feathers alone would very likely mount up to ten roubles in the year. But he had wasted his time, he had done nothing of this. What losses! Ah! What losses! And if he had gone in for all those things at once—catching fish and playing the fiddle, and running boats and killing geese—what a fortune he would have made! But nothing of this had happened, even in his dreams; life had passed uselessly without any pleasure, had been wasted for nothing, not even a pinch of snuff; there was nothing left in front, and if one looked back—there was nothing there but losses, and such terrible ones, it made one cold all over. And why was it a man could not live so as to avoid these losses and misfortunes? One wondered why they had cut down the birch copse and the pine forest. Why was he walking with no reason on the grazing ground? Why do people always do what isn't needful? Why had Yakov all his life scolded, bellowed, shaken his fists, ill-treated his wife, and, one might ask, what necessity was there for him to frighten and insult the Jew that day? Why did people in general hinder each other from living? What losses were due to it! what terrible losses! If it were not for hatred and malice people would get immense benefit from one another.

In the evening and the night he had visions of the baby, of the willow, of fish, of slaughtered geese, and Marfa looking in profile like a bird that wants to drink, and the pale, pitiful face of Rothschild, and faces moved down from all sides and muttered of losses. He tossed from side to side, and got out of bed five times to play the fiddle.

In the morning he got up with an effort and went to the hospital. The same Maxim Nikolaitch told him to put a cold compress on his head, and gave him some powders, and from his tone and expression of face Yakov realized that it was a bad case and that no powders would be any use. As he went home afterwards, he reflected that death would be nothing but a benefit; he would not have to eat or drink, or pay taxes or offend people, and, as a man lies in his grave not for one year but for hundreds and thousands, if one reckoned it up the gain would be enormous. A man's life meant loss: death meant gain. This reflection was, of course, a just one, but yet it was bitter and mortifying; why was the order of the world so strange, that life, which is given to man only once, passes away without benefit?

He was not sorry to die, but at home, as soon as he saw his fiddle, it sent a pang to his heart and he felt sorry. He could not take the fiddle with him to the grave, and now it would be left forlorn, and the same thing would happen to it as to the birch copse and the pine forest. Everything in this world was wasted and would be wasted! Yakov went out of the hut and sat in the doorway, pressing the fiddle to his bosom. Thinking of his wasted, profitless life, he began to play, he did not know what, but it was plaintive and touching, and tears trickled down his cheeks. And the harder he thought, the more mournfully the fiddle wailed.

The latch clicked once and again, and Rothschild appeared at the gate. He walked across half the yard boldly, but seeing Yakov he stopped short, and seemed to shrink together, and probably from terror, began making signs with his hands as though he wanted to show on his fingers what o'clock it was.

"Come along, it's all right," said Yakov in a friendly tone, and he beckoned him to come up. "Come along!"

Looking at him mistrustfully and apprehensively, Rothschild began to advance, and stopped seven feet off.

"Be so good as not to beat me," he said, ducking. "Moisey Ilyitch has sent me again. 'Don't be afraid,' he said; 'go to Yakov again and tell him,' he said, 'we can't get on without him.' There is a wedding on Wednesday. . . . Ye—-es! Mr. Shapovalov is marrying his daughter to a good man. . . . And it will be a grand wedding, oo-oo!" added the Jew, screwing up one eye.

"I can't come," said Yakov, breathing hard. "I'm ill, brother."

And he began playing again, and the tears gushed from his eyes on to the fiddle. Rothschild listened attentively, standing sideways to him and folding his arms on his chest. The scared and perplexed expression on his face, little by little, changed to a look of woe and suffering; he rolled his eyes as though he were experiencing an agonizing ecstasy, and articulated, "Vachhh!" and tears slowly ran down his cheeks and trickled on his greenish coat.

And Yakov lay in bed all the rest of the day grieving. In the evening, when the priest confessing him asked, Did he remember any special sin he had committed? straining his failing memory he thought again of Marfa's unhappy face, and the despairing shriek of the Jew when the dog bit him, and said, hardly audibly, "Give the fiddle to Rothschild."

"Very well," answered the priest.

And now everyone in the town asks where Rothschild got such a fine fiddle. Did he buy it or steal it? Or perhaps it had come to him as a pledge. He gave up the flute long ago, and now plays nothing but the fiddle. As plaintive sounds flow now from his bow, as came once from his flute, but when he tries to repeat what Yakov played, sitting in the doorway, the effect is something so sad and sorrowful that his audience weep, and he himself rolls his eyes and articulates "Vachhh! . . ." And this new air was so much liked in the town that the merchants and officials used to be continually sending for Rothschild and making him play it over and over again a dozen times.

## IVAN MATVEYITCH

BETWEEN five and six in the evening. A fairly well-known man of learning—we will call him simply the man of learning—is sitting in his study nervously biting his nails.

"It's positively revolting," he says, continually looking at his watch. "It shows the utmost disrespect for another man's time and work. In England such a person would not earn a farthing, he would die of hunger. You wait a minute, when you do come . . . ."

And feeling a craving to vent his wrath and impatience upon someone, the man of learning goes to the door leading to his wife's room and knocks.

"Listen, Katya," he says in an indignant voice. "If you see Pyotr Danilitch, tell him that decent people don't do such things. It's abominable! He recommends a secretary, and does not know the sort of man he is recommending! The wretched boy is two or three hours late with unfailing regularity every day. Do you call that a secretary? Those two or three hours are more precious to me than two or three years to other people. When he does come I will swear at him like a dog, and won't pay him and will kick him out. It's no use standing on ceremony with people like that!"

"You say that every day, and yet he goes on coming and coming."

"But to-day I have made up my mind. I have lost enough through him. You must excuse me, but I shall swear at him like a cabman."

At last a ring is heard. The man of learning makes a grave face; drawing himself up, and, throwing back his head, he goes into the entry. There his amanuensis Ivan Matveyitch, a young man of eighteen, with a face oval as an egg and no moustache, wearing a shabby, mangy overcoat and no goloshes, is already standing by the hatstand. He is in breathless haste, and scrupulously wipes his huge clumsy boots on the doormat, trying as he does so to conceal from the maidservant a hole in his boot through which a white sock is peeping. Seeing the man of learning he smiles with that broad, prolonged, somewhat foolish smile which is seen only on the faces of children or very good-natured people.

"Ah, good evening!" he says, holding out a big wet hand. "Has your sore throat gone?"

"Ivan Matveyitch," says the man of learning in a shaking voice, stepping back and clasping his hands together. "Ivan Matveyitch."

Then he dashes up to the amanuensis, clutches him by the shoulders, and begins feebly shaking him.

"What a way to treat me!" he says with despair in his voice. "You dreadful, horrid fellow, what a way to treat me! Are you laughing at me, are you jeering at me? Eh?"

Judging from the smile which still lingered on his face Ivan Matveyitch had expected a very different reception, and so, seeing the man of learning's countenance eloquent of indignation, his oval face grows longer than ever, and he opens his mouth in amazement.

"What is . . . what is it?" he asks.

"And you ask that?" the man of learning clasps his hands. "You know how precious time is to me, and you are so late. You are two hours late! . . . Have you no fear of God?"

"I haven't come straight from home," mutters Ivan Matveyitch, untying his scarf irresolutely. "I have been at my aunt's name-day party, and my aunt lives five miles away. . . . If I had come straight from home, then it would have been a different thing."

"Come, reflect, Ivan Matveyitch, is there any logic in your conduct? Here you have work to do, work at a fixed time, and you go flying off after name-day parties and aunts! But do make haste and undo your wretched scarf! It's beyond endurance, really!"

The man of learning dashes up to the amanuensis again and helps him to disentangle his scarf.

"You are done up like a peasant woman, . . . Come along, . . . Please make haste!"

Blowing his nose in a dirty, crumpled-up handkerchief and pulling down his grey reefer jacket, Ivan Matveyitch goes through the hall and the drawing-room to the study. There a place and paper and even cigarettes had been put ready for him long ago.

"Sit down, sit down," the man of learning urges him on, rubbing his hands impatiently. "You are an unsufferable person. . . . You know the work has to be finished by a certain time, and then you are so late. One is forced to scold you. Come, write, . . . Where did we stop?"

Ivan Matveyitch smooths his bristling cropped hair and takes up his pen. The man of learning walks up and down the room, concentrates himself, and begins to dictate:

"The fact is . . . comma . . . that so to speak fundamental forms . . . have you written it? . . . forms are conditioned entirely by the essential nature of those principles . . . comma . . . which find in them their expression and can only be embodied in them . . . . New line, . . . There's a stop there, of course. . . . More independence is found . . . is found . . . by the forms which have not so much a political . . . comma . . . as a social character . . "

"The high-school boys have a different uniform now . . . a grey one," said Ivan Matveyitch, "when I was at school it was better: they used to wear regular uniforms."

"Oh dear, write please!" says the man of learning wrathfully. "Character . . . have you written it? Speaking of the forms relating to the organization . . . of administrative functions, and not to the regulation of the life of the people . . . comma . . . it cannot be said that they are marked by the nationalism of their forms . . . the last three words in inverted commas. . . . Aie, aie . . . tut, tut . . . so what did you want to say about the high school?"

"That they used to wear a different uniform in my time."

"Aha! . . . indeed, . . . Is it long since you left the high school?"

"But I told you that yesterday. It is three years since I left school. . . . I left in the fourth class."

"And why did you give up high school?" asks the man of learning, looking at Ivan Matveyitch's writing.

"Oh, through family circumstances."

"Must I speak to you again, Ivan Matveyitch? When will you get over your habit of dragging out the lines? There ought not to be less than forty letters in a line."

"What, do you suppose I do it on purpose?" says Ivan Matveyitch, offended. "There are more than forty letters in some of the other lines. . . . You count them. And if you think I don't put enough in the line, you can take something off my pay."

"Oh dear, that's not the point. You have no delicacy, really. . . . At the least thing you drag in money. The great thing is to be exact, Ivan Matveyitch, to be exact is the great thing. You ought to train yourself to be exact."

The maidservant brings in a tray with two glasses of tea on it, and a basket of rusks. . . . Ivan Matveyitch takes his glass awkwardly with both hands, and at once begins drinking it. The tea is too hot. To avoid burning his mouth Ivan Matveyitch tries to take a tiny sip. He eats one rusk, then a second, then a third, and, looking sideways, with embarrassment, at the man of learning, timidly stretches after a fourth. . . . The noise he makes in swallowing, the relish with which he smacks his lips, and the expression of hungry greed in his raised eyebrows irritate the man of learning.

"Make haste and finish, time is precious."

"You dictate, I can drink and write at the same time. . . . I must confess I was hungry."

"I should think so after your walk!"

"Yes, and what wretched weather! In our parts there is a scent of spring by now. . . . There are puddles everywhere; the snow is melting."

"You are a southerner, I suppose?"

"From the Don region. . . . It's quite spring with us by March. Here it is frosty, everyone's in a fur coat, . . . but there you can see the grass . . . it's dry everywhere, and one can even catch tarantulas."

"And what do you catch tarantulas for?"

"Oh! . . . to pass the time . . ." says Ivan Matveyitch, and he sighs. "It's fun catching them. You fix a bit of pitch on a thread, let it down into their hole and begin hitting the tarantula on the back with the pitch, and the brute gets cross, catches hold of the pitch with his claws, and gets stuck. . . . And what we used to do with them! We used to put a basinful of them together and drop a bihorka in with them."

"What is a bihorka?"

"That's another spider, very much the same as a tarantula. In a fight one of them can kill a hundred tarantulas."

"H'm! . . . But we must write, . . . Where did we stop?"

The man of learning dictates another twenty lines, then sits plunged in meditation.

Ivan Matveyitch, waiting while the other cogitates, sits and, craning his neck, puts the collar of his shirt to rights. His tie will not set properly, the stud has come out, and the collar keeps coming apart.

"H'm! . . ." says the man of learning. "Well, haven't you found a job yet, Ivan Matveyitch?"

"No. And how is one to find one? I am thinking, you know, of volunteering for the army. But my father advises my going into a chemist's."

"H'm! . . . But it would be better for you to go into the university. The examination is difficult, but with patience and hard work you could get through. Study, read more. . . . Do you read much?"

"Not much, I must own . . ." says Ivan Matveyitch, lighting a cigarette.

"Have you read Turgenev?"

"N-no. . . ."

"And Gogol?"

"Gogol. H'm! . . . Gogol. . . . No, I haven't read him!"

"Ivan Matveyitch! Aren't you ashamed? Aie! aie! You are such a nice fellow, so much that is original in you . . . you haven't even read

Gogol! You must read him! I will give you his works! It's essential to read him! We shall quarrel if you don't!"

Again a silence follows. The man of learning meditates, half reclining on a soft lounge, and Ivan Matveyitch, leaving his collar in peace, concentrates his whole attention on his boots. He has not till then noticed that two big puddles have been made by the snow melting off his boots on the floor. He is ashamed.

"I can't get on to-day . . ." mutters the man of learning. "I suppose you are fond of catching birds, too, Ivan Matveyitch?"

"That's in autumn, . . . I don't catch them here, but there at home I always did."

"To be sure . . . very good. But we must write, though."

The man of learning gets up resolutely and begins dictating, but after ten lines sits down on the lounge again.

"No. . . . Perhaps we had better put it off till to-morrow morning," he says. "Come to-morrow morning, only come early, at nine o'clock. God preserve you from being late!"

Ivan Matveyitch lays down his pen, gets up from the table and sits in another chair. Five minutes pass in silence, and he begins to feel it is time for him to go, that he is in the way; but in the man of learning's study it is so snug and light and warm, and the impression of the nice rusks and sweet tea is still so fresh that there is a pang at his heart at the mere thought of home. At home there is poverty, hunger, cold, his grumbling father, scoldings, and here it is so quiet and unruffled, and interest even is taken in his tarantulas and birds.

The man of learning looks at his watch and takes up a book.

"So you will give me Gogol?' says Ivan Matveyitch, getting up.

"Yes, yes! But why are you in such a hurry, my dear boy? Sit down and tell me something . . ."

Ivan Matveyitch sits down and smiles broadly. Almost every evening he sits in this study and always feels something extraordinarily soft, attracting him, as it were akin, in the voice and the glance of the man of learning. There are moments when he even fancies that the man of learning is becoming attached to him, used to him, and that if he scolds him for being late, it's simply because he misses his chatter about tarantulas and how they catch goldfinches on the Don.

## ZINOTCHKA

THE party of sportsmen spent the night in a peasant's hut on some newly mown hay. The moon peeped in at the window; from the street came the mournful wheezing of a concertina; from the hay came a sickly sweet, faintly troubling scent. The sportsmen talked about dogs, about women, about first love, and about snipe. After all the ladies of their acquaintance had been picked to pieces, and hundreds of stories had been told, the stoutest of the sportsmen, who looked in the darkness like a haycock, and who talked in the mellow bass of a staff officer, gave a loud yawn and said:

"It is nothing much to be loved; the ladies are created for the purpose of loving us men. But, tell me, has any one of you fellows been hated—passionately, furiously hated? Has any one of you watched the ecstasies of hatred? Eh?"

No answer followed.

"Has no one, gentlemen?" asked the staff officer's bass voice. "But I, now, have been hated, hated by a pretty girl, and have been able to study the symptoms of first hatred directed against myself. It was the first, because it was something exactly the converse of first love. What I am going to tell, however, happened when I knew nothing about love or hate. I was eight at the time, but that made no difference; in this case it was not *he* but *she* that mattered. Well, I beg your attention. One fine summer evening, just before sunset, I was sitting in the nursery, doing my lesson with my governess, Zinotchka, a very charming and poetical creature who had left boarding school not long before. Zinotchka looked absent-mindedly towards the window and said:

"'Yes. We breathe in oxygen; now tell me, Petya, what do we breathe out?'

"'Carbonic acid gas,' I answered, looking towards the same window.

"'Right,' assented Zinotchka. 'Plants, on the contrary, breathe in carbonic acid gas, and breathe out oxygen. Carbonic acid gas is contained in seltzer water, and in the fumes from the samovar. . . . It is a very noxious gas. Near Naples there is the so-called Cave of

Dogs, which contains carbonic acid gas; a dog dropped into it is suffocated and dies.'

"This luckless Cave of Dogs near Naples is a chemical marvel beyond which no governess ventures to go. Zinotchka always hotly maintained the usefulness of natural science, but I doubt if she knew any chemistry beyond this Cave.

"Well, she told me to repeat it. I repeated it. She asked me what was meant by the horizon. I answered. And meantime, while we were ruminating over the horizon and the Cave, in the yard below, my father was just getting ready to go shooting. The dogs yapped, the trace horses shifted from one leg to another impatiently and coquetted with the coachman, the footman packed the waggonette with parcels and all sorts of things. Beside the waggonette stood a brake in which my mother and sisters were sitting to drive to a name-day party at the Ivanetskys'. No one was left in the house but Zinotchka, me, and my eldest brother, a student, who had toothache. You can imagine my envy and my boredom.

"'Well, what do we breathe in?' asked Zinotchka, looking at the window.

"'Oxygen...'

"'Yes. And the horizon is the name given to the place where it seems to us as though the earth meets the sky.'

"Then the waggonette drove off, and after it the brake. . . . I saw Zinotchka take a note out of her pocket, crumple it up convulsively and press it to her temple, then she flushed crimson and looked at her watch.

"'So, remember,' she said, 'that near Naples is the so-called Cave of Dogs. . . .' She glanced at her watch again and went on: 'where the sky seems to us to meet the earth. . . .'

"The poor girl in violent agitation walked about the room, and once more glanced at her watch. There was another half-hour before the end of our lesson.

"'Now arithmetic,' she said, breathing hard and turning over the pages of the sum-book with a trembling hand. 'Come, you work out problem 325 and I . . . will be back directly.'

"She went out. I heard her scurry down the stairs, and then I saw her dart across the yard in her blue dress and vanish through the garden gate. The rapidity of her movements, the flush on her cheeks and her excitement, aroused my curiosity. Where had she run, and what for? Being intelligent beyond my years I soon put two and two together, and understood it all: she had run into the garden, taking advantage of the absence of my stern parents, to steal in among the raspberry bushes, or to pick herself some cherries. If that were so, dash it all, I would go and have some cherries too. I threw aside the sum-book and ran into the garden. I ran to the cherry orchard, but she was not there. Passing by the raspberries, the gooseberries, and the watchman's shanty, she crossed the kitchen garden and reached the pond, pale, and starting at every sound. I stole after her, and what I saw, my friends, was this. At the edge of the pond, between the thick stumps of two old willows, stood my elder brother, Sasha; one could not see from his face that he had toothache. He looked towards Zinotchka as she approached him, and his whole figure was lighted up by an expression of happiness as though by sunshine. And Zinotchka, as though she were being driven into the Cave of Dogs, and were being forced to breathe carbonic acid gas, walked towards him, scarcely able to move one leg before the other, breathing hard, with her head thrown back. . . . To judge from appearances she was going to a rendezous for the first time in her life. But at last she reached him. . . . For half a minute they gazed at each other in silence, as though they could not believe their eyes. Thereupon some force seemed to shove Zinotchka; she laid her hands on Sasha's shoulders and let her head droop upon his waistcoat. Sasha laughed, muttered something incoherent, and with the clumsiness of a man head over ears in love, laid both hands on Zinotchka's face. And the weather, gentlemen, was exquisite. . . . The hill behind which the sun was setting, the two willows, the green bank, the sky—all together with Sasha and Zinotchka were reflected in the pond . . . perfect stillness . . . you can imagine it. Millions of butterflies with long whiskers gleamed golden above the reeds; beyond the garden they were driving the cattle. In fact, it was a perfect picture.

"Of all I had seen the only thing I understood was that Sasha was kissing Zinotchka. That was improper. If *maman* heard of it they would both catch it. Feeling for some reason ashamed I went back to the nursery, not waiting for the end of the rendezvous. There I sat over the sum-book, pondered and reflected. A triumphant smile strayed upon my countenance. On one side it was agreeable to be the possessor of another person's secret; on the other it was also very agreeable that such authorities as Sasha and Zinotchka might at any moment be convicted by me of ignorance of the social proprieties. Now they were in my power, and their peace was entirely dependent on my magnanimity. I'd let them know.

"When I went to bed, Zinotchka came into the nursery as usual to find out whether I had dropped asleep without undressing and whether I had said my prayers. I looked at her pretty, happy face and grinned. I was bursting with my secret and itching to let it out. I had to drop a hint and enjoy the effect.

"'I know,' I said, grinning. 'Gy—y.'

"'What do you know?'

"'Gy—y! I saw you near the willows kissing Sasha. I followed you and saw it all.'

"Zinotchka started, flushed all over, and overwhelmed by 'my hint' she sank down on the chair, on which stood a glass of water and a candlestick.

"'I saw you . . . kissing . . .' I repeated, sniggering and enjoying her confusion. 'Aha! I'll tell mamma!'

"Cowardly Zinotchka gazed at me intently, and convincing herself that I really did know all about it, clutched my hand in despair and muttered in a trembling whisper:

"'Petya, it is low. . . . I beg of you, for God's sake. . . . Be a man . . . don't tell anyone. . . . Decent people don't spy . . . . It's low. . . . I entreat you.'

"The poor girl was terribly afraid of my mother, a stern and virtuous lady—that was one thing; and the second was that my grinning countenance could not but outrage her first love so pure and poetical, and you can imagine the state of her heart. Thanks to me, she did not sleep a wink all night, and in the morning she appeared at breakfast with blue rings round her eyes. When I met Sasha after breakfast I could not refrain from grinning and boasting:

"'I know! I saw you yesterday kissing Mademoiselle Zina!'

"Sasha looked at me and said:

"'You are a fool.'

"He was not so cowardly as Zinotchka, and so my effect did not come off. That provoked me to further efforts. If Sasha was not frightened it was evident that he did not believe that I had seen and knew all about it; wait a bit, I would show him.

"At our lessons before dinner Zinotchka did not look at me, and her voice faltered. Instead of trying to scare me she tried to propitiate me in every way, giving me full marks, and not complaining to my father of my naughtiness. Being intelligent beyond my years I exploited her secret: I did not learn my lessons, walked into the schoolroom on my head, and said all sorts of rude things. In fact, if I had remained in that vein till to-day I should have become a famous blackmailer. Well, a week passed. Another person's secret irritated and fretted me like a splinter in my soul. I longed at all costs to blurt it out and gloat over the effect. And one day at dinner, when we had a lot of visitors, I gave a stupid snigger, looked fiendishly at Zinotchka and said:

"'I know. Gy—y! I saw! . . .'

"'What do you know?' asked my mother.

"I looked still more fiendishly at Zinotchka and Sasha. You ought to have seen how the girl flushed up, and how furious Sasha's eyes were! I bit my tongue and did not go on. Zinotchka gradually turned pale, clenched her teeth, and ate no more dinner. At our evening lessons that day I noticed a striking change in Zinotchka's face. It looked sterner, colder, as it were, more like marble, while her eyes gazed strangely straight into my face, and I give you my word of honour I have never seen such terrible, annihilating eyes, even in hounds when they overtake the wolf. I understood their expression perfectly, when in the middle of a lesson she suddenly clenched her teeth and hissed through them:

"'I hate you! Oh, you vile, loathsome creature, if you knew how I hate you, how I detest your cropped head, your vulgar, prominent ears!'

"But at once she took fright and said:

"'I am not speaking to you, I am repeating a part out of a play. . . .'

"Then, my friends, at night I saw her come to my bedside and gaze a long time into my face. She hated me passionately, and could not exist away from me. The contemplation of my hated pug of a face had become a necessity to her. I remember a lovely summer evening . . . with the scent of hay, perfect stillness, and so on. The moon was shining. I was walking up and down the avenue, thinking of cherry jam. Suddenly Zinotchka, looking pale and lovely, came up to me, she caught hold of my hand, and breathlessly began expressing herself:

"'Oh, how I hate you! I wish no one harm as I do you! Let me tell you that! I want you to understand that!'

"You understand, moonlight, her pale face, breathless with passion, the stillness . . . little pig as I was I actually enjoyed it. I listened to her, looked at her eyes. . . . At first I liked it, and enjoyed the novelty. Then I was suddenly seized with terror, I gave a scream, and ran into the house at breakneck speed.

"I made up my mind that the best thing to do was to complain to *maman*. And I did complain, mentioning incidentally how Sasha had kissed Zinotchka. I was stupid, and did not know what would follow, or I should have kept the secret to myself. . . . After hearing my story *maman* flushed with indignation and said:

"'It is not your business to speak about that, you are still very young. . . . But, what an example for children.'

"My *maman* was not only virtuous but diplomatic. To avoid a scandal she did not get rid of Zinotchka at once, but set to work gradually, systematically, to pave the way for her departure, as one does with well-bred but intolerable people. I remember that when Zinotchka did leave us the last glance she cast at the house was directed at the window at which I was sitting, and I assure you, I remember that glance to this day.

"Zinotchka soon afterwards became my brother's wife. She is the Zinaida Nikolaevna whom you know. The next time I met her I was already an ensign. In spite of all her efforts she could not recognize the hated Petya in the ensign with his moustache, but still she did not treat me quite like a relation. . . . And even now, in spite of my good-humoured baldness, meek corpulence, and unassuming air, she still looks askance at me, and feels put out when I go to see my brother. Hatred it seems can no more be forgotten than love. . . .

"Tchoo! I hear the cock crowing! Good-night. Milord! Lie down!"

## BAD WEATHER

BIG raindrops were pattering on the dark windows. It was one of those disgusting summer holiday rains which, when they have begun, last a long time—for weeks, till the frozen holiday maker grows used to it, and sinks into complete apathy. It was cold; there was a feeling of raw, unpleasant dampness. The mother-in-law of a lawyer, called Kvashin, and his wife, Nadyezhda Filippovna, dressed in waterproofs and shawls, were sitting over the dinner table in the dining-room. It was written on the countenance of the elder lady that she was, thank God, well-fed, well-clothed and in good health, that she had married her only daughter to a good man, and now could play her game of patience with an easy conscience; her daughter, a rather short, plump, fair young woman of twenty, with a gentle anæmic face, was reading a book with her elbows on the table; judging from her eyes she was not so much reading as thinking her own thoughts, which were not in the book. Neither of them spoke. There was the sound of the pattering rain, and from the kitchen they could hear the prolonged yawns of the cook.

Kvashin himself was not at home. On rainy days he did not come to the summer villa, but stayed in town; damp, rainy weather affected his bronchitis and prevented him from working. He was of the opinion that the sight of the grey sky and the tears of rain on the windows deprived one of energy and induced the spleen. In the town, where there was greater comfort, bad weather was scarcely noticed.

After two games of patience, the old lady shuffled the cards and took a glance at her daughter.

"I have been trying with the cards whether it will be fine to-morrow, and whether our Alexey Stepanovitch will come," she said. "It is five days since he was here. . . . The weather is a chastisement from God."

Nadyezhda Filippovna looked indifferently at her mother, got up, and began walking up and down the room.

"The barometer was rising yesterday," she said doubtfully, "but they say it is falling again to-day."

The old lady laid out the cards in three long rows and shook her head.

"Do you miss him?" she asked, glancing at her daughter.

"Of course."

"I see you do. I should think so. He hasn't been here for five days. In May the utmost was two, or at most three days, and now it is serious, five days! I am not his wife, and yet I miss him. And yesterday, when I heard the barometer was rising, I ordered them to kill a chicken and prepare a carp for Alexey Stepanovitch. He likes them. Your poor father couldn't bear fish, but he likes it. He always eats it with relish."

"My heart aches for him," said the daughter. "We are dull, but it is duller still for him, you know, mamma."

"I should think so! In the law-courts day in and day out, and in the empty flat at night alone like an owl."

"And what is so awful, mamma, he is alone there without servants; there is no one to set the samovar or bring him water. Why didn't he engage a valet for the summer months? And what use is the summer villa at all if he does not care for it? I told him there was no need to have it, but no, 'It is for the sake of your health,' he said, and what is wrong with my health? It makes me ill that he should have to put up with so much on my account."

Looking over her mother's shoulder, the daughter noticed a mistake in the patience, bent down to the table and began correcting it. A silence followed. Both looked at the cards and imagined how their Alexey Stepanovitch, utterly forlorn, was sitting now in the town in his gloomy, empty study and working, hungry, exhausted, yearning for his family. . . .

"Do you know what, mamma?" said Nadyezhda Filippovna suddenly, and her eyes began to shine. "If the weather is the same to-morrow I'll go by the first train and see him in town! Anyway, I shall find out how he is, have a look at him, and pour out his tea."

And both of them began to wonder how it was that this idea, so simple and easy to carry out, had not occurred to them before. It was only half an hour in the train to the town, and then twenty minutes in a cab. They said a little more, and went off to bed in the same room, feeling more contented.

"Oho-ho-ho. . . . Lord, forgive us sinners!" sighed the old lady when the clock in the hall struck two. "There is no sleeping."

"You are not asleep, mamma?" the daughter asked in a whisper. "I keep thinking of Alyosha. I only hope he won't ruin his health in town. Goodness knows where he dines and lunches. In restaurants and taverns."

"I have thought of that myself," sighed the old lady. "The Heavenly Mother save and preserve him. But the rain, the rain!"

In the morning the rain was not pattering on the panes, but the sky was still grey. The trees stood looking mournful, and at every gust of wind they scattered drops. The footprints on the muddy path, the ditches and the ruts were full of water. Nadyezhda Filippovna made up her mind to go.

"Give him my love," said the old lady, wrapping her daughter up. "Tell him not to think too much about his cases. . . . And he must rest. Let him wrap his throat up when he goes out: the weather— God help us! And take him the chicken; food from home, even if cold, is better than at a restaurant."

The daughter went away, saying that she would come back by an evening train or else next morning.

But she came back long before dinner-time, when the old lady was sitting on her trunk in her bedroom and drowsily thinking what to cook for her son-in-law's supper.

Going into the room her daughter, pale and agitated, sank on the bed without uttering a word or taking off her hat, and pressed her head into the pillow.

"But what is the matter," said the old lady in surprise, "why back so soon? Where is Alexey Stepanovitch?"

Nadyezhda Filippovna raised her head and gazed at her mother with dry, imploring eyes.

"He is deceiving us, mamma," she said.

"What are you saying? Christ be with you!" cried the old lady in alarm, and her cap slipped off her head. "Who is going to deceive us? Lord, have mercy on us!"

"He is deceiving us, mamma!" repeated her daughter, and her chin began to quiver.

"How do you know?" cried the old lady, turning pale.

"Our flat is locked up. The porter tells me that Alyosha has not been home once for these five days. He is not living at home! He is not at home, not at home!"

She waved her hands and burst into loud weeping, uttering nothing but: "Not at home! Not at home!"

She began to be hysterical.

"What's the meaning of it?" muttered the old woman in horror. "Why, he wrote the day before yesterday that he never leaves the flat! Where is he sleeping? Holy Saints!"

Nadyezhda Filippovna felt so faint that she could not take off her hat. She looked about her blankly, as though she had been drugged, and convulsively clutched at her mother's arms.

"What a person to trust: a porter!" said the old lady, fussing round her daughter and crying. "What a jealous girl you are! He is not going to deceive you, and how dare he? We are not just anybody. Though we are of the merchant class, yet he has no right, for you are his lawful wife! We can take proceedings! I gave twenty thousand roubles with you! You did not want for a dowry!"

And the old lady herself sobbed and gesticulated, and she felt faint, too, and lay down on her trunk. Neither of them noticed that patches of blue had made their appearance in the sky, that the clouds were more transparent, that the first sunbeam was cautiously gliding over the wet grass in the garden, that with renewed gaiety the sparrows were hopping about the puddles which reflected the racing clouds.

Towards evening Kvashin arrived. Before leaving town he had gone to his flat and had learned from the porter that his wife had come in his absence.

"Here I am," he said gaily, coming into his mother-in-law's room and pretending not to notice their stern and tear-stained faces. "Here I am! It's five days since we have seen each other!"

He rapidly kissed his wife's hand and his mother-in-law's, and with the air of a man delighted at having finished a difficult task, he lolled in an arm-chair.

"Ough!" he said, puffing out all the air from his lungs. "Here I have been worried to death. I have scarcely sat down. For almost five days now I have been, as it were, bivouacking. I haven't been to the flat once, would you believe it? I have been busy the whole time with the meeting of Shipunov's and Ivantchikov's creditors; I had to work in Galdeyev's office at the shop. . . . I've had nothing to eat or to drink, and slept on a bench, I was chilled through . . . . I hadn't a free minute. I hadn't even time to go to the flat. That's how I came not to be at home, Nadyusha. . . And Kvashin, holding his sides as though his back were aching, glanced stealthily at his wife and mother-in-law to see the effect of his lie, or as he called it, diplomacy. The mother-in-law and wife were looking at each other in joyful astonishment, as though beyond all hope and expectation they had found something precious, which they had lost. . . . Their faces beamed, their eyes glowed. . . .

"My dear man," cried the old lady, jumping up, "why am I sitting here? Tea! Tea at once! Perhaps you are hungry?"

"Of course he is hungry," cried his wife, pulling off her head a bandage soaked in vinegar. "Mamma, bring the wine, and the savouries. Natalya, lay the table! Oh, my goodness, nothing is ready!"

And both of them, frightened, happy, and bustling, ran about the room. The old lady could not look without laughing at her daughter who had slandered an innocent man, and the daughter felt ashamed. . . .

The table was soon laid. Kvashin, who smelt of madeira and liqueurs and who could scarcely breathe from repletion, complained of being hungry, forced himself to munch and kept on talking of the meeting of Shipunov's and Ivantchikov's creditors, while his wife and mother-in-law could not take their eyes off his face, and both thought:

"How clever and kind he is! How handsome!"

"All serene," thought Kvashin, as he lay down on the well-filled feather bed. "Though they are regular tradesmen's wives, though they are Philistines, yet they have a charm of their own, and one can spend a day or two of the week here with enjoyment. . . ."

He wrapped himself up, got warm, and as he dozed off, he said to himself:

"All serene!"

## A GENTLEMAN FRIEND

THE charming Vanda, or, as she was described in her passport, the "Honourable Citizen Nastasya Kanavkin," found herself, on leaving the hospital, in a position she had never been in before: without a home to go to or a farthing in her pocket. What was she to do?

The first thing she did was to visit a pawn-broker's and pawn her turquoise ring, her one piece of jewellery. They gave her a rouble for the ring . . . but what can you get for a rouble? You can't buy for that sum a fashionable short jacket, nor a big hat, nor a pair of bronze shoes, and without those things she had a feeling of being, as it were, undressed. She felt as though the very horses and dogs were staring and laughing at the plainness of her dress. And clothes were all she thought about: the question what she should eat and where she should sleep did not trouble her in the least.

"If only I could meet a gentleman friend," she thought to herself, "I could get some money. . . . There isn't one who would refuse me, I know. . . ."

But no gentleman she knew came her way. It would be easy enough to meet them in the evening at the "Renaissance," but they wouldn't let her in at the "Renaissance" in that shabby dress and with no hat. What was she to do?

After long hesitation, when she was sick of walking and sitting and thinking, Vanda made up her mind to fall back on her last resource: to go straight to the lodgings of some gentleman friend and ask for money.

She pondered which to go to. "Misha is out of the question; he's a married man. . . . The old chap with the red hair will be at his office at this time. . . ."

Vanda remembered a dentist, called Finkel, a converted Jew, who six months ago had given her a bracelet, and on whose head she had once emptied a glass of beer at the supper at the German Club. She was awfully pleased at the thought of Finkel.

"He'll be sure to give it me, if only I find him at home," she thought, as she walked in his direction. "If he doesn't, I'll smash all the lamps in the house."

Before she reached the dentist's door she thought out her plan of action: she would run laughing up the stairs, dash into the dentist's room and demand twenty-five roubles. But as she touched the bell, this plan seemed to vanish from her mind of itself. Vanda began suddenly feeling frightened and nervous, which was not at all her way. She was bold and saucy enough at drinking parties, but now, dressed in everyday clothes, feeling herself in the position of an ordinary person asking a favour, who might be refused admittance, she felt suddenly timid and humiliated. She was ashamed and frightened.

"Perhaps he has forgotten me by now," she thought, hardly daring to pull the bell. "And how can I go up to him in such a dress, looking like a beggar or some working girl?"

And she rang the bell irresolutely.

She heard steps coming: it was the porter.

"Is the doctor at home?" she asked.

She would have been glad now if the porter had said "No," but the latter, instead of answering ushered her into the hall, and helped her off with her coat. The staircase impressed her as luxurious, and magnificent, but of all its splendours what caught her eye most was an immense looking-glass, in which she saw a ragged figure without a fashionable jacket, without a big hat, and without bronze shoes. And it seemed strange to Vanda that, now that she was humbly dressed and looked like a laundress or sewing girl, she felt ashamed, and no trace of her usual boldness and sauciness remained, and in her own mind she no longer thought of herself as Vanda, but as the Nastasya Kanavkin she used to be in the old days. . . .

"Walk in, please," said a maidservant, showing her into the consulting-room. "The doctor will be here in a minute. Sit down."

Vanda sank into a soft arm-chair.

"I'll ask him to lend it me," she thought; "that will be quite proper, for, after all, I do know him. If only that servant would go. I don't like to ask before her. What does she want to stand there for?"

Five minutes later the door opened and Finkel came in. He was a tall, dark Jew, with fat cheeks and bulging eyes. His cheeks, his eyes, his chest, his body, all of him was so well fed, so loathsome and repellent! At the "Renaissance" and the German Club he had usually been rather tipsy, and would spend his money freely on women, and be very long-suffering and patient with their pranks (when Vanda, for instance, poured the beer over his head, he simply smiled and shook his finger at her): now he had a cross, sleepy expression and looked solemn and frigid like a police captain, and he kept chewing something.

"What can I do for you?" he asked, without looking at Vanda.

Vanda looked at the serious countenance of the maid and the smug figure of Finkel, who apparently did not recognize her, and she turned red.

"What can I do for you?" repeated the dentist a little irritably.

"I've got toothache," murmured Vanda.

"Aha! . . . Which is the tooth? Where?"

Vanda remembered she had a hole in one of her teeth.

"At the bottom . . . on the right . . ." she said.

"Hm! . . . Open your mouth."

Finkel frowned and, holding his breath, began examining the tooth.

"Does it hurt?" he asked, digging into it with a steel instrument.

"Yes," Vanda replied, untruthfully.

"Shall I remind him?" she was wondering. "He would be sure to remember me. But that servant! Why will she stand there?"

Finkel suddenly snorted like a steam-engine right into her mouth, and said:

"I don't advise you to have it stopped. That tooth will never be worth keeping anyhow."

After probing the tooth a little more and soiling Vanda's lips and gums with his tobacco-stained fingers, he held his breath again, and put something cold into her mouth. Vanda suddenly felt a sharp pain, cried out, and clutched at Finkel's hand.

"It's all right, it's all right," he muttered; "don't you be frightened! That tooth would have been no use to you, anyway . . . you must be brave. . ."

And his tobacco-stained fingers, smeared with blood, held up the tooth to her eyes, while the maid approached and put a basin to her mouth.

"You wash out your mouth with cold water when you get home, and that will stop the bleeding," said Finkel.

He stood before her with the air of a man expecting her to go, waiting to be left in peace.

"Good-day," she said, turning towards the door.

"Hm! . . . and how about my fee?" enquired Finkel, in a jesting tone.

"Oh, yes!" Vanda remembered, blushing, and she handed the Jew the rouble that had been given her for her ring.

When she got out into the street she felt more overwhelmed with shame than before, but now it was not her poverty she was ashamed of. She was unconscious now of not having a big hat and a fashionable jacket. She walked along the street, spitting blood, and brooding on her life, her ugly, wretched life, and the insults she had endured, and would have to endure to-morrow, and next week, and all her life, up to the very day of her death.

"Oh! how awful it is! My God, how fearful!"

Next day, however, she was back at the "Renaissance," and dancing there. She had on an enormous new red hat, a new fashionable jacket, and bronze shoes. And she was taken out to supper by a young merchant up from Kazan.

## A TRIVIAL INCIDENT

IT was a sunny August midday as, in company with a Russian prince who had come down in the world, I drove into the immense so-called Shabelsky pine-forest where we were intending to look for woodcocks. In virtue of the part he plays in this story my poor prince deserves a detailed description. He was a tall, dark man, still youngish, though already somewhat battered by life; with long moustaches like a police captain's; with prominent black eyes, and with the manners of a retired army man. He was a man of Oriental type, not very intelligent, but straightforward and honest, not a bully, not a fop, and not a rake—virtues which, in the eyes of the general public, are equivalent to a certificate of being a nonentity and a poor creature. People generally did not like him (he was never spoken of in the district, except as "the illustrious duffer"). I personally found the poor prince extremely nice with his misfortunes and failures, which made up indeed his whole life. First of all he was poor. He did not play cards, did not drink, had no occupation, did not poke his nose into anything, and maintained a perpetual silence but yet he had somehow succeeded in getting through thirty to forty thousand roubles left him at his father's death. God only knows what had become of the money. All that I can say is that owing to lack of supervision a great deal was stolen by stewards, bailiffs, and even footmen; a great deal went on lending money, giving bail, and standing security. There were few landowners in the district who did not owe him money. He gave to all who asked, and not so much from good nature or confidence in people as from exaggerated gentlemanliness as though he would say: "Take it and feel how *comme il faut* I am!" By the time I made his acquaintance he had got into debt himself, had learned what it was like to have a second mortgage on his land, and had sunk so deeply into difficulties that there was no chance of his ever getting out of them again. There were days when he had no dinner, and went about with an empty cigar-holder, but he was always seen clean and fashionably dressed, and always smelt strongly of ylang-ylang.

The prince's second misfortune was his absolute solitariness. He was not married, he had no friends nor relations. His silent and reserved character and his *comme il faut* deportment, which became the more conspicuous the more anxious he was to conceal his poverty, prevented him from becoming intimate with people. For love affairs he was too heavy, spiritless, and cold, and so rarely got on with women. . . .

When we reached the forest this prince and I got out of the chaise and walked along a narrow woodland path which was hidden among huge ferns. But before we had gone a hundred paces a tall, lank figure with a long oval face, wearing a shabby reefer jacket, a straw hat, and patent leather boots, rose up from behind a young fir-tree some three feet high, as though he had sprung out of the ground. The stranger held in one hand a basket of mushrooms, with the other he playfully fingered a cheap watch-chain on his waistcoat. On seeing us he was taken aback, smoothed his waistcoat, coughed politely, and gave an agreeable smile, as though he were delighted to see such nice people as us. Then, to our complete surprise, he came up to us, scraping with his long feet on the grass, bending his whole person, and, still smiling agreeably, lifted his hat and pronounced in a sugary voice with the intonations of a whining dog:

"Aie, aie . . . gentlemen, painful as it is, it is my duty to warn you that shooting is forbidden in this wood. Pardon me for venturing to disturb you, though unacquainted, but . . . allow me to present myself. I am Grontovsky, the head clerk on Madame Kandurin's estate."

"Pleased to make your acquaintance, but why can't we shoot?"

"Such is the wish of the owner of this forest!"

The prince and I exchanged glances. A moment passed in silence. The prince stood looking pensively at a big fly agaric at his feet, which he had crushed with his stick. Grontovsky went on smiling agreeably. His whole face was twitching, exuding honey, and even the watch-chain on his waistcoat seemed to be smiling and trying to impress us all with its refinement. A shade of embarrassment passed over us like an angel passing; all three of us felt awkward.

"Nonsense!" I said. "Only last week I was shooting here!"

"Very possible!" Grontovsky sniggered through his teeth. "As a matter of fact everyone shoots here regardless of the prohibition. But once I have met you, it is my duty . . . my sacred duty to warn you. I am a man in a dependent position. If the forest were mine, on the word of honour of a Grontovsky, I should not oppose your agreeable pleasure. But whose fault is it that I am in a dependent position?"

The lanky individual sighed and shrugged his shoulders. I began arguing, getting hot and protesting, but the more loudly and impressively I spoke the more mawkish and sugary Grontovsky's face became. Evidently the consciousness of a certain power over us afforded him the greatest gratification. He was enjoying his condescending tone, his politeness, his manners, and with peculiar relish pronounced his sonorous surname, of which he was probably very fond. Standing before us he felt more than at ease, but judging from the confused sideway glances he cast from time to time at his basket, only one thing was spoiling his satisfaction—the mushrooms, womanish, peasantish, prose, derogatory to his dignity.

"We can't go back!" I said. "We have come over ten miles!"

"What's to be done?" sighed Grontovsky. "If you had come not ten but a hundred thousand miles, if the king even had come from America or from some other distant land, even then I should think it my duty . . . sacred, so to say, obligation . . ."

"Does the forest belong to Nadyezhda Lvovna?" asked the prince.

"Yes, Nadyezhda Lvovna . . ."

"Is she at home now?"

"Yes . . . I tell you what, you go to her, it is not more than half a mile from here; if she gives you a note, then I. . . . I needn't say! Ha—ha . . . he—he—!"

"By all means," I agreed. "It's much nearer than to go back. . . . You go to her, Sergey Ivanitch," I said, addressing the prince. "You know her."

The prince, who had been gazing the whole time at the crushed agaric, raised his eyes to me, thought a minute, and said:

"I used to know her at one time, but . . . it's rather awkward for me to go to her. Besides, I am in shabby clothes. . . . You go, you don't know her. . . . It's more suitable for you to go."

I agreed. We got into our chaise and, followed by Grontovsky's smiles, drove along the edge of the forest to the manor house. I was not acquainted with Nadyezhda Lvovna Kandurin, née Shabelsky. I had never seen her at close quarters, and knew her only by hearsay. I knew that she was incredibly wealthy, richer than anyone else in the province. After the death of her father, Shabelsky, who was a landowner with no other children, she was left with several estates, a stud farm, and a lot of money. I had heard that, though she was only twenty-five or twenty-six, she was ugly, uninteresting, and as insignificant as anybody, and was only distinguished from the ordinary ladies of the district by her immense wealth.

It has always seemed to me that wealth is felt, and that the rich must have special feelings unknown to the poor. Often as I passed by Nadyezhda Lvovna's big fruit garden, in which stood the large, heavy house with its windows always curtained, I thought: "What is she thinking at this moment? Is there happiness behind those blinds?" and so on. Once I saw her from a distance in a fine light cabriolet, driving a handsome white horse, and, sinful man that I am, I not only envied her, but even thought that in her poses, in her movements, there was something special, not to be found in people who are not rich, just as persons of a servile nature succeed in discovering "good family" at the first glance in people of the most ordinary exterior, if they are a little more distinguished than themselves. Nadyezhda Lvovna's inner life was only known to me by scandal. It was said in the district that five or six years ago, before she was married, during her father's lifetime, she had been passionately in love with Prince Sergey Ivanitch, who was now beside me in the chaise. The prince had been fond of visiting her father, and used to spend whole days in his billiard room, where he played pyramids indefatigably till his arms and legs ached. Six months before the old man's death he had suddenly given up visiting the Shabelskys. The gossip of the district having no positive facts to go upon explained this abrupt change in their relations in various ways. Some said that the prince, having observed the plain daughter's feeling for him and being unable to reciprocate it, considered it the duty of a gentleman to cut short his visits. Others maintained that old Shabelsky had discovered why his daughter was pining away, and had proposed to the poverty-stricken prince that he should marry her; the prince, imagining in his narrow-minded way that they were trying to buy him together with his title, was indignant, said foolish things, and quarrelled with them. What was true and what was false in this nonsense was difficult to say. But that there was a portion of truth in it was evident, from the fact that the prince always avoided conversation about Nadyezhda Lvovna.

I knew that soon after her father's death Nadyezhda Lvovna had married one Kandurin, a bachelor of law, not wealthy, but adroit, who had come on a visit to the neighbourhood. She married him not from love, but because she was touched by the love of the legal gentleman who, so it was said, had cleverly played the love-sick swain. At the time I am describing, Kandurin was for some reason living in Cairo, and writing thence to his friend, the marshal of the district, "Notes of Travel," while she sat languishing behind lowered blinds, surrounded by idle parasites, and whiled away her dreary days in petty philanthropy.

On the way to the house the prince fell to talking.

"It's three days since I have been at home," he said in a half whisper, with a sidelong glance at the driver. "I am not a child, nor a silly woman, and I have no prejudices, but I can't stand the bailiffs. When I see a bailiff in my house I turn pale and tremble, and even have a twitching in the calves of my legs. Do you know Rogozhin refused to honour my note?"

The prince did not, as a rule, like to complain of his straitened circumstances; where poverty was concerned he was reserved and exceedingly proud and sensitive, and so this announcement surprised me. He stared a long time at the yellow clearing, warmed by the sun, watched a long string of cranes float in the azure sky, and turned facing me.

"And by the sixth of September I must have the money ready for the bank . . . the interest for my estate," he said aloud, by now regardless of the coachman. "And where am I to get it? Altogether, old man, I am in a tight fix! An awfully tight fix!"

The prince examined the cock of his gun, blew on it for some reason, and began looking for the cranes which by now were out of sight.

"Sergey Ivanitch," I asked, after a minute's silence, "imagine if they sell your Shatilovka, what will you do?"

"I? I don't know! Shatilovka can't be saved, that's clear as daylight, but I cannot imagine such a calamity. I can't imagine myself without my daily bread secure. What can I do? I have had hardly any education; I have not tried working yet; for government service it is late to begin, . . . Besides, where could I serve? Where could I be of use? Admitting that no great cleverness is needed for serving in our Zemstvo, for example, yet I suffer from . . . the devil knows what, a sort of faintheartedness, I haven't a ha'p'orth of pluck. If I went into the Service I should always feel I was not in my right place. I am not an idealist; I am not a Utopian; I haven't any special principles; but am simply, I suppose, stupid and thoroughly incompetent, a neurotic and a coward. Altogether not like other people. All other people are like other people, only I seem to be something . . . a poor thing. . . . I met Naryagin last Wednesday—you know him?—drunken, slovenly . . . doesn't pay his debts, stupid" (the prince frowned and tossed his head) . . . "a horrible person! He said to me, staggering: 'I'm being balloted for as a justice of the peace!' Of course, they won't elect him, but, you see, he believes he is fit to be a justice of the peace and considers that position within his capacity. He has boldness and self-confidence. I went to see our investigating magistrate too. The man gets two hundred and fifty roubles a month, and does scarcely anything. All he can do is to stride backwards and forwards for days together in nothing but his underclothes, but, ask him, he is convinced he is doing his work and honourably performing his duty. I couldn't go on like that! I should be ashamed to look the clerk in the face."

At that moment Grontovsky, on a chestnut horse, galloped by us with a flourish. On his left arm the basket bobbed up and down with the mushrooms dancing in it. As he passed us he grinned and waved his hand, as though we were old friends.

"Blockhead!" the prince filtered through his teeth, looking after him. "It's wonderful how disgusting it sometimes is to see satisfied faces. A stupid, animal feeling due to hunger, I expect. . . . What was I saying? Oh, yes, about going into the Service, . . . I should be ashamed to take the salary, and yet, to tell the truth, it is stupid. If one looks at it from a broader point of view, more seriously, I am eating what isn't mine now. Am I not? But why am I not ashamed of that. . . . It is a case of habit, I suppose . . . and not being able to realize one's true position. . . . But that position is most likely awful. . ."

I looked at him, wondering if the prince were showing off. But his face was mild and his eyes were mournfully following the movements of the chestnut horse racing away, as though his happiness were racing away with it.

Apparently he was in that mood of irritation and sadness when women weep quietly for no reason, and men feel a craving to complain of themselves, of life, of God. . . .

When I got out of the chaise at the gates of the house the prince said to me:

"A man once said, wanting to annoy me, that I have the face of a cardsharper. I have noticed that cardsharpers are usually dark. Do you know, it seems that if I really had been born a cardsharper I should have remained a decent person to the day of my death, for I should never have had the boldness to do wrong. I tell you frankly I have had the chance once in my life of getting rich if I had told a lie, a lie to myself and one woman . . . and one other person whom I know would have forgiven me for lying; I should have put into my pocket a million. But I could not. I hadn't the pluck!"

From the gates we had to go to the house through the copse by a long road, level as a ruler, and planted on each side with thick, lopped lilacs. The house looked somewhat heavy, tasteless, like a façade on the stage. It rose clumsily out of a mass of greenery, and caught the eye like a great stone thrown on the velvety turf. At the chief entrance I was met by a fat old footman in a green swallow-tail coat and big silver-rimmed spectacles; without making any announcement, only looking contemptuously at my dusty figure, he showed me in. As I mounted the soft carpeted stairs there was, for some reason, a strong smell of india-rubber. At the top I was enveloped in an atmosphere found only in museums, in signorial mansions and old-fashioned merchant houses; it seemed like the smell of something long past, which had once lived and died and had left its soul in the rooms. I passed through three or four rooms on my way from the entry to the drawing-room. I remember bright yellow, shining floors, lustres wrapped in stiff muslin, narrow, striped rugs which stretched not straight from door to door, as they usually do, but along the walls, so that not venturing to touch the bright floor with my muddy boots I had to describe a rectangle in each room. In the drawing-room, where the footman left me, stood old-fashioned ancestral furniture in white covers, shrouded in twilight. It looked surly and elderly, and, as though out of respect for its repose, not a sound was audible.

Even the clock was silent . . . it seemed as though the Princess Tarakanov had fallen asleep in the golden frame, and the water and the rats were still and motionless through magic. The daylight, afraid of disturbing the universal tranquillity, scarcely pierced through the lowered blinds, and lay on the soft rugs in pale, slumbering streaks.

Three minutes passed and a big, elderly woman in black, with her cheek bandaged up, walked noiselessly into the drawing-room. She bowed to me and pulled up the blinds. At once, enveloped in the bright sunlight, the rats and water in the picture came to life and movement, Princess Tarakanov was awakened, and the old chairs frowned gloomily.

"Her honour will be here in a minute, sir . . ." sighed the old lady, frowning too.

A few more minutes of waiting and I saw Nadyezhda Lvovna. What struck me first of all was that she certainly was ugly, short, scraggy, and round-shouldered. Her thick, chestnut hair was magnificent; her face, pure and with a look of culture in it, was aglow with youth; there was a clear and intelligent expression in her eyes; but the whole charm of her head was lost through the thickness of her lips and the over-acute facial angle.

I mentioned my name, and announced the object of my visit.

"I really don't know what I am to say!" she said, in hesitation, dropping her eyes and smiling. "I don't like to refuse, and at the same time...."

"Do, please," I begged.

Nadyezhda Lvovna looked at me and laughed. I laughed too. She was probably amused by what Grontovsky had so enjoyed—that is, the right of giving or withholding permission; my visit suddenly struck me as queer and strange.

"I don't like to break the long-established rules," said Madame Kandurin. "Shooting has been forbidden on our estate for the last six years. No!" she shook her head resolutely. "Excuse me, I must refuse you. If I allow you I must allow others. I don't like unfairness. Either let all or no one."

"I am sorry!" I sighed. "It's all the sadder because we have come more than ten miles. I am not alone," I added, "Prince Sergey Ivanitch is with me."

I uttered the prince's name with no *arrière pensée*, not prompted by any special motive or aim; I simply blurted it out without thinking, in the simplicity of my heart. Hearing the familiar name Madame Kandurin started, and bent a prolonged gaze upon me. I noticed her nose turn pale.

"That makes no difference..." she said, dropping her eyes.

As I talked to her I stood at the window that looked out on the shrubbery. I could see the whole shrubbery with the avenues and the ponds and the road by which I had come. At the end of the road, beyond the gates, the back of our chaise made a dark patch. Near the gate, with his back to the house, the prince was standing with his legs apart, talking to the lanky Grontovsky.

Madame Kandurin had been standing all the time at the other window. She looked from time to time towards the shrubbery, and from the moment I mentioned the prince's name she did not turn away from the window.

"Excuse me," she said, screwing up her eyes as she looked towards the road and the gate, "but it would be unfair to allow you only to shoot. . . . And, besides, what pleasure is there in shooting birds? What's it for? Are they in your way?"

A solitary life, immured within four walls, with its indoor twilight and heavy smell of decaying furniture, disposes people to sentimentality. Madame Kandurin's idea did her credit, but I could not resist saying:

"If one takes that line one ought to go barefoot. Boots are made out of the leather of slaughtered animals."

"One must distinguish between a necessity and a caprice," Madame Kandurin answered in a toneless voice.

She had by now recognized the prince, and did not take her eyes off his figure. It is hard to describe the delight and the suffering with which her ugly face was radiant! Her eyes were smiling and shining, her lips were quivering and laughing, while her face craned closer to the panes. Keeping hold of a flower-pot with both hands, with bated breath and with one foot slightly lifted, she reminded me of a dog pointing and waiting with passionate impatience for "Fetch it!"

I looked at her and at the prince who could not tell a lie once in his life, and I felt angry and bitter against truth and falsehood, which play such an elemental part in the personal happiness of men.

The prince started suddenly, took aim and fired. A hawk, flying over him, fluttered its wings and flew like an arrow far away.

"He aimed too high!" I said. "And so, Nadyezhda Lvovna," I sighed, moving away from the window, "you will not permit . . ."—Madame Kandurin was silent.

"I have the honour to take my leave," I said, "and I beg you to forgive my disturbing you. . ."

Madame Kandurin would have turned facing me, and had already moved through a quarter of the angle, when she suddenly hid her face behind the hangings, as though she felt tears in her eyes that she wanted to conceal.

"Good-bye. . . . Forgive me . . ." she said softly.

I bowed to her back, and strode away across the bright yellow floors, no longer keeping to the carpet. I was glad to get away from this little domain of gilded boredom and sadness, and I hastened as though anxious to shake off a heavy, fantastic dream with its twilight, its enchanted princess, its lustres. . . .

At the front door a maidservant overtook me and thrust a note into my hand: "Shooting is permitted on showing this. N. K.," I read.

Copyright © 2023 Esprios Digital Publishing. All Rights Reserved.

Milton Keynes UK
Ingram Content Group UK Ltd.
UKHW050722010724
444982UK00014B/1015

9 798331 220488